Doctor Of The Lost

LONDON BOOKS

FLYING THE FLAG FOR
FREE-THINKING LITERATURE

www.london-books.co.uk

PLEASE VISIT OUR WEBSITE FOR

- Current and forthcoming books
  - Author and title profiles
- A lively, interactive message board
  - Events and news
  - Secure on-line bookshop
  - Recommendations and links
- An alternative view of London literature

London Classics

The Angel And The Cuckoo *Gerald Kersh*
The Gilt Kid *James Curtis*
Jew Boy *Simon Blumenfeld*
May Day *John Sommerfield*
Night And The City *Gerald Kersh*
A Start In Life *Alan Sillitoe*
They Drive By Night *James Curtis*
Wide Boys Never Work *Robert Westerby*

Doctor Of The Lost
Simon Blumenfeld

With an introduction by Paolo Hewitt

LONDON BOOKS CLASSICS

LONDON BOOKS
39 Lavender Gardens
London SW11 1DJ
www.london-books.co.uk

First published 1938 by Jonathan Cape
This edition published by London Books 2013

A catalogue record for this book
is available from the British Library

ISBN 978-0-9568155-2-1

Printed and bound by CPI Group (UK) Ltd
Croydon, CR0 4YY

Typeset by Octavo Smith Ltd in Plantin 10.5/13.5
www.octavosmith.com

INTRODUCTION

Some years ago, The Sohemian Society (motto 'join the rebel set') asked me to deliver a lecture to their members on The London Orphan. The idea was to trace the history of London's relationship with abandoned children, those unfortunates who had been forced to face life in one of the world's greatest and most imposing cities without parental guidance, love or wisdom. It was a talk I had been preparing for years.

That is because London is my home and I am an orphan. Two days after my birth, I was removed from my mother and placed in care. Four years later, I was fostered out to a family. At age ten, I went back into care. I spent my teenage years in a children's home in Woking, Surrey.

To steal from the master, it was the best of times, it was the worst of times. Certainly, it was a unique experience that, for *most* of the time, I am highly grateful to have received. If there was one constant throughout this whole period, it was my love of books and music. Both instantly took me out of the difficult world I inhabited.

At the age of fourteen I was shown a copy of the music paper *New Musical Express*. I knew straight away what path I had to follow. In 1983, the *NME* employed me as a staff writer. In 1990, I left the paper and began writing a series of books based around music, football (another passion that instantly lifted me out of the dark) and fashion. That discipline led me towards social history. I absorbed the 1960s, Italian-Americans, various youth cults.

Soon, I began wondering about the history of orphans . . . My first important discovery was a man named Sir Thomas Coram. In 1742, he opened The Foundling Hospital in Holborn,

London. It was, as far as I can tell, Britain's first children's home. My second discovery was the subject of the book you now hold in your hand – Thomas John Barnardo. Of course, I had heard of Barnardo's homes, but I was totally unaware of Simon Blumenfeld's wonderful novel *Doctor Of The Lost*, his vivid but fictional account of Barnardo's incredible achievements.

Before I encountered this book, I had gathered facts on Barnardo. He was born in 1845, Dublin, the son of a furrier. At school, he marked himself out as an independent thinker, a fine pupil highly influenced by the works of Rousseau and Tom Paine. At sixteen, Barnardo converted to Protestant evangelicalism and began teaching bible classes in a Dublin ragged school. These schools were charitable institutions that provided free education for destitute children. They began in Scotland in 1841 and over the next three years spread to the rest of Britain and Ireland. (It is said that the visit author Charles Dickens made to a ragged school in Field Lane in 1842 subsequently inspired him to write his classic novel *A Christmas Carol*.)

In 1866, after turning twenty-one, Barnardo decided to go to London and train as a doctor. He hoped to eventually help the poor in China and began his training at the London Hospital, Whitechapel. A few months later cholera swept through the East End, killing three thousand people in its wake. This was a tragedy waiting to happen. London's poorer districts were massively over-populated and ruled by corrupt councils. Thousands of children slept in the street, many crippled or disfigured from work in factories.

Unlike the majority of his English contemporaries Barnardo could not stand by and do nothing. He set out to beat away the disease from the streets he walked. Then, in 1867, he set up his own ragged school in Whitechapel. One of the boys who attended was a Jim Jarvis. It was he who took Barnardo around the East End and showed his teacher sights so distressing that Barnardo was galvanized into further action.

After three years of fundraising and petitioning, Barnardo opened his first home for boys in London's Stepney Causeway. Unlike The Foundling Hospital, no child was ever turned away from its doors. Barnardo created this policy after reluctantly refusing entry to an eleven-year-old boy, John Somers (nickname Carrots), as the shelter was full. Carrots was found dead on the streets two nights later.

From then on, Barnardo regularly went out at night to seek destitute boys and offer them shelter and protection. He was soon persuaded that family life was the best possible environment for the abandoned child, and established the first fostering scheme by persuading well-off families to take in destitute children. He also introduced a scheme to board out babies to potential adoptive parents.

At the Stepney Boys' Home, another innovation, Barnardo opened a photographic department. When children arrived they were photographed twice in the space of a few months to illustrate their progress. These pictures were then made into cards and sold in packs of twenty for five shillings, or singly for sixpence.

Barnardo led a God-driven life marked by generosity and courage. As one of his biographers noted: 'In the short space of forty years, starting without patronage or influence of any kind, this man had raised the sum of three-and-a-quarter million pounds sterling, established a network of homes of various kinds such as never existed before for the reception, care and training of homeless, needy and afflicted children, and had rescued no fewer than sixty thousand destitute boys and girls.'

Those then are the facts.

What Simon Blumenfeld's novel does is give you the man, and in the most compelling fashion.

Doctor Of The Lost is Blumenfeld's third novel. At the time of its publication, 1938, he was already a celebrity novelist, having acquired great fame (and notoriety) with his novels

Jew Boy (also reprinted by London Books as part of its London Classics series) and *Phineas Kahn: Portrait Of An Immigrant.*

Blumenfeld was greatly suited for public attention. The son of Sicilian refugees, he dressed strikingly and was once described as 'a Jew who was proud of his race but remained aloof from its religion, a confirmed Marxist happy to mingle when necessary with royalty and capitalists, a lover of the fine arts at home with pop stars and champion boxers.'

London's East End, the scene of his childhood days, fascinated him. It became the world he returned to on countless occasions. To his credit, Blumenfeld never romanticised the area. He saw in it horror as much as he did beauty. The work of Barnardo brought together both strands.

To research the book, Blumenfeld sat down with Serena, Barnardo's wife, and drew from her the salient facts of her husband's life. He then applied his own imagination and knowledge to recreate Barnardo's life in vivid fictional terms. If there is a template for the work then it is surely that of the work of Charles Dickens. Blumenfeld has the same effortless ability to create a world full of life and colour and smell and taste. Within the first few pages the reader literally feels as if they are walking next to Barnardo, experiencing the very same sights and sounds of the London he inhabits.

Doctor Of The Lost opens with the young Barnardo arriving in the East End, an area filled with poverty, disease and vice. When Barnardo looks out of his window he sees steam rising from rotting heaps of rubbish. There is vermin everywhere. Dirt is a constant character in the novel.

Barnardo is here to study medicine before he travels to China to work as a missionary. He is a young man driven by two certainties: God exists and man's role on this earth is to perform His will. Yet here in the East End, he soon realises that he is living in a kind of hell. Early on in the novel, then, Blumenfeld lays out Barnardo's mission to bring God to the people: 'The only way he (Barnardo) would be able to do that was to enter more fully into their lives, and this he determined to embark upon without any further delay.'

Soon, cholera will enter the East End and kill many. We are informed of this impending crisis through Barnardo's relationship with Jonathan Haddock – the Black Doctor – a major figure in the book. Haddock is portrayed as a universally respected character – he judges the donkey contest where Barnardo first meets him – and his presence wonderfully blurs the line between fact and fiction. Did he actually exist, or is he a part of the author's imagination?

The facts would tell us that he is a creation. By 1800, there were at least 10,000 Africans and Caribbeans living in London, many of them in the East End, the immigrant's traditional first port of call. Most, unlike Haddock, were poor and subject to great racial abuse. Moreover, Haddock, as we shall see later, is politically opposed to Barnardo's work. He states that it does not solve the huge problems, based around poverty and disease, that the locals face on a daily basis, a position Blumenfeld as a Marxist would have adopted. It is Haddock who warns Barnardo of the impending outbreak of cholera, aggravated in part by a corrupt local council, and it is he that Barnardo helps to beat the terrible disease.

By the end of Act One we have met many of the local residents. Moreover, we are highly impressed by Blumenfeld's brilliant and totally faithful rendering of the Cockney dialect.

In Blumenfeld's hands, 'you' becomes 'yer 'and 'he is' becomes ''e's'. 'Nothing' is 'nuffing'. 'Don't you' is 'doncher'. 'Anyone can' translates as 'anyone kin'. The Spicer character is born in 'Marrerbone Lane', not 'Marylebone Lane'. 'Hands' are ''ands' and 'now' is 'naow'. A character never 'goes out', he or she 'goes aout'. And so on . . .

His faithful rendering of the dialect gives the book a vital authenticity so necessary in placing the reader at the very heart of the action. If you can trust these voices, you can see the characters' streets.

In Act Two we meet Barnardo's university contemporaries, in particular his nemesis Brad, who we discover is 'too interested in gambling, drinking and its associated vices to be able to spare much attention to study'.

We also meet Phillip Comyns, who Barnardo will brilliantly manipulate into helping with his missions. When Comyns is given the terrible facts surrounding the almost non-existent education of East End children at that time, he quickly exclaims that they must start a ragged school, not realizing that Barnardo has inoculated him 'with the proselytizing germ . . .'

The school opens and Barnardo is soon admired by all for his efforts. Yet Blumenfeld is never rose-tinted about the community. Spicer cruelly dismisses the abandoned kids as 'little thieves, that's all they are', while many believe 'they should go to the workhouse'. The view of the rich, mainly expressed through the dissolute Brad, is that poverty is the result of a natural order and therefore excusable, a view even held by some local religious folk.

Barnardo's strength is that he has no time for the whys and wherefores of poverty. As Blumenfeld lets him firmly state at one point: 'When I see hungry children, I want to give them food. When I see them homeless, I want to give them shelter.'

Blumenfeld regularly directs us to Barnardo's deep conviction that God will always provide. However big the obstacle, Barnardo believes if it be the Lord's will then mountains will be moved. Which they are. Money always comes in when most needed. Faith and conviction therefore act as this novel's subtext.

As Barnardo immerses himself in the fate of his children, China recedes like a dream, as do his ambitions in the field of medicine. Daringly, it is only on page 154 that our hero finally falls for a woman, the understanding and courageous Serena, who provides her husband with much needed protection as the forces of darkness and envy gather around him.

If you hold this book, then you will soon know its ending.

Therefore, I have no wish to reveal it. What interests is just why would Blumenfeld be so attracted to this story? Two reasons, the first of which is expressed most forcibly by the Black Doctor. Towards the end of the novel, tending once more to an exhausted Barnardo, Haddock calls his patient a revolutionary.

'Me?' Tom's keen eyes gazed through his pince-nez at the negro in surprise. 'I don't meddle in politics, how in heaven's name can you call me a revolutionary?'

'Of course you are a revolutionary,' Haddock asserted. 'You could hardly be otherwise. You come from the land of revolutionaries. You are the countryman of Bronterre O'Brien and Feargus O'Connor and you follow a master who was the earliest of the revolutionaries, He who whipped the money-changers from the Temple. That was an act just as revolutionary as your determination to save the outcast children from the streets.'

Yet Haddock himself disagrees with Barnardo's actions. He believes that only political action will change the status quo. As far as he is concerned, what Barnardo is doing is applying a plaster to a poison that needs removing. Haddock therefore allows Blumenfeld, a strident Marxist, to start the debate on how best to eradicate poverty.

The second reason is the book's nature. I think Blumenfeld must have been artistically excited to create a biography within the form of a novel. It is a hard task, one beset with potential pitfalls. Facts allow the biographer to create a world and then place their chosen subject within that environment. Blumenfeld's approach allows the author much more scope – you can create your own characters, invent conversations that never took place – but the author has to convey an emotional truth that pertains to both subject and his environment. Blumenfeld does not fail us.

Moreover, *Doctor Of The Lost* beautifully chimes with his personal conviction as to the point of the novel. It is a view he expressed to the author Aldous Huxley, a conversation captured by Blumenfeld in an unpublished work, kindly lent to me by his son Eric.

The occasion of this meeting – which would lead to a great friendship – was in a West End ballroom. Blumenfeld and his wife were on a night out when they spotted Huxley standing on his own. They approached the novelist, fell into conversation. During their talk, Blumenfeld laid bare his literary convictions. He told Huxley that he 'refused to regard as literature anything that existed in a world of its own . . . a contemporary tale had to fit in with the framework of contemporary society, which had to be scientifically postulated or implied in the book, and a period piece had to have its roots in the reality of that period.'

Doctor Of The Lost lives up to that credo. It is a great novel, one I simply could not live without while in the process of reading it, and it wonderfully confirms the last line of my London Orphan talk. I wrote and then declared: 'Thomas Barnardo was nothing less than a true hero.'

Paolo Hewitt
London 2013

PREFACE

This is a novel, and should be read as such. Several of the incidents really did occur in real life, and for them I am indebted to Doctor Wesley Breedy's biography, Barnardo and Marchant's *Memoirs*, and to Mrs Barnardo herself. For the rest of the novel, by far the greater portion of it, I have attempted to give my own conception of the man Barnardo and a rounded picture of those early years in East London. The portrait of Thomas J Barnardo is based on fact, but the rest is fiction.

Simon Blumenfeld

Dedicated to
my very good friends
Charles Barclay
and
L Sterling

CHAPTER I

The young man stood on the quay and watched the *Lammer-muir* sail down the river. He strained his eyes till the fluttering handkerchiefs became blurred specks of white. There they went, all his friends, off to China and he was left alone in London. Not quite alone, for he had his work, his preparation for the great adventure, but the brothers Fiske and John McCarthy and his mentor, Hudson Taylor, they were all gone before him, and it might be years before he would see them again.

In a few weeks they would be sailing up the Yangtse, changing into junks and sampans to reach the stations of the China Inland Mission, while he would be cooped up in the stuffy lecture halls of the medical college. A lump came into his throat as he thought of his stark loneliness. On this hot May morning it would be very pleasant in his native Dublin, beside the Liffey, where everybody knew him, and he knew everybody. Here, a stranger in gargantuan, smoky, sprawling London, he was an anonymous ant amongst myriads of dirty, quarrelsome, equally anonymous insects. He removed his pince-nez and wiped away the tears that were clouding his eyes. There was a big job ahead of him, he could not afford to stumble now.

As he made his way homewards to his lodgings off the Commercial Road he reviewed the events of the past few years. The great religious revival of 1859 and 1861 that, starting in Belfast, had swept over Ireland right to the south had passed him untouched. With his mother and brothers he had attended Richard Weaver's missions in the Metropolitan Hall, once the home of the circus, but the mass hysteria of thousands of converts had affected him not at all. His mind was well stocked and fortified by years of omnivorous reading, although he had only been seventeen at the time. He knew the works of Tom Paine and Voltaire, Godwin and Shelley, and the arguments of *The Rights Of Man* and *The Age Of Reason* were proof against the emotion of the evangelist. Then he had suddenly been swept into the fold by John Hambleton, a converted actor, at a private gathering. And he had met the missionary Hudson Taylor, home on furlough from China, and read his pamphlet *China's Spiritual Needs And Claims*. That had decided his future course; at seventeen he felt the call for China and here he was at the age of twenty-one, a candidate for work in foreign fields, commencing on his studies at the London Hospital.

Tom Barnardo was a little over five feet in height, but, to retrieve his figure from personal insignificance, endowed with massive shoulders and a leonine head. He was always immaculately dressed, a moustache was just beginning to sprout on his upper lip, and despite his shortness of stature, his general appearance gave the impression of a man, a foreigner much older than his years. This foreign strain came from his father, a well-to-do merchant of Spanish-Jewish stock, who had travelled a good deal in his youth, until he settled permanently in Ireland. On his mother's side he was English, descended from an old Quaker family that had settled in Dublin. The early promise of business ability and organizational power that Hudson Taylor had discerned in him was inherited from his father, and his mother had passed on the burning religious spirit that was leading him on his proselytizing mission to those teeming millions at the other end of the world. Yet in spite of himself, on this brilliant summer morning, with his friends already en route for the Orient, he felt some doubts as to the direction in which he was travelling. There was so much deprivation and misery around him. He lived in Dempsey Street, a stone's throw from the hospital, and the narrow alleys of the district were cesspools of disease and vice. He had encountered intense poverty before in the 'Libertys' of Dublin, but never such extremes of degradation as confronted him on his very door-step.

In this year of grace 1866, it seemed incredible that human beings could live under such conditions; side by side with an enlightened constitution, Houses of Parliament, a democratic monarchy, and enormously wealthy industrial undertakings, an army of homeless, propertyless wretches existed in almost unimaginable squalor. Not so many years ago, a boy of eight out of these same streets had been hanged for stealing, and in defiance of Parliamentary law children still climbed with brushes up soot-laden chimneys, and were sometimes suffocated by the fumes from the fires their masters burned below them to hasten their progress. And these were not heathen Chinese, but Christians, his brothers. While his friends were with him, everything except the study of the Bible and the attraction of China was forgotten, but now they were gone the innumerable abuses to which his fellow men were subjected struck home with full force.

The house in which he lived was quite a respectable building and of recent structure, but the majority of the houses in the street were dirty, dark, tumbledown cottages, some of them shored up with huge splints of timber, the rest looking as though they would be unable to withstand the very next wind. And yet people lived in them, and compared with some hovels he had seen not a great distance away, they were veritable palaces. The summer day should have intensified in his young blood the joy of living, but as he unlocked the front door and climbed the stairs to his room, his heart was heavy and he felt unbearably sad. He sat down at the table and opened his Bible, but for once he was unable to immerse himself in the Scriptures.

He became conscious of a foul stench in the room. The single window was open at the top. He crossed over to it and looked down into the yard. Just beneath his room was the square brick garbage receptacle built against the back wall of the house. It was filled with a fortnight's rubbish, and a thin vapour, milky like steam, rose to his nostrils. Hurriedly he closed the window, but the stench had taken possession of the room and seemed to linger in every corner. Some time today the dustmen should call, but if they had collected a full load of refuse elsewhere, this suppurating, smoking mess would have to wait over the weekend, since they never worked later than six on Saturdays. The young man hoped devoutly that the dustmen would call; he did not relish the prospect of sleeping tonight and spending most of Sunday in such an atmosphere. A warm day, the first sunny day of the year, and instead of welcoming the harbinger of summer he found himself worrying about the pests and maggots that were the natural concomitant of nakedly exposed filth.

He closed the door behind him. He did not lock it, although the necessity had constantly been impressed upon him since his arrival. Mrs Perrot, his landlady, seemed an honest Christian woman, and as for the other lodgers he did not know them but he trusted them. There were so many other, more important things in life he would have to take on trust, that leaving his few items of personal property unsecured and unguarded appeared as a mere gesture of belief in humanity that did not warrant a second thought. He went out into the street again. London. He would have to stay here for five years until he got his degree and was ready for China. London, so vast, so over-whelming, so antagonistic and inhospitable. Yet the Bible said, 'Son, go work this day in My vineyard.' For him it was an express injunction, but he felt himself too insignificant to make any impression on this ungainly giant as a whole. For five years he would have to labour in these mean streets, and he determined to make this unsightly festering corner of the city his own, the East End and its inhabitants his vineyard.

The rest of the afternoon he spent wandering about the streets. He did not penetrate deep into the labyrinth of slums, but kept fairly close to the main roads. First he wanted to get an idea of the topographical situation, where the roads led to and where they came from. Those small, short-sighted eyes behind the thick lenses missed very little, they noted the preponderance of public-houses and the almost complete absence of schools. Ragged women with babies in their arms tried to sell him matches; tattered dirty men at street corners stared at him sullenly with open hostility; urchins ran beside him turning cartwheels in the gutter, hoping that the swell would toss them a copper. 'I must remember this,' thought Barnardo, 'and this, and this.' He was like an artist drawing unrelated sketches – a man leaning against a lamp-post, a sobbing woman, a group of children playing. He saw them as individuals, perfectly etched and standing alone, but later he would be able to fuse them all into the pattern of a broad canvas.

In the evening he found himself walking towards Limehouse, through the Ratcliff Highway that ran parallel to the river. Some special dispensation must have guarded him, for he passed through the dimly lit street unmolested. Every other house was a tavern, and every other tavern a brothel with a sort of dance hall at the back, where the prostitutes decoyed unsuspecting sailors. When the ships put in at the docks the first stop of the seafarers was Ratcliff Highway, and the wages of a six-months' voyage could easily be spent there in one night's carousal. And the denizens of the Highway did not stop at wages, they would remove a drunken sailor's clothes and leave him naked in the street, or, if he was stubborn, with a knife in his back. The Peelers themselves gave the Highway a wide berth after dark, but Barnardo did not know that, and if he had it would not have made any difference. In serene ignorance of his danger he walked as far as Stepney Causeway and cutting through the turning found himself in Commercial Road again.

On the opposite side of the road he saw a coffee shop. Scrawled in roughly imitated copper-plate across the facia was the name Spicer, and written in whitewash over the steaming window the invitation 'Good pull-up for car-men!' Barnardo crossed the road and stopped outside the coffee shop. Now that he was close to it the grubby and unwholesome appearance of the shop revolted him. He was as fastidious about food as about his personal appearance, and the prospect of touching anything in this unsavoury place, even a cup of tea, was nauseating. He felt half-inclined to return home, but suddenly remembering his mission he pulled himself together and entered the shop.

Lit by a single oil-lamp over the counter at the far end of the room, it appeared at first so dingy that Barnardo could discern nothing at all, neither people, nor furniture, and it was as if he had stumbled into the riverside fog. Gradually, however, his eyes grew accustomed to the gloom, and he found himself in a narrow lane between two rows of high-backed untenanted pews. He passed down the gangway and seated himself on a bench facing the counter. Like a jack-in-the-box a head and shoulders suddenly appeared before him, a moon-shaped face with an oiled coif plastered over the low forehead, and a spread of dirty brocade waistcoat with a pair of hairy arms shown off by cotton shirt-sleeves tightly rolled almost to the armpits.

'Yes, guv'nor?' said the apparition.

'Er – I'll have a cup of tea, please,' Barnardo replied.

'Wotcher want, a cup or a mug?'

'A cup will do,' said Barnardo.

'Sorry, matey, ain't got no cups in this plice. If I gave one of me coalies or car-men a cup they'd chuck it in me fice. They want their money's worth, they do – somefink ter drink, not fimbles-full like some blokes gives 'em. Kin I get yer a mug?'

'Very well then, a mug.'

'Anyfing to eat?' said Spicer cheerfully.

Barnardo thought for a moment. He was not hungry and nothing short of starvation would have driven him at this moment to touch Mr Spicer's food, but he felt it would be churlish of him not to order anything more, apart from leaving a bad impression on the proprietor, and that was the last thing he desired. He asked for bread and butter, which seemed the most innocuous dish, and a few minutes later a huge mug of steaming brown brew and a thick slice of bread smeared with a yellowish paste were on the scarred dark table before him.

'Tuppence, please,' said Spicer.

He paid out the coppers, and the stout little man waddled back to his nook behind the counter. The door opened and a tall labourer in a long derby-tweed jacket, his corduroy trousers belted below the knees, swaggered into the shop. He halted before the counter, and Barnardo watched him rummage in his pockets until he selected a thick new coin. Without a word the man tossed the penny into the empty scales on the counter and waited.

'Usual, Splodger?' said Spicer.

'Yus,' the man replied, "Less yer wanter trust me.'

'Don't trust nobody in business,' said Spicer. 'Not even me own muvver.'

'Don' blame yer,' Splodger answered with a guffaw. 'Yer own farver couldn't trust 'er.'

Spicer grinned and, half-turning, reached up for a jar of tobacco on the shelf behind him. Bringing it down with a sweep of his arm he placed it on the counter and removed the lid. His hand dipped into the coarse brown shag and dragged from it unwillingly the thick strands of tobacco, dropping it carefully on the scales until the tobacco balanced the penny. With the dark strings trembling like a parasitic growth from his suspended fingers, it seemed as though he were reluctant to part with his goods and conferring on his client a tremendous favour by serving him at all.

'Careful, old cock-sparrer,' jeered the labourer. 'Yer 'ands shakin' somefing awful. I bet yer chucked on a 'air too much fer me mouldy – Blimey! I'd like ter see yer weigh gold.'

'This baccy's more precious than gold,' said Spicer sententiously. 'Fat lot I git outer you and yer 'aporths and pennorths.'

'Course not!' Splodger returned, taking up his flimsy package. 'Yer losing money like every shopkeeper in the Commercial Road. 'Ow yer manage ter keep going at all beats me.'

'Beats me too,' Spicer answered. 'Still I gotter keep going. H'ain't nuffing else fer me to do.'

The labourer made a shallow trough in a strip of rice-paper and, tipping in some tobacco from the package, rolled it with a deft, circular movement of his thumb and forefinger. Then sealing it with a swift lick of his tongue he stuck it behind his ear, and thrusting his hands into his trousers pockets swaggered towards the door. When he reached it he turned as if he had thought of something to cap the conversation.

'Nuffing else ter do!' he said ironically. 'Yer don't want ter do nuffing else. All yer want ter do is sit in yer shop an' pison yer customers, the likes of them as is makin' yer rich!'

He pulled the peak of his deerstalker cap disdainfully over his eyes, stooped at the doorway, and disappeared. Spicer did not seem at all put out by this tirade. He carefully replaced the tobacco jar on the shelf and turned to face Barnardo again. Apparently he thought some explanation was necessary.

'Drunk,' he said.

'Eh?' Barnardo looked up.

'Drunk. Drunk as a lord.'

'Who? That man? I confess I could not notice it.'

'Course yer couldn't,' said Spicer. ''E's always drunk. Yer'd notice it soon enough if 'e wasn't. Makin' me rich, 'e is, wiv 'is pennorths of baccy an' corfee and bloaters fer dinner every day. Rich! And me 'aving ter stand on me pore feet from five in the morning till eleven at night.'

'Every day?'

'Course every day. People's gotter eat and 'ave their baccy, ain't they?'

'I suppose they have,' said Barnardo.

He was learning rapidly. Men bought pennyworths of tobacco and had coffee and bloaters for lunch, and were more often drunk than sober. And even the shopkeepers, a higher caste, had to work eighteen hours a day. These were just two of the millions on the fringe; what suffering and tragedies he would unearth as he probed further he could not guess. The ungainly giant seemed magnified already to the size of a colossus, and he himself futilely hammering against it, a maggot on the nail of a graven toe.

'Yer a stranger in these parts, ain't yer, guv'nor?'

'Eh?' said Barnardo. Engrossed in his thoughts he had not noticed Spicer lean his elbows on the counter in the attitude of the born gossip. 'Pardon me, I did not hear you.'

'Stranger 'ere, ain't yer?'

'Yes indeed,' he replied. 'How did you know?'

'Easy,' said Spicer. 'By yer clobber. Anyone kin tell yer a gent. Do yer come from the West End?'

'Oh dear no! I live here in Stepney. But I've only been in London three weeks. I come from Dublin.'

'Do yer really!' Spicer's face broke into a delighted grin. 'I'm from Dublin meself. Born in Marrerbone Lane. But I was took over when I was a kid, so I'm as yer might say three parts Cockney. Wot brings yer dahn 'ere, though? Come ter see the old moke give away?'

'I don't understand,' said Barnardo. 'What moke?'

'It's like this 'ere,' Spicer explained patiently. 'There used ter be a market in Three Colt Street, fer years an' years as fer back as I kin remember. And the costers did a pretty bit o' trading too. On a Sattirdy night the crowds was so thick yer couldn't shoot a pea through 'em. Well, the shopkeepers fancied the barrer-men was taking all their trade away, so they got their pals on the vestry board ter 'ave 'em shifted to another street. First there was a bit er trouble, fights with the coppers an' sichlike, but arterwards the costers 'ad to go and what 'appened was the public went wiv 'em. Then the old codgers of shopkeepers came round crying ter 'ave 'em back, and naow they're giving away a donkey and cart to the barrerman with the best stall. As if that's going ter 'elp 'em. It's too late. The public's like a flighty 'ussy. Before, you couldn't keep 'em outer Three Colt Street, now yer can't get 'em to go there. That's why they're giving the moke away free. They ruined the market, naow they're trying to work it up agin, but one donkey ain't enough fer that. They need thousands ter give ter customers fer nuffing.'

'That sounds interesting, anyhow,' the young man said. 'Three Colt Street, is it?'

'Yus. That's right.'

'How do I get there?'

'Easy enough,' Spicer answered. 'Jest walk ter the next turning, then foller the crowd.'

Barnardo rose to his feet. 'Thanks,' he said.

'Don't mention it, guv'nor,' said Spicer jovially.

Barnardo walked to the door, but before he could leave Spicer called to him again. He turned, gazing towards the coffee-shop proprietor who, with his bare arms resting on the counter and his podgy face set off by the tuft of hair on top, looked like the upper half of a grinning Buddha bathed in a cloud of incense.

'Anuvver fing, guv,' he said. 'I'll give yer a tip. When yer go dahn the market keep yer 'ands in yer pockets.'

'Thank you,' said Barnardo. 'I will indeed. I will.'

CHAPTER 2

The young man walked to the corner of the next street, and as he turned left found himself amongst a stream of people all going in the same direction, towards the market. It was strange and significant that the most constant enjoinders he had received since his settling in this part of London were warnings against robbery in one form or another. At home he was to have his door locked, here to keep his hands in his pockets. It was as if the level of income determined morality as well as respectability; above a certain limit of earnings people were honest and could be trusted, below that line of demarcation were to be found only thieves and rogues. That such a state of affairs was common in the East End, he found it difficult to believe, yet Spicer's words had borne the imprint of truth, and as the shrill distant cries of vendors from the market reached his ears, he imagined himself to be in the position of a merchant from Jerusalem venturing unprotected through Samaria.

The moment he reached the market it seemed as though he had stepped into another world. The grey drabness of the gloomy street through which he has passed erupted into a riot of light and colour and an unceasing babble of tongues. In a side-turning he detected a patent Aunt Sally and a moveable shooting gallery, and perched on the back of a stationary dogcart a florid gentleman dressed in loud, flashy clothes selling priceless racing tips in sealed envelopes. The fumes from the smoky paraffin flares penetrated his lungs and seemed to spread rasping bubbles in his throat, while the sudden glare of the lights hammered at his head until he felt sick and faint. He felt himself tottering and would have fallen but for a strong arm that curled itself protectingly round his shoulders.

'Steady on, guv,' said a familiar voice.

Barnardo looked up and recognized the lean form of Splodger stooping over him. The labourer opened his mouth with a reassuring grin, and a gust of stale beer and tobacco fumes seemed to envelop Barnardo so that he felt like retching again.

'You . . . you've been drinking!' Barnardo said weakly.

'That's right!' Splodger answered ironically. 'I bin drinking, an' you're drunk!'

The young man straightened himself and shook the other's arm from his shoulders.

'Thank you,' he said. 'I feel much better now.'

''At's old Spicer's grub, 'at is,' Splodger returned irrepressibly.

'I didn't eat anything – the noise – the flares . . .'

He passed his hand across his forehead, and made as if to move away, but again Splodger's strong arm clamped round the top of his back.

'Oh, no yer don't,' said Splodger. 'Yer look as if yer gonna spew yer guts aout, yer face is green – 'at's number one. Number two, it ain't safe fer a toff ter show 'is mug rahnd 'ere arter dark, 'specially in the market – Wotcher doing dahn 'ere, anyways. Come ter see 'ow the other 'arf lives?'

'I . . . I've heard about the donkey,' said Barnardo.

'The donkey, eh! Well they're all a proper parcel of mokes rahnd 'ere. It's the blooming shopkeepers wot's done it, they ruined the market, Spicer's pals – Be somefing ter see if they 'itched their fat bellies ter the barrers instead.'

'You don't seem to like the shopkeepers,' Barnardo remarked.

'No one does,' said Splodger. 'Some on 'em ain't bad, but the rest finks 'emselves too 'igh an' mighty fer the likes of us working coves. All men was born free and equal I says, an' I don't see why some 'as to give 'emselves airs more'n uvvers.'

'Quite right,' Barnardo replied. 'All men are brothers.'

Splodger nodded. ''At's it, matey. 'At's wot I says – 'at's wot I says.'

They took a few paces down the market. Splodger seemed quite an intelligent man, and Barnardo was now more pleased than otherwise at this encounter. True, the labourer stank of liquor, his face and hands were thick with grime, and his clothes stiff with beer stains and accumulated dirt, but he was the native in his native haunt, and as such one of the keys to this monstrous warped puzzle of the East End. It was obvious to the young man that he could not talk down to Splodger, even if he would have desired to do so, for there was a sturdy air of independence about the labourer in spite of his shabby clothes and the hint of liquor in his flushed cheeks.

'Tell me,' said Barnardo, 'why should it be unsafe for me to walk down here alone, if as you say all men are brothers?'

Splodger grinned. 'I fink so, an' you fink so, but there's uvvers as don't. You see, they ain't got nuffink, no money, no decent clobber, no sort of 'omes, and when they meets someone wot's got all those, they picks on 'em ter git some of their own back orf the swells.'

'But surely it isn't the fault of the "Swells" that they're so poor?'

'No?' said Splodger. 'Then 'oos fault is it?'

Barnardo did not answer. On the surface the question seemed quite simple, but posed in this manner, to reply was not so ridiculously easy. Whose fault *was* it? That was one of the things he had never troubled to think about seriously. Another of the shortcomings that he would have to remedy if his work in this wasted vineyard were to bear fruit. But one thing was wrong about Splodger, on his own confession he drank too much, surely there could be no excuse for that.

'And drinking?' Barnardo inquired. 'Is that our fault too?'

'It is, an' it ain't,' said Splodger. ''Ave you ever worked dahn a coal-'ole?' he asked, rather irrelevantly, Barnardo thought.

'I can't say I have,' the young man replied.

'Well, you oughter try it one day, matey. If the lights an' smells dahn 'ere makes yer sick, a couple 'er 'ours shovelling coal would kill yer, an' if yer 'ad ter spend fifteen 'ours a day wiv the dust getting' in yer froat an' chokin' yer lungs so's yer can't breave, yer'd fetch a gallon of beer wiv yer, soon enough.'

'But surely there's something else you could drink?'

'Is there?' said Splodger. 'Tell me wot?'

Again Barnardo lapsed into silence. These questions seemed a long way removed from Jesus and the Chinese, which were his chief interests in life, but he knew he would have to find the answers before he was qualified to approach these people on a basis of common understanding in order to lead them to God. The only way he would be able to do that was to enter more fully into their lives, and this he determined to embark upon without any further delay.

He began to take an interest in the double row of stalls that lined the gutters on either side of the road. Most of them were push-carts propped up with empty packing cases. Usually, they were a drab enough sight, but tonight there was something festive about even the meanest of them. Coloured paper camouflaged the fronts of the packing cases, and the uprights of those stalls that boasted a tarpaulin roof were entwined with streamers. The tripe stall that sold offal not fit for dogs to housewives at 3d a pound, was gaily bedecked with strings of sausages painted red, white and blue, and all except the most impoverished stall-holders were in their flashiest costumes – pearly kings, women with enormous boa-mounted hats, the more sedate costers resplendent in quilted tail-coats and beaver top-hats that had last been aired at the coronation of Queen Victoria. There was the most heterogeneous collection of goods on display – linen sheetings, rolls of American cloth, old clothes for renovating, boots seemingly in the last stages of decay, that even so would find buyers to 'translate' them, damaged oil-lamps, chipped ornaments, mildewed locks, hinges and door-handles. And side by side with these heaped-up, rusty, worm-eaten relics were stalls with edibles, fish, meat, vegetables and fruit, the costers jostling cheek by jowl as incongruously as their goods, the butchers, fat, well-fed, bull-necked, rubbing elbows with half-starved, itinerant gutter-scavengers, scarecrows of men that scraped an existence from the cast-off rubbish of wretches only a few shillings removed from the gutter themselves.

Splodger was the complete cicerone, and before the astonished eyes of Barnardo a section of society exposed itself to view, as different in its habits and outlook from the young man's middle-class *milieu* as he was himself from the shiftless bloods of the nobility. Yet there were sub-strata of castes in this section of slum-life, too, among the customers as well as the stall-holders. Splodger pointed out coalies, men of his own calling, easily recognizable by the inlaid seams of dust on their faces, and the sparkles of coal splinters that caught the light on their clothes. Dock labourers, stevedores, pilots, shipwrights – the latter amongst the aristocrats of the riverside, who had their private bars in public-houses, and their own festival day once a year, when they carried the wooden effigy of a ship in procession along the Mile End Road to their favourite tavern at Bow.

He poked his thumb towards two women outstanding in the neatness of their clothes from the beshawled harridans of the market, sailing down the narrow street with the swish of carefully starched petticoats and the glint of red silk stockings, like a couple of admiral's barges nosing through a lane of coastal tramps. Shipwright's wives, Queens of the waterfront, bringing their opulence and sense of superiority into the most mundane things of everyday life, golden guineas omnipresent in their purses and put to such uses as chipping off tiny pats of butter from the slabs at the grocer's for their Royal Highnesses to taste before purchasing.

Suddenly, towards the upper end of the market, a crowd began to gather opposite the steps of the old church. The stalls became denuded of their owners, and in a body the costers moved towards the church. Splodger and his companion were carried along by the crowd, and the young man, handicapped by his short stature, became pressed like a small boy in a throng of adults, against a moving wall of backs, until it came to a swaying halt that gave him a glimpse of enormous coloured feathers waving over the heads of the costers. Again Splodger came to the rescue. Barnardo found himself being drawn to the side of the road until he was rubbing against a hardware stall. The labourer bent down and unearthed an empty box. Straightening himself, he shifted it into position with his foot, and pinning the young man's arms to his sides lifted him bodily on to the wooden perch.

From his new vantage point, Barnardo was able to discern the prize, the cause of all the excitement, a sleek brown donkey attached to a cart, drawn up against the steps. The crowd surged all round it, but the donkey remained aloof and disinterested and slightly superior, as if it realized that it was the centre of attention and far removed in station from these other undignified, clamorous animals. The box seemed to sag beneath the young man's weight, and appeared to tilt at one end. To preserve his balance he rested his fingertips on the pearl-studded shoulders of the coster in front and shifted his feet so that his weight was more evenly distributed. The coster did not even look round. He was staring at the donkey and cart. A fine moke! A grand little carriage. He and the missus wouldn't half cut a dash in a spanking contraption like that!

A narrow lane formed in the crowd, and a smiling negro passed down it and mounted the steps. As soon as the upper part of his body became visible to the mass of costers, a burst of huzzas and shrill, piercing whistles greeted him. The negro waited for the clamour to subside, still with the smile on his face, like a favoured music-hall performer holding the stage before an indulgent and adoring audience. Barnardo half-turned towards Splodger.

'Who's that?' he asked.

'Doncher know '*im*?' The incredulous expression on the labourer's face showed the extent of the young man's ignorance; he shrugged his shoulders like a parent humouring a backward child and spoke in a voice tinged with affection and pride – ''At's the Black Doctor, 'at is,' he said.

CHAPTER 3

The negro was a tall man, his magnificent torso seeming to swell from beneath the tight lines of his outer garments, the silk-faced frock-coat and yellow waistcoat embossed with golden dandelions. Such a man, stripped, thought Barnardo, would have the figure of an ancient god, and to him it seemed almost blasphemy to girdle this physique with misshapen modern clothes. There was something of a military bearing in his carriage, indeed it was rumoured in the neighbourhood that the negro had once held high rank in Her Majesty's army, but the truth of that, like most else about the origin of the Black Doctor, was shrouded in mystery. Several things about the negro, however, were no mystery, and those his prowess as a healer and his reputation for honesty and fairness. The ten years he had spent in this East End slum had endeared him even to the roughest characters amongst the inhabitants; he had become one of them, a neighbour and a friend as though born within the sound of Bow Bells. For that reason he had been elected to adjudicate the winner, since any other person's choice must have ended eventually in a riot, but with the Black Doctor as judge, the costers knew the decision would be a just one, and without rancour all would abide by it.

The negro raised his hands for silence, and Barnardo noticed the curved palms incongruously pale against the blackness of his face and the deeper black of his coat.

'Mah friends,' he said . . . 'Mah friends' . . .

He waited again until the faintest whispers died down. His deep voice was soft but penetrating, and rolled musically with a slight foreign intonation. Just the sort of voice for such a man. A subdued throbbing bass, pregnant with strength and, it seemed to Barnardo, an inherent gentleness like the superhuman goodness, almost saintliness that glowed in his face.

'Mah friends. You have honoured mah person by asking me to adjudicate in this contest. When Ah walked through Three Colt Street, Ah could hardly recognize it, and Ah have passed through it many times a day for more years then Ah like to remembah . . . Ah wish Ah could always see it like this. Alive with brightness and colour. There's too little of that in our lives, mah friends, far too little. Now there's the question of the donkey and cart. It has been the hardest task of mah life to decide. Ah would like to give a donkey and cart to every one of you – you all deserve it – but as Ah must choose Ah name as the winners – Jim and Ethel Moody!'

After a split second's silence a roar of approbation rose in the air, and above the heads of the crowd a man and woman were rapidly passed by brawny arms till they landed beside the negro on the steps. Jim Moody's face was flushed and his hat askew over his ears, and in one hand he flourished a beer bottle, having apparently been celebrating his success in advance. He was a skinny little man, dressed in the tightly fitting black clothes of a pearly king, shining with a thousand milky buttons. His wife, bedecked in all her feathers and finery, blew a handful of kisses to the crowd and executed a little jig in the few inches of space on the steps, then she flung her arms round the negro's neck, and to the delight of the spectators planted a spanking kiss on each cheek. The Black Doctor did not lose his poise for an instant. Courteously he took Ethel Moody's hand and helped her into the open carriage. Her husband proudly seated himself beside her, and, grasping the reins with one hand, waved the beer bottle over his head with the other in response to the ovation of the crowd. He clicked his tongue between his teeth and tugged at the reins, but the donkey twitched its ears lazily and remained sublimely indifferent. At once half a dozen Cockneys put their shoulders behind the cart and, finding itself propelled along, the donkey slyly glanced back and commenced the procession with a leisurely walk. One of the costers had taken possession of the gaily feathered whip that went with the prize; twirling it in his hands like a drum-major's baton he went before the donkey, and laughing and singing and yelling at the top of their voices, the hilarious crowd followed.

Barnardo found himself high and dry on top of the wooden box. Even Splodger had deserted him, following behind the triumphant procession. The negro watched the costers with a good-humoured grin, then descended the steps. At once Barnardo jumped from his perch, and as the Black Doctor stepped into the gutter the young man accosted him.

'Excuse me, sir,' said Barnardo.

'Excuse you? – Why?' asked the negro.

'I mean . . . Well . . . That is to say – After all, I'm talking to you, and I don't know you.'

The Black Doctor smiled.

'That's easily remedied, mah young friend,' he said. 'Mah name is Jonathan Haddock. Born somewhere on the continent of Africa. MD. Graduate of Edinburgh University.'

'I'm Tom Barnardo. Student at London Hospital.'

The Black Doctor clasped his hands. 'Ah hope you feel more comfortable,' he said, 'now etiquette has been satisfied. But surely you don't have to know a man's name or have him know yours before you talk to him? . . .'

'It does seem rather silly . . .' Barnardo admitted.

'It is. The way you've been brought up, mah friend . . . so you're a new worshipper at the shrine of Æsculapius . . . Difficult, mah friend, difficult for a conscientious devotee . . . But tell me, what are you doing here?'

Barnardo felt himself flushing. Again that same barrier cropping up, as though he were an interloper. He knew Splodger felt it, that was natural to him, yet this man, obviously from his speech a comparative newcomer, and not even the same colour as himself or the people he lived amongst, regarded him as a stranger from another world, one who had no business in these parts.

'I live in Stepney,' said Barnardo. 'I shall be living here for five years, and while I *am* here I want to get to know these people and help them.'

'A most laudable ambition.' The Black Doctor shook his head gravely. 'And after those five years?' he asked.

'Then I go to China, to work amongst the heathen.'

'But are there no heathen closer than China? These same men and women in Three Colt Street, for example, do they not need us as much as the Chinese?'

'You misunderstand me, sir,' said Barnardo. 'I am going to China not primarily as a doctor, but as a missionary to spread the word and light of God in dark places.'

'Hum! Mah friend, when you get to know these parts better, you will find no lack of dark places. Surely there is room for God there too? When Ah first graduated, Ah wanted to go back to Africa to work amongst mah own people, then Ah came here, and here Ah have stayed. Now these are mah people. In Africa they have the sun, here they have nothing – nothing at all except disease and poverty, mah friend.'

The negro lifted up his head, dilating his broad nostrils.

'Smell, mah friend, can you smell?'

They had passed across Three Colt Street, and were walking down one of the narrow dark turnings leading away from Commercial Road. Barnardo stopped and, intrigued by the suddenness of this strange question, sniffed at the air. Beyond an elusive faint stench he could smell nothing to differentiate this street from any of the others through which he had passed. He had grown accustomed to the peculiar smell of London streets, and had come to associate it with London itself. When he had first arrived the atmosphere had seemed unbearably foul, but he had become inured to it, and since then an incipient form of catarrh had partly blocked his nose, and temporarily robbed him of the faculty for detecting any but the most noxious odours. He shook his head.

'I am sorry,' he replied. 'Since I came to town I seem to have lost all the finer gradations of smell. The whole of East London seems to smell the same to me.'

'That may be so,' said the Black Doctor. 'It smells the same to most people. But Ah was born in Africa. Mah ancestors lived on the fringe of the desert, and Ah have inherited their olfactory organs. You see these nostrils, broad and hairy inside, there's a reason for them, mah friend; nature rarely works in the dark in these things. In a desert storm that would smother most white men Ah would be able to breathe with ease because mah nostrils would act as a sort of filter for the fine particles of sand. Here in London there are no sandstorms, but Ah have retained mah sense of smell. And do you know what Ah can smell, mah friend, you'll never guess – it's cholera!'

'Cholera! But how?'

'You're right. No person can smell the plague, but Ah can smell the rubbish that is accumulating in people's yards, and sure as fate, as soon as the sun starts blazing in the summer heat there will be an epidemic – or mah name's not Jonathan Haddock.'

At once the open brick rubbish container in the backyard of the house in which he lived jumped to the young man's mind. Truly, as the doctor hinted, such depositories were the ideal breeding places for festering germs. But cholera seemed too drastic a conclusion to deduce from the presence of accumulated rubbish and the action of the sun's heat; the negro, surely, must have collected some additional data to account for the conclusiveness of his speech.

'You seem very positive,' said Barnardo.

'Ah am, mah friend. Ah am. There have already been several cases amongst mah patients. Ah know cholera when Ah see it. Ah have met it before. High fever, nausea, vomiting, the skin drying up through water absorbed from the tissues, a tendency for blood to clot, and in advanced cases, relapsing into a state of coma. Those are the symptoms, mah friend, and they are unmistakable. Already three of mah patients have died. Three. That is only the beginning. You saw those laughing crowds down Three Colt Street – well, before we are a great deal older, a good many of those will be unable to laugh any more.'

'But why isn't something done?' the young man asked.

'Why! Why!' the doctor exclaimed. 'Why! I'll tell you why, because this borough is rotten with corruption. Because the vestry board is packed with nominees of the rich shop-keepers and factory owners. They were elected to look after the interests of the public, but all they are interested in are their own pockets. Ah have reported the cases of cholera, they have laughed at me. Ah have told them what should be done – they have reviled me as an interfering black busybody. Soon they will have reason to curse their own shortsightedness; the plague is no respecter of persons or fat bellies – and wherever they hide in London it will reach them. The cholera will start here in the slums, but like a fire it will sweep through the city and the West End right to their very doorsteps.'

The smouldering indignation of the doctor that had erupted in his bitter words seemed to die down reluctantly, only to live on in his face with a sort of hopeless, silent resentment. As the young man walked beside him through the dark, narrow street, the misshapen little houses appeared to rear over them like lines of crooked tombstones. Barnardo was bewildered by the torrent of accusation that had been loosed before him. This compact, geographical East End that he had set out to understand so determinedly was swelling into an Albrecht Dürer underworld where every step was burdened with diabolically fantastic implications.

'You mean, they're neglecting even the most elementary precautions?'

'That's just what Ah do mean,' said the Black Doctor. 'The refuse should be cleared, if not every day, at least once a week, whereas now we are lucky to have it shifted once in three weeks. Do you know why that is, mah friend? Because that duty is farmed out to private contractors, and those not the most efficient ones, but the contractors who give the biggest bribe to the gentlemen on the vestry board.'

'But the doctors. They could certainly make an effective joint protest?'

'Even the doctors are divided amongst themselves,' answered the negro. 'Some of them laugh at the idea of dirt, lack of air, and bad sanitation precipitating a plague, others would almost welcome one for the clients it would bring. Prejudice, mah friend, dies hard in every profession. Why, even when Ah was a student at Edinburgh, the lecturer had only to say "Close the door, gentlemen, before one of Mr Lister's germs comes in" to raise a certain laugh. Doctors laughing at the giant Lister! And you wonder why they pay no attention to a poor negro descended from African savages.'

'And the Church?' Barnardo asked. 'Surely the clergy are not so blind?'

'None so blind as those who will not see,' Haddock returned sombrely. 'Twenty years ago honest, pious churchmen opposed the introduction of anaesthetics on the grounds that the abolition of pain by man interfered with the prerogative of God . . . No, there is no help, excepting perhaps from the people themselves, and they are too ignorant and too obsessed by the struggle for food and shelter to pay any attention to new-fangled notions like health and hygiene. If they have any time or money to spare it goes on drink – and alcohol lowers the resistance to disease. Poverty – drink – disease. It is a vicious circle, mah friend, that Ah am very much afraid will, before very long, turn this part of London into a gigantic charnel house.'

The negro sighed and shook his head. He seemed like an ancient prophet, his shoulders weighted with the tribulations of a whole people. Barnardo was deeply impressed, it was impossible to be otherwise when confronted with this burning sincerity, but he still felt somehow that the negro was exaggerating the state of affairs. Unwittingly, perhaps, but nevertheless exaggerating, and more important still, leaving out the dominant factor – God. To the young man this was a most significant omission, for the Lord surely would not countenance such a holocaust. The Lord was just and merciful, unless in His wider justice and mercy He would blot out the undeserving among these people as He had punished the sins of Sodom and Gomorrah. The Black Doctor stopped at the corner of a street, where three other narrow roads converged to form a scrubby little triangular island of pavement in between. Opposite the apex of the triangle stood a large public-house, brightly illuminated like a sentinel of light and merriment amidst the grim darkness of the squat irregular lines of cottages that surrounded it. Snatches of laughter and song burst from the tavern as if the volume of joy and high spirits engendered there was too great to be compressed within its walls. A few knots of swaying men stood beneath the lighted windows and people dribbled out to join them like a trickle of water from a cup that is over-full, only to be replaced by lurching shadows that hugged the walls until the brightness of the entrance engulfed them.

'Is it always so busy here?' asked the young man innocently.

'Always,' said the Black Doctor. 'Every evening it is crammed to the doors. And on Sunday afternoons a German band comes here to this triangle and serenades the tipplers.'

'It shouldn't be allowed!' Barnardo exclaimed indignantly. 'Even on the Lord's day! Desecrating the Sabbath!'

The negro took the young man gently by the arm and led him across the road to the opposite pavement.

'Don't be too hard on these people,' he said. 'The tavern is part of their lives. For the workman it is a sort of club, almost the only place of social interaction available to him, the one spot where he can enjoy a laugh with his mates and forget the dreary round of his days. Like most young people, you jump to extremes too quickly. The public-house is not entirely bad; almost the only thing Ah have against it is the beer. Taken in moderation beer can be a tonic, at least it makes life bearable for a while, but when the publican takes what should go to the butcher and the grocer . . .'

'The undertaker steps in soon enough to complete the process.'

The Black Doctor nodded. Barnardo had followed the trend of his thoughts and aptly completed the sentence he had left intentionally unfinished. He led the young man to a corner house a little larger than its neighbours, the shutter of the windows reaching almost to the ground, as if they covered the frontage of a shop.

'This is mah surgery,' he said.

Before the negro could knock at the door, it opened and a stubby figure appeared in the doorway. He was of medium height, and sturdy build, with extraordinarily long arms, and a face that in the darkness defied any attempt to pin an exact age on it possessor. A shock of matted hair fell over a low brow, he had wide-set eyes, a small childish nose and thin lips.

'Glad yer've come, guv'nor,' said the apparition.

'Why, what is it, Ernest?' asked the doctor.

'Number 16 Marchant,' said Ernest. 'They sent for you. Fink she's a gonner.'

'Sixteen . . . Sixteen . . .' The doctor seemed to be trying to place the name of the patient; then, as if he had suddenly remembered it, his voice assumed a tone of urgency.

'Fetch Rachel out at once,' he said.

Ernest tipped his forefinger to his head and stepped on to the pavement. Now that he was close to Barnardo his age was still problematical, and might have been anything from twenty-five to fifty. He gave the young man an inquisitive stare, and turning on his heels shuffled round the corner with a peculiar slouching gait, his long hands brushing against his knees like a captive gorilla.

'Mah factotum, Ernest,' said the Black Doctor. 'A worthy fellow.' He gave one or two impatient strides along the pavement. 'Ah wanted to invite you to mah house, but there is an urgent case I must attend . . . Another one.'

'Not cholera?' asked Barnardo.

'Afraid so. Ah have done all Ah could. Injected pints of normal saline – but the woman had not the ghost of a chance from the very first moment of contracting the disease. Cholera and malnutrition. A deadly combination, and more than a match for anything the modern miracles of science can devise.'

At that moment came the sound of a horse's hooves and round the corner Ernest appeared, leading a huge dappled grey mare by the halter. The horse whinnied with delight as she saw the negro and thrust her nose playfully beneath his armpits. The Black Doctor, giving ground before her forceful approach, fondly stroked her outstretched head, while Ernest rapidly tightened the saddle straps and attached a big carpet bag to the pommel.

'Ready, guv,' said Ernest, shambling away from the restive horse.

The negro thrust one foot in the stirrups and vaulted lightly on to the horse's back. Rachel reared exuberantly at the feel of her master, but the doctor sat up gracefully and, holding the reins tightly with one hand, patted her head soothingly with the other. When the horse's excitement had subsided, the Black Doctor turned to Barnardo, and Rachel stood immobile as if she were listening and approving, with an occasional whisk of her beautiful head.

'Ah have to go now,' the negro said. 'But Ernest will escort you to Commercial Road.'

'There really is no need for that,' Barnardo replied. 'I know the way.'

'The side-streets are dark, and drunken men are dangerous,'

said Haddock. 'With Ernest by your side no one will dare molest you.'

He slapped the horse smartly on the haunches. Again it gave a turbulent rear, then set off at a brisk canter down the street, its iron hooves striking sparks of light and a rumbling cannonade of sound from the flinty cobbles. Near the corner, the negro turned in the saddle without slackening his pace, and waved to Barnardo. The young man returned his salute, and with a last glimpse of flying coat-tails the doctor vanished on his hopeless errand.

Barnardo turned to the servant.

'Are you coming?' he asked.

Ernest looked intently at the student, and from the contemptuously mocking expression on that ageless face it seemed as though the 'young swell' did not meet with his entire approval. He shrugged his shoulders, as if the doctor's affairs were no business of his, but duty was duty, however trivial or unpleasant. Shuffling on to the pavement he pulled-to the door of the surgery, then he looked again at Barnardo, and clearing his throat spat expostulatorily on the pavement.

'Foller me,' he said, with a wry gesture of resignation.

Half a pace ahead of Barnardo, Ernest crossed the road to the apex of the triangle. Following the shuffling, ape-like figure, the young man walked mechanically, his mind coursing round the bizarre events of the past few hours, and trying to strike a tentative evaluation. He found that the bewilderment had worn off and given place to a series of clear-cut impressions, and it seemed to him that he was a stranger here no longer. He felt drawn to these slum-dwellers, and he would make them accept him, in spite of his fashionable clothes, as they had accepted the Black Doctor, and made him one of their own. But above all, within their acceptance, he would still remain Tom Barnardo, the student of medicine, the servant of God, incorruptible by man or Devil, even in these outposts of the Black Kingdom itself.

CHAPTER 4

It was an early summer. An exceptionally hot May blazed into a scorching June, but in the East End of London the inhabitants cursed the heat and cursed the sun. At first the dread name had been whispered furtively, but now Cholera was shouted from the housetops; it was no longer a secret since every street had its own tokens of death nailed across the shutters. After dark and in the early hours of the morning, the death-carts rumbled in the streets like tumbrils dragging doomed aristocrats to the guillotine, only these carts bore no aristocrats, neither had the silent, wasted bodies any fear of execution. Cholera . . . Cholera . . . The Black Doctor had predicted it and at least one of these vestrymen that had laughed at Haddock was himself on the way to the cemetery. The vestry board was alarmed and waited for the Black Doctor to come to them again; but he did not come, so they came to him; and now he laughed at them bitterly, for he could not tell them how to assuage the plague that, but for their cupidity, might have been prevented altogether, or at least kept within bounds . . . Cholera . . . Men dropped dead in the streets, women babbled incoherently with fever, clasping babies in their arms, and children sank into stupors with parchment-like faces, the moisture sucked from their delicate skins as if vampires had left them like wizened little mummies . . . Cholera . . . Cholera . . .

At the hospital the lectures were temporarily discontinued. There was so much pressure of work in the wards and amongst the outpatients that most of the students volunteered to help in the hospital until the epidemic had abated. A few, of course, went home into the country, and one or two welcomed the excuse for prolonged visits to the West End gaming-houses. Barnardo spent several weeks in the hospital, but all the time felt somehow vaguely dissatisfied. When the patients came in they assumed an anonymity, they were no longer men and women, but numbered beds, and though he was doing useful work, the young man felt unfulfilled. Even in this epidemic his mother's old Quaker obstinacy pricked at the student. He was doing good work here, but he was sure he could do better at the other end of Stepney with the Black Doctor, where he could meet his patients as man to man, without a number to cover up the grisly background of each individual tragedy. The people would get to know him and respect him, and perhaps he would be able to win some of them for God, even if his own life were forfeit in the houses of the plague.

Already, according to semi-official reports in the columns of the staid *Thunderer*, the victims numbered close on six thousand, to which the district east of Aldgate contributed no less than two-thirds of the fatalities. Four thousand human lives forfeit in that comparatively small segment of London, where the young student lived and worked. In one week, sixty-seven out of a hundred and twenty-four patients admitted to the hospital died, and in one afternoon Barnardo counted thirty bodies in the dead-room waiting for men to be found to bury them. Apart from those cases the cholera wards could accommodate, nearly five thousand people had visited the hospital as outpatients from the commencement of the outbreak, and still they came, tottering and half-dazed, like drug addicts, a never-ending stream of fever-racked bodies.

Most piteous sights of all were the children. It hurt the young man to watch the agonies of the adults, but the spectacle of the sufferings of the infants and toddlers made him weak, and drove him close to the verge of a breakdown himself. Grown men and women had perhaps had an opportunity to get something out of life, but the scores of innocent babies whose vitality he watched flickering out feebly, like dwindling fires, excited his compassion almost to the exclusion of any pity for the adults.

A man can stand just so much and no more, either as a sufferer or as an observer of suffering, and Barnardo had reached that pitch where his sensitiveness to the spectacle of adult distress had become numbed, yet the sight of a groaning child never failed to evoke his deepest sympathy and a sense of baffled rebellious helplessness. To sustain himself in the knowledge that a beneficent power still ruled over the world, he had constantly to return at home to the solace of the Bible, and when he walked through the wards where the seemingly insensate agony was spread before him, he had to fortify his spirit with his favourite hymns –

> 'I *do* believe, I *will* believe
> That Jesus died for me.
> That on the cross He gave His blood
> From sin to set me free.'

On a Saturday afternoon during a rest period he suddenly made up his mind to offer his services to the Black Doctor. Leaving the hospital, he cut through a back turning to Sidney Street, and from there walked down to the Commercial Road. The sun, mocking the season of growth and fertility, blazed down on acres of sweltering streets where even the voices of children were subdued, and where men and women shunned their neighbours in the fear of contracting the rampant illness that struck so suddenly and with such devastating effect.

Although he did not know the name of the street, he reached the triangle without difficulty, and located the doctor's surgery at once. The shutters were still drawn over the front of the house, and the heavy door was shut. Barnardo knocked timidly and waited. In a few moments a grille opened above the knocker and a pair of small watery blue eyes peered out. Without a word from the person behind the door the grille closed again. The student had recognized Ernest's hostile expression even from the small portion of his face that had been visible, and wondered why the doctor's factotum took so long to admit him. He heard the heavy lumbering tread move away from the door and after a brief interval approach again, and hands fumbling at the lock. When the door opened, Ernest stepped aside to allow Barnardo to enter, then securely bolted the massive door behind him. Looking at the young man with ill-concealed distrust, Ernest pointed a finger down the narrow dark passage.

'Straight froo,' he said.

'Thank you,' Barnardo answered politely.

His friendly smile found no welcoming response on the dull face of the doctor's shabby servant, so he turned his back on Ernest, and blinking a little in the sudden darkness of the passage made his way towards the block of light that showed an open door at the other end. Passing through, he found himself in the tiny kitchen which Haddock had rigged up as a dispensary. The doctor himself, in his shirt-sleeves, was pounding some gritty mixture in a mortar, but as soon as he saw Barnardo he laid his work aside to greet him, and motioned Ernest, who had followed immediately behind, to take his place at the table.

'Ah am sorry you were kept waiting, mah friend,' the negro apologized. 'The fact is, Ah have been so overworked, Ah have had to close up the surgery to keep out the patients. For two days and two nights Ah have not slept, and Ah cannot afford to be ill mahself, not for half a day – there are too many dependent on me.'

He sank down on to an easy chair, his long athletic body stooped beneath the strain the unremitting labours of the past few weeks had imposed upon him. His eyes were bloodshot, and there was a grey stubble on his cheeks and his jutting chin. As he sat he involuntarily leaned forward and closed his eyes. For a moment his head drooped, but he quickly recovered himself, and sat upright, his eyes opened, and his mouth twisted into a tired smile.

'Pardon me,' he said.

'That's quite all right,' Barnardo answered. 'You should get some sleep – at once!'

'There's no time for sleep,' Haddock said. 'Ah have to start rounds in half an hour.'

'Then you must rest for that period,' Barnardo insisted. 'You know you are indispensable, at least give your body a chance.'

The tired smile flickered again across the doctor's unshaven face. He spread his arms in an apologetic gesture.

'Ah am a bad host – but you always seem to visit me at such inopportune moments.'

'Never mind,' said Barnardo. 'I am not in a hurry this time. I have come to help you in whatever capacity I can.'

'But your work at the hospital –' Haddock protested.

'The hospital is full – and they have sufficient helpers. I am sure I could be of more use to you – that is, if you want me.'

'Of course Ah want you,' said Haddock, trying to force some of the gratefulness he felt into his voice. 'Ah need someone like you very badly indeed, but –'

'There are no buts about it,' Barnardo interrupted forcefully. '*J'y suis. J'y reste.*'

'Thank you,' said Haddock simply.

The negro tried to rise, but the young student pushed him gently back into the chair. From the other chair in the corner he took a cushion and placed it behind the negro's head, then he shifted up a stool and sat on it, facing Haddock with an expression of mock gravity.

'Now sleep!' he said severely. 'I shall wake you in exactly half an hour.'

With a sigh of contentment, the Black Doctor nestled back in the chair, and closed the heavy, scorching lids of his eyes. Ernest, with a practised hand, softly handled the pestle till he judged the mixture to be sufficiently fine, then, completely ignoring the student, he tiptoed with surprising gentleness out of the kitchen, bent on some unknown duty about the house. Barnardo watched the golden dandelion pattern on the negro's waistcoat heaving like powerful bellows, and subsiding with his heavy breathing. This was a man, he thought. About him there was no bitterness, no recriminations, no desire to impress as a seer. He had clearly foretold the plague and the consequences, and now that it was endemic, he was bending every effort to combat it. There had been no triumphant 'I told you this would happen' about his attitude, merely a desire to serve even beyond his physical capacity. A man . . . Truly one of the righteous. In this world respected by his fellow-men, and in the next, surely destined to sit at the right hand of Jehovah Himself.

For an hour the doctor lay in a deep sleep, without stirring once to change his position. Occasionally a few words burst from his lips or a sigh that showed he was battling the plague even in slumber. From time to time Ernest peeped in and quietly vanished after a glance at the doctor, and Barnardo was half-convinced when he met his eyes that his face had assumed a softer expression. At last the doctor sat up with a start.

'What's the time?' he exclaimed.

Without waiting for a reply from the student he pulled out a huge silver watch, and after glancing at it jumped to his feet in alarm.

'Heavens! Ah'm late! Why didn't you wake me?'

'I hadn't the heart,' said Barnardo. 'You were so sound asleep.'

'Asleep! Ah have no right to sleep when people may be dying because Ah am not there to save them!' He noticed the hurt look on the young man's face, and crossing over to him, the doctor laid his hand gently on his arm. 'There now, Ah didn't mean to scold you, mah friend.'

He turned away from him.

'Ernest!' he called. 'Ernest.'

At once the ungainly figure of his servant shuffled into the room. There was a look of animal devotion in his eyes as he gazed at the doctor and Barnardo knew that this man would cut off his right arm for Haddock.

'Rachel's ready, guv'nor,' he said.

'Good!' Haddock replied. He flung on his coat that had been tossed carelessly over a chair, and picked up the carpet bag that contained his drugs and instruments. Then he reminded himself of Barnardo.

'Are you coming?' he asked.

'That's what I'm here for,' said the student.

'Then we'll walk,' the doctor announced. 'Ernest – put Rachel back in her stall.'

Their first call was a house in the next turning. They passed through a narrow, evil-smelling passage to a back-room that, windowless, had to be lit by a smoky oil-lamp even during the long summer day. In this one room a family of four lived, a widow and her three children. When Haddock and the student entered, the woman was sewing some new garments, seated directly beneath the lamp to catch the maximum light. She raised her head as the doctor entered, and across her haggard face flitted a smile of recognition. On the floor lay Haddock's patient, a boy of five, dead. His scarecrow figure was garbed in the only rags he had worn during life, his dirty little feet bare as when he had roamed the alley-ways. His arms were folded in prayer, the peaked little face puckered, and a ghastly yellow. The woman continued her labour. She knew her child was dead, but she had not time to mourn him.

Haddock knelt beside the infant. One touch told him that the child had not been laid out before his time. He rose gravely to his feet and crossing to the woman patted her comfortingly on the shoulder.

'Ah'll see he gets buried,' he said.

'Thank yer, yer a toff,' the woman replied wearily in a toneless voice, without raising her head.

A sob broke from the corner, and for the first time they noticed a small girl half-concealed in the darkness. She was thirteen, but looked no more than ten, her shabby print apron covering a physique that seemed all skin and bones. She lifted her face towards the doctor and burst into a torrent of tears.

'Quiet, Daisy! Quiet!' said the sempstress harshly, afraid that the girl's emotion might set loose the flood that she controlled so rigidly. Dead was dead. She loved her son, but he was better gone than starving and suffering. There was this work to do. It had to be finished on time or the whole family would have no food. Let those weep who could afford it. Perhaps when she went to bed she also might give way to the luxury of tears . . .

The sobs died down and the girl buried her head in her apron, emitting a choked, intermittent snuffling. Barnardo had been close to her in the corner, and noticed that the girl's gums were black, showing a few decayed teeth, the lower part of the sagging jaws being covered with an ugly eruption. When he left the house with the doctor Barnardo drew Haddock's attention to what he had seen.

'Something's wrong with the girl too,' he remarked.

'Phosphorus necrosis – better known as Phossy-Jaw,' said the doctor unemotionally. 'A common complaint.'

'Is there no cure?'

'There is,' said Haddock, 'and certain of our statesmen are seeking to apply it.'

'Statesmen? – But surely you mean doctors?'

'Statesmen are just what Ah *do* mean,' Haddock repeated. 'Sane statesmen can be the only possible doctors for these diseases. A girl of thirteen working under vile conditions in a match factory, dipping sticks of pine into poisonous phosphorus, without any protection whatsoever from the fumes. What use are doctors? We relieve one case of Phossy-

Jaw only to be faced with a dozen others. Believe me, mah friend, that child is crying for her brother, but if only she realized it she should be saving those tears for herself.'

A few minutes' walk brought them to the house of the next patients, and Barnardo almost dreaded entering the forbidding hovel. Death in the mass held a sombre majesty, but these ugly single corpses were terrifying in their repulsiveness. He had wanted to become acquainted with each individual tragedy, but he had not been prepared for the toll these stark revelations made on his nervous resistance. In this home, one room and a tiny scullery, there were four sufferers. Two children and two adults were sprawled about the room, on the bed and on the chairs, an inert, fogged look on their faces as though all of them were incapably drunk. The doctor examined the children first, then turned his attention to the man and his wife. The woman appeared to be in a bad condition. Her eyes were sunk deeply in her head, her dishevelled hair hanging in matted tufts over her shoulders, while her skin seemed crusty as the hide of a pachyderm. She was practically in a state of coma, and Haddock and the young man felt no resilience in her body as they lifted her onto the bed. Puncturing the median cubital vein, the doctor injected a flow of saline through a thin glass tube, and when the operation was completed, the woman stirred, opened her eyes and thanked the negro mutely. Packing his carpet bag, the doctor left instructions about the medicine with a shy young woman who had been hiding in the scullery during his visit, and departed with Barnardo.

When the round concluded some hours later, they had left behind nine dead bodies in various houses, with the certainty that the morrow would add at least as many more to their number. In silence, each obsessed by his own thoughts, the doctor and Barnardo walked back to the surgery. Of all the abysmal sights the young man had seen that evening, none struck him more forcibly than the spectacle of one gaunt mother at the tub, washing all the garments her children possessed, while the infants, naked as the day they were born, huddled, like slabs of dirty fish, beneath the coverlet, the infected child mingling its puny limbs with the embraces of the other three.

Ernest was waiting for them, supper being ready in the kitchen. Barnardo could not eat, he could hardly stand, and while making excuses for his lack of appetite, he suddenly collapsed. At first the doctor feared the plague, but the young man had no sign of fever, and almost immediately opened his eyes and apologized for his weakness. Haddock, correctly assessing his momentary collapse as the inevitable result of prolonged nervous tension, refused to allow the young man to return to his lodgings, but made a bed for him in his own room. In a day, Barnardo recovered, and after returning to Dempsey Street to explain matters to his landlady, he went back to the Black Doctor's surgery, and remained there, sharing the negro's labours until the epidemic had passed.

CHAPTER 5

East London breathed freely again. The deathly sickness was conquered, and the unquenchable spirit of the Cockney burst forth once more on to the streets. The usual knots gathered noisily outside the public-houses in the evenings, and the vestry boards went on in the same old way, completely forgetting the frantic promises of reform they had made during the panic of the plague.

The cholera wards emptied, and the London Hospital went back to normal routine. The students, within a week or so, found their bearings, and settled down more or less willingly to the humdrum business of learning to become doctors, all except Barnardo, whose continual absence had by this time excited the curiosity even of those of his contemporaries who were notorious for their own lack of interest in the tasks of the curriculum.

A group of first year students gathered noisily in their own common-room after a lecture. They were most of them about Barnardo's age, but one, a tall handsome fellow, with dark side-burns and thick waxed mustachios, seemed several years older than the rest, although that might possibly have been due to the striking attraction of his presence. He singled out for himself the most comfortable chair, and filling his pipe with tobacco lit it, and balanced his long legs on the edge of the table, while four or five of his henchmen gathered eagerly around him.

'Viva Voce tomorrow,' he announced.

'No need for you to worry about that, Brad,' a slim, curly-headed young fellow replied. 'You'll do the usual – you won't show up.'

'Can't do that tomorrow,' said Brad glumly. 'The Pater's

on the trail. He's threatening to come down and interview the Dean . . . He seems to think I'm slacking, so I've got to show up for one Viva at least. Fine prospect! Dash it all, I'll be lucky to get two per cent.'

There was a general laugh at this sally, Brad himself joining in, although he was reflecting ruefully that he had not unduly belittled his prospective marks in tomorrow's oral anatomy examination.

'Never mind,' the curly-headed youth consoled him, 'if that Barnardo fellow turns up, he'll probably get two per cent less than you.'

'I can't allow that!' said Brad. 'I have my honour to consider as the biggest duffer in the college!'

'You'll have to look to your laurels, then,' a chubby youngster broke in. 'Barnardo will give you a run for your money – and if it comes to a wager my cash is on Barnardo.'

Brad drew his feet down from the table. He bore the reputation of being the slackest student of the year, and he had worked hard at other pursuits to attain that distinction. He was one of those gentlemen who purposely cultivate an atrocious handwriting to stamp them as infinitely removed from those persons who have to write well for a living, and for a clerk to write badly without affectation he regarded almost as an insult. For himself he was too interested in gambling, drinking and its associated vices to be able to spare much attention to study, but that the middle-class Barnardo, whom he never met at any of the brothels or gaming houses, fell below him without effort seemed unbelievable.

'That's right, Brad,' said Smith Junior, the curly-headed boy. 'Barnardo's got you whacked. All the months I've been here, I've hardly seen him at a single lecture.'

'Nor me,' chimed in another, and with grins and nods of the head the rest of the group concurred.

Brad, however, was determined not to shed his laurels without a struggle.

'Nonsense!' he said spiritedly. 'He's up to something we don't know of . . . Yes, that Barnardo's a dark horse.'

'Something *is* wrong with that fellow,' the chubby student admitted. 'He's always walking about as if there are terribly important things on his mind. And he's no fool. He's got brains, you know.'

'There!' said Brad triumphantly. 'That's his little game. I'll bet all the tea in China he's burning the midnight oil reading on the sly!'

'You're wrong there, Brad,' the chubby youth insisted. 'The other week he couldn't find the brachial plexus – and even *you* know where that is.'

'At least, with all my faults,' said Brad, 'I am a gregarious animal, always prepared to join my fellow-men in a game of cards or footer, but our friend Barnardo does none of these things, or does them where nobody can see him. And he walks about with a preoccupied air. Has brains and doesn't use them. Those are the symptoms, gentlemen – and my diagnosis is a woman!'

'Rubbish!' expostulated Smith Junior. 'Not Barnardo. I'll stake my skeleton he's not that sort.'

'Perhaps he's a betting man,' suggested the chubby student.

'No,' said Brad. 'I mix in all the betting circles from the highest to the very low, and I can state definitely that the specimen under dissection is never to be found there.'

'I hope you'll excuse me butting in, Brad,' ventured a meek, bespectacled boy, who, tolerated on the fringe of the group, had learned it best never to have any opinions of his own, 'but I think I can solve the mystery.'

'You, Johnson!' Brad ejaculated with an incredulous smile. 'Come on then, out with it.'

'W-well . . .' the boy stammered, terribly embarrassed at thus finding himself for once the centre of attraction. '. . . He . . . he preaches in the street.'

'What!' the students yelled unanimously in a derisive chorus at the top of their voices.

The unhappy Johnson's face grew a deeper red. 'It . . . It's true,' he repeated. 'I saw him myself the other n-night talking on a soap-box at the Mile End Waste.'

Brad was the first to recover himself.

'Well!' he said. 'I didn't expect it to be as bad as that. Preaching! And in the street, to those ignorant yahoos along the Mile End Waste! I can't believe it. I won't believe it till I see it!'

The spectacled youth's features assumed a pained expression. Johnson was half-sorry now that he had spoken.

'B-but, Brad,' he protested. 'I . . . I assure you *I* saw it.'

Brad threw up his hands in disgust. If that were so, then Barnardo was completely outside the pale. For a student to preach in the streets was nothing but arrant hypocrisy, a slimy fad. It was as though a first-year man were to join a sewing-circle run by the Dean's wife and pretend to like it.

'Well,' he said. 'He'd better keep his prayer meetings out in the street. If he tries that on in the college I know what *I* shall do. And when these religious cranks get a bee in their bonnets they go to extremes; our Mr Barnardo has probably developed into a brother of the Christian Mission or Ranter – or Heaven preserve us – a Holy Shaker!'

'The House Committee would do something about it if they knew,' said the chubby youth.

'There's no need for the House Committee to know,' replied Brad. 'We can take matters into our own hands. Let's have nothing to do with the fellow. We'll cut him dead!'

'That shouldn't be difficult,' remarked Smith Junior slyly, with a cynical grin. 'Up to now, he's practically been cutting us!'

Brad jumped to his feet. The conversation had left a nasty taste in his mouth, and a musty sacerdotal smell in the air, for which the obvious deodorant was several pints of beer. The others followed him, trouping out of the common-room with a gust of obscene laughter. Now the room was practically deserted, with the exception of two students, apparently so deeply immersed in medical books and magazines that a revolution might have raged about them without their being any the wiser. One of them, however, seated in a corner, had heard every word of the discussion. Phillip Comyns, a little younger than the others, and only more recently entered into the college roster, had purposely kept aloof. He did not object much to Brad and his friends – in fact, he had mixed willingly with them in the lecture-rooms and occasionally joined them at a tavern over a tankard of beer. The only thing that set him aside from the other students was an ingrained disability to appreciate and enjoy the libidinous witticisms that seemed to be the common medium of communication between first-year men, interlarded with blasphemous profanity that would not have disgraced the robust vocabularies of the Mile End Waste.

For the past two months Phillip had been lodging in the same house as Barnardo in Dempsey Street, but although his cheery greetings had always been answered by Barnardo with a friendly smile, his attitude did not seem to encourage the birth of an association that would go beyond 'Good morning' and 'Good evening'. Comyns had been quite content with that; if a chap wanted to keep himself to himself, he wasn't the sort to seek to violate another's integrity, but the conversation he had overheard stamped Barnardo as a character. A man who could face the unscrupulous loungers of the Mile End Waste on their own Tom Tiddlers' Ground deserved respect for his courage, even though he might be a crack-brained eccentric. The more he thought about it, the more puzzled Comyns became. Eccentric, yes, but there was an air of resoluteness and quiet determination about Barnardo that dispelled the notion of a scatterbrain.

That same evening Phillip Comyns went up to Barnardo's landing. There was a light showing beneath the door, so he knocked gently and in a moment heard Barnardo's voice bidding him enter. He found Barnardo seated at the table studying his Bible. The room, unlike Comyns' own quarters, was scrupulously tidy, the books carefully stacked on home-made shelves, and whatever clothes there were in his wardrobe hidden away out of sight, showing an orderliness of mind and habit that went ill with the conception of an irresponsible fanatic.

'I hope I'm not interrupting,' said Comyns.

'Not at all,' Barnardo replied. 'Is there anything I can do for you?'

'There is,' said Comyns. 'There's a Viva on tomorrow. I'd like to polish up my anatomy. I loaned my *Gray's* to someone, I forget who, but it hasn't been returned, so I'd like to borrow yours.'

'With pleasure. Help yourself. It's on the shelf.'

Comyns went across the room and took down the bulky medical volume. A glance at the uncut leaves showed that it had been very little handled, if at all. That was one facet of the peculiar story corroborated – reading the Bible while *Gray's*, the ABC of the medical student, lay neglected on the shelf – and another was entrusting a valuable book to a person Barnardo only knew by sight. Comyns began to feel uncomfortable about the whole matter. He had hit on the subterfuge of borrowing a book that he already possessed to strike up some sort of acquaintance with the recluse, but it looked as if he would have to remain content simply with the volume, for Barnardo was impatiently turning the leaves of his Bible as if eager to get back again to the story of the Prophets.

'Thank you very much,' he said. At the door he turned. 'By the way, my name is Comyns.'

'Mine is Barnardo,' the other answered with a smile.

'I know,' Comyns said. 'But dash it all, man,' he burst out irrepressibly, 'we live in the same house, go to the same college; we're neighbours, colleagues; why should we be strangers?'

'Quite right,' Barnardo replied. 'I hope you won't think I

am a snob. It's very wrong of me to be so unfriendly, especially as I want to live in the Lord, and have the whole world as my neighbour.' He rose from the table and walking towards Comyns extended his hand. 'My name is Tom,' he said.

'That's better!' Comyns answered cheerfully. 'I'm Phillip.' He held out the book. 'Here. You'd better take this back. It looks as if you need it more than I do.'

'No,' said Barnardo. 'At the moment there is only one book I need – the word of God.'

'But dash it, Tom,' Comyns protested. 'You're trying to become a doctor, not training for the ministry.'

'That's true,' said Barnardo. His face grew serious again. 'I fear I have been neglecting my studies, but I have been in Limehouse during the plague, and the work I have been doing there has seemed vastly more important than the medical college. To obtain a degree takes so long, so many years, while every day, people are hungry, people are starving, children are dying – and few of them know God. I would like to tear myself in two and send one half to the London Hospital and the other half to Limehouse, but as I cannot do that I shall have to apportion my time to the best possible advantage.'

'You know,' Comyns said quizzically, 'I can't make head or tail of what you're driving at.'

Barnardo drew his neighbour close to the table and invited him to be seated. He liked Phillip's frank, open face, and felt sure he would be a sympathetic listener. The misery he had seen in Limehouse had burned in him so deeply that it monopolized his thoughts almost to the exclusion of everything else. His goal was still China, but that seemed so distant, whereas the grim horrors he had witnessed were so fresh in his mind that he felt he must do something about them now. The plague was over, but the beastly hovels still stood and ghastly wretches still crowded them, helpless material for whatever disaster was coming their way. The vestry boards had returned to their smug old complacency, leaving the survivors to pick up what was to those unfortunates the norm of life. Now that he had been intimately accepted into those houses, and seen the conditions under which whole families struggled, the young student could not cast them altogether out of his life as though they were an episode, closed.

He walked about the room with quick, nervous movements, telling Comyns what he had seen. It seemed he had only to talk to get others to feel as he felt himself. To erase the slums was a national problem, quite beyond his meagre conception of economics, but the human flotsam could somehow be salvaged, and not by statesmen, but by people close to the derelicts, men like Haddock and himself, and perhaps this Comyns too. The older generation was doomed, but it was essential to rescue the children. They would have to start with the children, start with them from the bottom, teach them to read, to write, to understand the meaning of life and God. He shot a quick glance at Comyns who was listening seriously and, he thought, sympathetically. From his pocket, Barnardo drew a book in which he had started to make an inventory of a single slum street. He placed it before Comyns and opened it at the first page. If these cold facts did not convince him, all his talking had been in vain.

Comyns looked closely at the paper that bore evidence of Barnardo's early mercantile training. It had been neatly ruled off with the name of the street on top, and the numbers of the houses on the extreme left. Near the numerals were details of rooms occupied, the names of the tenants, and across the page was a summary of each family's history and circumstances. Comyns glanced down it at random, and read a few entries.

'BOWKER'S RENTS

Number 1. Bootmaker (journeyman). One room. Wife chars.
Three school-children. Two over school age, one a cripple.
Terribly poor. Man deaf, almost decrepit, suffering from
rheumatism.

Number 2. Sweep. One room. Wife dead. Four school-children. The eldest girl looks after the others while father is at work.

Number 7. Hawker. One room. Four children of school age and one infant. Makes and sells flower-stands. Income always behind expenditure.

Number 13. Greengrocer's. One room and small shop. Two children of school age and one infant. Very old grandmother, almost a cripple, lives with them.

Number 14. Match-box maker. Two rooms. Three children of school age, two over age. Man and wife and whole family work at this terribly underpaid trade. Pawns same set of garments every week.

Number 15. Casual dock labourer. In poor health, wife consumptive. Son of 17 earns six shillings weekly as carman's boy. Two girls of school age. Father and son eat midday meal out, father taking 3d and son taking 2d per day.

(For these three houses, Numbers 14, 15 and 16, inhabited by eight families, one small yard, one water-tap, and one lavatory.) . . .'

Comyns put the book down. He had seen enough. He could not cavil at these thumbnail descriptions, for they were so obviously authentic. Each tiny slum house subdivided into rooms, each room averaging less than ten feet square, holding a complete family, misery multiplied and magnified in the least possible space.

'It seems incredible,' he admitted at last.

'Did you note the number of children?' asked Barnardo, relentlessly pressing his point. 'Two, three, or more in almost every family. Can you imagine what is happening to them, how they grow up? Why, I met in Limehouse lads of sixteen and seventeen that could not read or write, could not even spell their names.'

'But surely there are schools,' said Comyns.

Barnardo laughed, a little bitterly.

'Schools!' he exclaimed. 'There are the Dame schools, but you couldn't find a casual dock labourer who could afford to send his children there – and as for the ordinary schools, he might as well save the penny a week each child cost him for all the education they give. Why, a good proportion of the masters themselves are unable to write and some have even been known to mark their reports with a cross. As for the poor pupils who are unable to pay their pennies at the end of the week, they are branded with red ink on the thumbnail, and dare not obliterate it until the due is made good.'

Comyns jumped to his feet.

'That's monstrous!' he said. 'Something certainly ought to be done about that. About slums, I don't know, perhaps there is a reason for them; about poverty I can't help – I have barely enough to support myself. Those things I don't understand, I am afraid to meddle with them; but schools – that's right in my province. Look here Barnardo, why don't we open a school of our own?'

'You mean something on the lines of a ragged school, with voluntary helpers?'

'That's right,' Comyns answered eagerly. 'There's me and you, to begin with.'

'I was hoping you would say something of the sort, Phillip. We two are enough for a start, and we can get the children if we can find the school.'

'Yes . . .' said Comyns. 'There'll probably be some difficulty about that.'

His sense of justice had flared spontaneously at the chance of helping the children, but now his easy-going habits baulked at the first fence. In his enthusiasm he had thrown out the ragged school as a suggestion, but not only did Barnardo take it seriously, he actually set out at once making plans for carrying it into operation. Phillip was all for letting the matter simmer a little longer, but Barnardo's mind had fastened on the idea with a relentless driving force that swept all objections aside. The only concession Comyns could obtain was one day's grace, and he had to promise to join his colleague in the search for a suitable classroom on the morning after that period expired.

Barnardo had some experience of voluntary teaching in an East End ragged school, to which he had been recommended on his arrival in London by members of the Open Brethren who had their headquarters in Sidney Street. The young student, however, was too ambitious to work within set rules, and the long rounds he had trudged in Haddock's company revealed the vast field in Limehouse that was practically barren so far as secular and religious education were concerned. If Comyns had not suggested the venture he would sooner or later have started a ragged school on his own; as it was, Phillip accepted the credit for the idea without realizing that Barnardo had skilfully inoculated him with the proselytizing germ.

They spent the whole morning searching for premises without any success. Wherever they went the two students were regarded with suspicion and the bare mention of a school was sufficient to nullify any prospects of a deal. At last Tom and his companion went to Haddock, and the Black Doctor, who had every street in the district at his finger-tips, sent them to a Mr Martin at a place called Donkey Row, which turned out to be a narrow blind-alley a stone's throw from Three Colt Street Market.

Mr Martin was a flabby mountain of a man. Originally a barge-owner, his right leg had been clamped between the side of his boat and the wharf and amputated above the knee. Hopping about on his wooden peg, he had given up the traffic of the waterway and, settling in Limehouse, had bought a few houses and lived on the income they brought him. His enormous frame filled the doorway of the house where the two young men accosted him, a peaked sailor's cap pulled over his small bleary eyes, the rest of his body undulating in a succession of bloated curves from his bristly chins to the lowest point of a stomach that seemed to sag between his fleshy thighs.

'We've come from the Black Doctor,' said Barnardo. 'He informs us you have some premises to let.'

'That I 'ave,' replied Martin. 'Though I don't know as 'ow it wor of any use to you gents.'

'Let's see the place first,' said Barnardo. 'Then we can talk about it.'

Martin, his flesh shaking like a disintegrating starfish at every tread, led them to a shack at the far end of the alley and unfastened the enormous padlock that secured the door.

''At's the plice, gents,' he said.

Barnardo and Comyns stepped inside. It was a large shed used by the costermongers to stable their donkeys in the affluent days of Three Colt Street Market. It had obviously been untenanted for a considerable period; cobwebs hung from the dark rafters and in the corners. The walls, originally white, were a dingy yellow and stained with vast patches of slime, where the damp had seeped through, and the floor was pounded cobblestones and earth. One horrified look was enough for Comyns, such a vile place was out of the question, but Barnardo, unperturbed, had rapidly taken stock and envisaged its possibilities. The walls and rafters whitewashed – they could do that themselves – a carpenter to lay a wooden floor for two or three pounds, and the donkey stable would become quite a respectable classroom. Then they would need benches and books, but that would come later. It would do, unless the rent were too prohibitive for their exchequer.

'Well?' asked Martin, as the two young men returned from their rapid survey.

'It will do,' said Barnardo, to his friend's amazement. 'What is the rent?'

The fat quivered on Martin's jowls as he raised a hand thoughtfully to scratch his bottom chin.

''Arf a crown a week,' he suggested. ''Ow's that?'

'Done,' said Barnardo. The young man took a half-sovereign

from his pocket and pressed it into Martin's hand. 'Here's the first month's rent in advance.'

Martin bent his huge frame over the padlock and fastened the door. These youngsters were too eager to get hold of his stable, had paid up too quickly. Somewhere there must be some funny business. Wheezing, as if he had just accomplished an extraordinarily tiring task, Martin stretched his layers of fat into the semblance of rigidity.

'Wotcher want it fer?' he asked suspiciously, holding the key tightly in his hand.

'A school. A ragged school for children.'

Martin shook his head. 'I f'ought it wor somefing fishy. No. sorry, gents, yer'll 'ave ter take the money back. Yer carn't 'ave it fer a school.'

'Why not?' said Barnardo agitatedly.

'Well, I gotter fink of the neighbours,' Martin replied. 'Donkeys only makes a bit of a stink; they ain't much trouble else, but kids is always a blooming nuisance. 'Sides, the blokes dahn 'ere don't care fer charity schools, they'd smash 'em ter pieces soon as look at 'em, an' I ain't takin' no chances wiv me stable!'

'But, Mr Martin!' Barnardo protested.

Again the crippled barge-master shook his head and tried to return the half-sovereign, but he had to deal with an exceptionally obstinate young fellow. He tilted his cap to the back of his bald head and attempted to pin the offender with a stern glare. To the fading retina a watery image percolated; surely he had seen these features before? . . . Of course! The Black Doctor had sent him. This would be that same young man who had watched half the night over Lucy before she died from the plague. To Barnardo's astonishment Martin gave up his attempt to return the money and instead put the key into the student's hand.

'There y'are, guv'nor,' said Martin. 'I recognize yer naow. As true as I'm standing 'ere on me one peg, yer the only man in London could 'ave me donkey stable fer a school.'

CHAPTER 6

They found a carpenter to put down a rough floor, and between them the two young men cleaned and whitewashed the rafters and the walls. Then they purchased a couple of second-hand lamps which they refurbished and suspended from the ceiling, some benches, and a few books. All this expense was met from their joint pockets, and when the classroom was ready they were both of them at the end of their resources, but, in spite of that, elated at having successfully accomplished the most difficult part of their task.

Getting the children was not so easy at first. On opening day Barnardo had two large posters printed and he and Comyns carried them about the mean streets. In some alleys they were met by shrill abuse, and in others volleys of garbage, and those same urchins they meant to educate showed their appreciation by following them around like howling dervishes, showering them with a continuous stream of unmentionable filth. Here and there a few people recognized him sympathetically as a friend of the Black Doctor's, but these were in the minority compared with those who resented this new intrusion by the upper class into their jealously guarded domain. Gradually the opposition died, and as the autumn darkened into winter the classroom was filled two nights a week and on Sundays with a crowd of children of all ages who came there as much for the comforting light and warmth as for the Bible lessons and readings from *Uncle Tom's Cabin* and Bunyan's *Pilgrim's Progress*.

Barnardo, having launched this venture successfully, turned his attention back to his studies. He did not forget that he was dedicated to the Chinese as doctor as well as preacher. The young student led a full life. Every day of the week except Sunday he spent in the lecture and dissecting rooms, and all his evenings were given over to study with the exception of those two he reserved for his ragged school. He had a lot of leeway to make up in the hospital, but he applied himself diligently to his books and practical work, until the end of the year found him advanced to the level of the other students.

This unceasing mental and physical labour laid a heavy toll on his bodily resources, but Barnardo came of healthy stock and had never unduly taxed his strength with excesses such as the vainglorious Brad delighted in. At the same time, those evenings he spent at the school left him limp at the end of every session, for it required the utmost effort of will and personality to control forty or more unruly children, each ready to take advantage of the most momentary lapse.

One chill November night he felt more exhausted than usual, for Comyns was out of town, and the conduct of the school devolved entirely on his own shoulders. Thankfully he watched the last child vanish into the darkness of Donkey Row, and with a sigh of relief he sank into a chair before the fire and luxuriously stretched his weary limbs. The flames still licked cheerily over the soft polished coal and caverns of grey ash, and the warmth that flowed towards him made him more than ever reluctant to exchange this comfortable seat for the cold winds of the late November streets. He gazed into the fire and seemed to see pictures of tropical vegetation and half-naked coolies straining at ropes and rickshaws. Whenever his vitality was at a low ebb, he conjured up visions of the colourful East that was his destination, and they always had the effect of comforting him on the way.

Suddenly he became conscious of another person in the room. He turned slowly and was confronted by the most ragged urchin he had ever seen. A boy about eight years of age stood meekly before him, dressed in a tattered jacket that reached almost to his calves and a pair of trousers that terminated below the knee in one leg and formed a loose jagged line round the ankle in the other. No shirt covered the pitifully thin chest, and his incredibly dirty feet were without the semblance of hose or boots. The emaciated face and limbs were too obviously genuine, and the garments too repulsively begrimed, or this scarecrow might have been a fancy-dress gamin, so badly did he compare with his own by no means well-clad pupils.

'Well, young man?' Barnardo said kindly. 'What can I do for you?'

The boy opened a pair of keen blue eyes. 'Please, sir,' he said eagerly, in a thin high-pitched voice, 'some on the boys told me ter come an' see yer. They said as 'ow the guv'nor might let me doss in front er the fire.'

'Doss in front of the fire?'

''Onist I won't do any 'arm, guv'nor,' the child assured him gravely. 'I f'ought yer might be so good . . . I'll be orf like a shot in the morning.'

'Nonsense!' said Barnardo. 'Be off with you now, my lad.' He rose from his chair. 'Come along, sonnie – I've got to be locking up.'

The boy stood his ground without attempting to move, staring up with appealing eyes at the student. Tom put his hand gently on his shoulder.

'Come along now,' he repeated. 'Go home to your mother.'

The boy shook his head without changing his expression. 'Ain't got no muvver,' he said.

'I'm sorry to hear that, my lad,' Barnardo answered commiseratingly. 'But it's getting late, really; you must go back to your father, or your family.'

'Ain't got no farver, ain't got no family,' the child said stubbornly.

'No father – no family . . . Then surely you have friends, you have a home?'

Again the boy shook his head and repeated dully his monotonous denials.

'Got no friends. Got no 'ome.'

Tom looked searchingly at the child, but those steady blue eyes did not flinch under the scrutiny. He looked like a moulting sparrow picked out of a puddle, only the pert little head seeming alive and responsive, the rest of its plumage heavy with mud.

'No friends? . . . No home? . . . Then where do you sleep?'

'I kips a ken when I gets money fer a bed, an' when I carn't I finds a lay somewhere in the street.'

'In the street!' exclaimed Barnardo, appalled.

''Course,' replied the child in a matter-of-fact tone. 'In the summer it's better nor the doss-'ouses, 'cause they ain't no bugs, but in the cold weather, sir, it's 'ard, werry 'ard.'

'And last night . . . Where did you sleep last night?' asked the student.

'In a cart at the 'Ay Market, nigh Aldgate Pump.'

Barnardo sat down on the chair, and drawing the child towards him perched the frail little body on his knees. He could feel the puny bones of the boy's ribs through the threadbare cloth of his jacket, and shuddered at the thought of this waif, with only these rags as protection from the biting east wind – that was, if the child's story were true – and in spite of its authentic ring, the student could hardly bring himself to believe that there were still depths of poverty, in this enormously wealthy London, lower than any he had yet plumbed. He set his face in a stern expression, determined to probe to the bottom of this fantastic tale.

'How old are you, my lad?' he asked.

'Ten, sir.' The reply came pat without any hesitation.

'I suppose you know what happens to little boys who don't tell the truth?' said Barnardo severely.

'But it wor the truth,' the urchin protested. ''Onist, guv'nor, it's true as I'm settin' 'ere.'

'Do you know of any more children sleeping in the streets?'

'Any more!' The child emitted a noise that sounded like a half contemptuous chuckle. 'Why there's million on 'em!'

'Millions?'

'Well . . . not 'xactly millions – f'ousands. A good lot on 'em, anyway – more'n I kin count!'

Still Tom was not convinced.

'Supposing I gave you food and something hot to drink,' he suggested, 'could you lead me to one of these "lays"?'

''Course!' said the arab emphatically, starting to his feet as if he were embarking on an errand that would give him nothing but the greatest of pleasure. ''Course I could, guv'nor.'

The tiny intruder followed Barnardo into the street, and waited patiently while he locked up the donkey stable, then his bare feet trotted behind the student on the pavement like a docile little dog while Tom led the way to his lodgings. As they passed down Commercial Road, the shivering waif poured out his history with the most ingenuous frankness in answer to the student's questions. He had never known his father and his mother died five years earlier. After her death he had been sent to a Union workhouse, where he had attended school along with perhaps a thousand other unfortunate children. The food had been bad and scanty, the superintendent continually asserting his authority by terrorizing the little paupers, to whom a high spot in their lives was a scrap of that pompous official's dinner, eaten from his own willow-pattern plate. Young Jimmy had quickly run away, and sought refuge in the house of a woman who had known his mother, sleeping in a shed in the back-yard. After that he had helped a barge-master, whose idea of a joke when in his cups was to set his dog on the helpless child, 'for fun'. Fortunately his persecutor took the Queen's Shilling while on a drinking bout, and Jimmy, free again, picked up a few coppers helping the costers in the market, or begging, or hiding as much as possible from the police, who were more severe on these youthful outlaws from society than the hardest of workhouse super-intendents.

At last they reached the student's lodgings in Dempsey Street. Barnardo made some hot coffee and supplied the little vagrant with bread and butter, and an astonishing number of cakes, which disappeared so miraculously that it hardly seemed possible for such an undeveloped digestive apparatus to absorb them all. When the boy's incredible appetite was appeased, Barnardo wrapped him in an old jacket and together they went into the street.

It was past midnight when they started down Whitechapel Road, the little arab walking close beside Barnardo, his tiny fist clasped protectingly in the student's hand. The hay-carts were absent from their usual stands in the High Street, so the boy led Barnardo a little way down to Houndsditch. Cutting through the 'Ditch' they passed through a narrow turning that led to a long barracks-like structure open at both ends, which on Sundays acted as an exchange mart for dealers in, and purchasers of, the old clothes that were the sole commodity handled in this little offshoot of nearby Petticoat Lane.

Passing through the shed, without encountering any signs of life, they came to a blind wall. The boy stopped.

''Ere we are, guv'nor,' he announced.

Barnardo looked around him in bewilderment. For a moment he thought he had been hoaxed.

'Here?' he said. 'I see no children here.'

For answer the boy wedged his hands and toes in cracks between the bricks, and agilely as a cat climbed to the top of the wall. With the aid of a stick he helped the student up to his perch, and as soon as Tom could balance himself comfortably on the narrow parapet, the boy pointed out triumph-antly eleven figures sprawled over the roof in ungainly postures of sleep. As if his companion needed further convincing, the lad wanted to awaken the awkward bundles, but Barnardo could not bear the thought of intruding his presence on the slumbers of these wretched little urchins, who had become so inured to their misery that they could sleep on lead tiles and without any covering beneath the grim November sky. His own comfortable bed seemed now like a silent reproach. He shook his head in reply to the youngster's repeated inquiry and as quickly as possible lowered himself to the ground. His guide followed sure-footedly, disappointed at not having been allowed to rouse his friends. The guv'nor had been good to him and he wanted to show him all he could in return.

'Shall I take you somewhere else, sir?' Jimmy asked eagerly.

'No, thank you,' said the student. A chill feeling clutched at his heart. If he were a woman he would at this moment have burst into tears . . .

'No, thanks,' he repeated, 'I have seen enough.'

CHAPTER 7

Tom found a home for the child with some friends, and whenever he could, made excursions to one or other of the various 'lays' and provided for as many of the little vagabonds as was within his power. Barnardo could not get them out of his mind. Surely other people must know of these derelicts, and if they knew, how could they reconcile the abandonment of scores of helpless children with the dictates of common humanity? In the cold weather they died like flies, and hundreds of those that did not die committed suicide to escape from horrors even they could no longer endure. They were buried in out-of-the-way spots, but the continuous stream of fragile little coffins became such a scandal that they had to be incarcerated in the dead of night in unmarked graves. People knew – it was impossible for them not to know – and yet this unending sacrifice of the innocents went on in the largest, the richest, the most Christian city in the world.

On his way to the ragged school, Barnardo often passed by Spicer's shop. Once he entered, and the shopkeeper, recognizing his compatriot, entered into conversation with him. As soon as he could lead the topic in the direction closest to his heart, Tom mentioned the homeless waifs, but Spicer dismissed them with a wave of his hairy arms.

'Little thieves, 'at's all they are,' he grunted. 'Allus comin' 'ere cadgin' fer crusts o' bread.'

To Spicer they were a nuisance, and he refused to hear any good about them, and when Barnardo tackled later some more responsible citizens, they too evaded the matter with the same reply – 'They should go to the workhouse.'

Members of the vestry board gave similar smug answers –

'The Union –' . . . 'The Workhouse –' . . . and the student, remembering how the Black Doctor's warnings of the plague had been disregarded, ceased to pursue that tack any further. The children became a gigantic responsibility that obsessed him, on top of his other self-imposed responsibilities, and his medical work by day and his teaching and studying in the evening led to the inevitable result. His health, that had withstood the rigours of the cholera epidemic, broke down; the culmination came one evening in a painful heart attack.

Next day, when he had slightly recovered, Barnardo wanted to return to what he considered his duty, but his friend Comyns took a firm stand. Phillip had rigged up sleeping accommodation for himself in Tom's room, and refused to budge from his friend's bedside. In vain the student protested that he was quite well again; Comyns insisted that he must see a doctor first and eventually persuaded Barnardo to let him call in Haddock. The negro came as quickly as Rachel could bring him, leaving Comyns to make his way back to Dempsey Street on foot, and after a thorough examination the Black Doctor diagnosed angina pectoris, though fortunately in a mild form. He put his stethoscope away and gazed at his patient reprovingly.

'Mah friend,' he said. 'Ah did not expect this of you.'

'Why?' asked Barnardo weakly. 'What have I done?'

'Done!' exclaimed Haddock. 'You lived and slept for months right in the middle of the plague – and the cholera couldn't kill you. Now you yourself have almost succeeded where the cholera failed.' He raised his finely shaped hand peremptorily in the air, to stifle the protests that he saw were about to come from his patient. 'No – no – don't talk. Just listen to me. Your bodily organs are mostly in good shape, but your heart is not strong. If you live carefully, without unduly exerting yourself, there is no reason why your span of life should not be prolonged to eighty or more, but continue the way you are going, and your years will fall short even of the Biblical three-score and ten. You are working too hard, Tom, you must relax. You need plenty of nourishment and, above all, rest.'

'But, doctor, how can I rest – those children –'

'Let me put it this way, mah friend,' said Haddock. 'Will it benefit your children if you were to die before you could do very much for them?'

'No – but . . .'

'There are no buts about it,' Haddock broke in severely. 'You are far too serious for a boy of twenty-one; you carry too many responsibilities on your shoulders. You must take things easy, for a while at any rate, laugh more, enjoy yourself without taxing your strength too much.'

The student smiled wanly. 'How can I enjoy myself,' he said, 'when I think of what I have seen so recently?'

'Then don't think about it,' Haddock replied. 'After all, there is so little you yourself can do. It is not a local problem, confined only to these streets, but a national question of extraordinary complexity. You see the results, children homeless on the streets, but have you sought to discover the reason for their being there? Why they have no homes? And if they had homes, why did they leave them? If they had parents, why did those adults ill-treat or desert them? You have to probe back to that primary "Why" mah friend.'

'I am sorry,' said the sick youth. 'The primary "Why" does not concern me. When I see hungry children I want to give them food, when I see them homeless I want to give them shelter.'

'There,' remarked Haddock quizzically, 'that is precisely the trouble with all you would-be reformers. You seek remedies only on the surface. Don't you see, mah friend, that if tonight you gathered all those arabs off the streets, tomorrow the conditions for creating fresh arabs would still remain?'

'I don't know about that,' Barnardo replied with a weary sigh. 'I only wish to God I *could* gather them all off the streets. That would be sufficient for me.'

Haddock rose from his chair resignedly and replaced his instruments in his carpet bag.

'When you get older, Tom,' he said, 'perhaps you will find Ah'm right.'

The sound of rapid footsteps bounded up the stairs, and Comyns burst into the room, followed a moment later by the buxom landlady, Mrs Perrott, puffing from the unaccustomed speed of her ascent.

'Well?' asked Phillip anxiously.

'Nothing very serious,' Haddock replied. 'All he needs is rest, nourishment, and more rest.'

'I'll see he gets rest,' said Comyns firmly.

'And you can leave nourishment to me,' Mrs Perrott added.

The Black Doctor put on his top hat.

'Ah know Ah'm leaving him in good hands,' he said. 'Ah'll send along a tonic, and if there are any further complications, call me in at once.'

Bidding them all 'Good day' the negro stooped to clear the doorway, and left the room. They heard his footsteps descend on the stairs, and soon afterwards the rhythmic metallic clop of Rachel's hooves dying down the street. Barnardo closed his eyes, and thinking he was asleep, Comyns and the landlady tiptoed quietly on to the landing.

Tom was not asleep. In spite of the doctor's strictures he was thinking. He realized that he had been overtaxing his strength, but he had uncovered a sore that would torment him for as long as it remained unhealed. Perhaps the negro was taking a long view, a correct view, but leaving out all the social complications the fact remained that meanwhile children were starving in the gutter. Haddock was older and certainly wiser than he, but the student consoled himself with the thought that God was older and wiser than both. If he made the Lord his guide, not even Haddock would be able to divert him from the path God pointed out.

In a short while Tom was on his feet again, apparently none

the worse for his illness. He resumed his studies and his duties at the ragged school, but although he no longer visited the midnight haunts of the homeless waifs they were never very far from his mind. One Sunday he decided to attend at the Agricultural Hall in Islington, where a minister with whom he was acquainted had inaugurated a series of missions. The Reverend Thain Davidson, a tall slim man with a sensitive face and a fine greying beard, was delighted to see him, and welcomed the young student on the platform. The hall was packed, and after a short prayer the meeting started off with a hymn. Then Davidson introduced the first speaker, who had just returned from Africa. Listening to the smooth voice of the young missionary, Barnardo thought again of those Chinese to whom he would one day be administering, and was carried by the rolling phrases into humid swamps and jungles, and face to face with the unsightly horrors of beri-beri and leprosy.

Other speakers followed, but Tom's mind had wandered to the East, and stayed there, and he was brought back to Islington with a start when he found the Reverend Davidson stooped over him during a hymn. The minister was in a quandary. Two of the most important speakers who had promised to attend had not shown up, and Davidson did not have an address ready. He did not trouble to inquire whether Barnardo had any experience of addressing public meetings, he took that for granted, and simply leaned over him and informed the student that he would be the next speaker.

'But, Mr Davidson, I have nothing to talk about,' Tom protested.

'Tell them about your ragged school,' said the minister in a quick whisper.

Without waiting for a reply Davidson returned to the chairman's table. As soon as the hymns finished and the audience settled expectantly on their benches, he rose again.

'And now,' he announced, 'we have Tom Barnardo, of the

London Hospital. He will tell us of his work among the poor children in Stepney . . . My friends, Tom Barnardo.'

As Tom walked towards the edge of the platform a cloud of white faces seemed to rise and hover before him. His tongue felt dry and his head completely devoid of any ideas except an overpowering desire to run away. He muttered a little prayer to fortify himself, and tried to concentrate on the things he was expected to say. Suddenly words came to him. The faces merged into a conglomerate blur and he felt as though his audience were no larger than a handful of stragglers on the Mile End Waste. He began to talk of his ragged school, of his first encounter with the arabs, and his visits to the various lays. The story carried him along confidently to the end of his speech, and as suddenly as the words came they dried up. Stammering a few embarrassed words of thanks to his auditors for their indulgence in listening to him, he half-stumbled back to his seat, accompanied by a thunder of applause. Tom was overwhelmed at his reception, and still in a daze at the end of the meeting. He received congratulations from all sides, but even on his way home, after tearing himself from his enthusiastic friends, he could hardly realize that he had made his debut before that enormous audience without making an exhibition of his shortcomings as an orator.

CHAPTER 8

Tom turned the envelope over again in his hands. There was no mistake. Incredible as it seemed the missive had been addressed to him and forwarded 'care of' the London Hospital. He took out the expensive hand-woven paper and read the letter once more. There it was in black and white, an invitation from the Earl of Shaftesbury to dine with him at Grosvenor House. Still puzzled, he descended to Comyns' room, hoping his friend would be at home. He caught Phillip in the nick of time, for, dressed in his smart new overcoat, Comyns was just about to leave.

'Ah!' said Phillip. 'Just the man I want. How does it look?'

He turned slowly so that Barnardo could appreciate the lines of the pinched waist and fluted skirts.

'Beautiful!' Tom answered. 'It looks just the same as it did yesterday, and the day before.'

'Oh – you've seen it on!' Phillip said, a trifle abashed, forgetting that there were very few in the college who hadn't. He was like a child with new clothes, and planned every fresh garment with the care of a débutante. Phillip had given the order for this topcoat to a strange tailor and had anxiously awaited its completion, but the resulting fit had even surpassed his expectations. He looked again in the mirror and gave his broad lapels a commendatory tug.

'He's a wizard, that fellow,' he commented.

'A wizard?' said Barnardo.

Phillip turned to his friend.

'The tailor,' he explained. 'A little Jew named Coleman. I found him in one of those turnings behind Whitechapel Road.'

'Oh,' said Barnardo dryly. At the moment he was not interested in clothes. He had been well stocked with new and expensive garments on his arrival from Dublin, and had since found no occasion to replenish his wardrobe. He pressed the letter into Phillip's hand.

'What d'you make of that?' he asked.

Comyns read the letter through rapidly, then gave a suspicious glance at Tom as though he suspected a practical joke. A scrutiny of the crest on the envelope and a second reading convinced him. He let out an involuntary whoop of excitement.

'Make of it!' he exclaimed. 'It's plain enough. What do you expect me to make of it? You're invited to dinner – mixing with the nobs, eh? You soon won't want to talk to any of your plebeian acquaintances.'

'Be serious, my dear fellow,' Tom expostulated. 'It seems genuine enough – in fact I have no doubt it is so. But why should Shaftesbury approach me of all people? Why not you, or Brad, or indeed anyone else?'

'Why? I'll tell you why, my good Doubting Thomas. Because I'm a nonentity, Brad's a nonentity, we're all of us nonentities at the college. Only you stand out, Mr Barnardo – you're somebody.'

'Me?' said Barnardo, puzzled at his friend's raillery. 'Me, Phillip?'

'Of course you!' Comyns answered. 'Why, Tom, you're a celebrity. Perhaps you haven't noticed it, but the other first-year men are beginning to rate you as something above an unamiable lunatic. They're beginning to see that you have something they haven't got.'

'I do wish you would explain yourself, Phillip,' said his friend. 'What has all that nonsense to do with this invitation?'

'Ah!' Comyns chuckled. 'For that you have to thank your reputation as an orator.'

'An orator? . . . Me? . . .'

'Well.' Comyns elaborated. 'Not so much your manner, as your matter. If you read the papers you would have noticed that the name of a certain young medical man keeps cropping up in their columns in connection with stories about homeless children. It may even interest you to know that one retired military gentleman hinted in *The Times* that you might not be telling the truth, and another sour old colonel wrote that it was a law of nature for humans to find their own level, and you had no business interfering anyway.'

'Yes, yes,' Barnardo interrupted impatiently. 'But I still don't follow the connection with Shaftesbury.'

'It's easy to see you're a provincial, Tom,' Phillip said, 'or you would know that you and old Shaftesbury have a lot in common. The Chimney-Sweeps Act was passed a couple of years ago to improve the conditions of the climbing boys – and who d'you think was responsible for that? Shaftesbury. True, it took him twenty-four years to get it through the House, in fact he started before either of us was born, and I've been reading about it ever since I knew how to read, but of course you wouldn't learn spelling so young in Dublin. Then there was the 1864 Commission of Inquiry about the employment of youngsters in mines, and earthenware, hosiery, and all the other factories. Who d'you think was the back of that? Shaftesbury. Wherever there's the question of kids, old Shaftesbury's got his nose in it, and I'll wager this new coat to a second-hand billycock hat that your Islington effort has got to his ears and His Lordship wants to know all about it.'

'You . . . you really think so?'

'Of course!' said Phillip emphatically. 'Why, man, there's nothing to be scared about. You look as if you've received an invitation to a hanging at Newgate, instead of having the chance to rub elbows with some of the greatest men in England. Don't look so glum, Tom. Why, man alive, I'd give my bottom teeth to go with you!'

'I . . . I probably won't be able to go myself,' said Tom dubiously.

'What!' Phillip ejaculated. 'Not go! In Heaven's name, why not?'

'Well . . . I haven't any evening clothes. By some peculiar oversight, I left them in Dublin.'

'That's nothing,' said Comyns. 'I'll lend you mine.'

'It's awfully nice of you,' Tom replied. 'But they'd need a bit of alteration first, and after we'd cut four inches off the sleeves and about eight inches off the legs, they wouldn't be of much more use to you.'

'That's right,' Phillip admitted. 'That's right.'

He lapsed into silence and involuntarily fondled the new stiff lapels of his coat. Every time he handled them he thought with gratitude of their creator. A great tailor, that little Jew, a wizard . . . A wizard . . . Yes . . . Yes . . . The very person. 'Look here, Tom,' he burst out excitedly. 'Come down to my tailor!'

'But I don't want to spend any money for that sort of thing,' Barnardo protested, 'when I have the clothes already.'

'I know you have,' said Phillip impatiently, 'but they're in Dublin. You need them now. You can't dress anyhow for Grosvenor House. You've got to be *de rigeur*, and I'm going to see that you are. Come and see my Nathan Coleman,' he urged. 'Nathan'll rig something up for you, or he loses the best customer he's got.'

'Shaftesbury again?' asked Barnardo with a sly grin.

'No one quite so old,' said his friend. 'Me, Phillip Comyns, MD, FRCS, some day, I hope.'

Mr Coleman, at first, was not of great assistance. He took a legitimate pride in his craft, and refused to run out anything botched that did not do justice to his skill. With the help of his wife and two children, working all day and half the night, he might have managed to produce the requisite garments within a week, but that would have been too late, even if Tom felt like spending any money on them. Eventually he unearthed a suit that had been left with him for alteration by a merchant who was on a visit to India; it was a comparatively easy matter to turn down the cuffs and shorten the trousers, and with Comyns as surety, Coleman hired out the suit to Tom for one evening on payment of five shillings.

The student came to the stately mansion in a condition bordering almost on panic. A line of smart broughams and beautifully equipped open carriages were drawn up outside the house, the coachmen gathered in laughing groups, probably discussing the shortcomings of their masters, a habit as old as servants themselves. Tom went up the broad stairs of the spacious Grecian porch and timorously lifted the beautifully wrought and polished bronze knocker. At the same moment his left hand felt in his pocket for the invitation, and to his horror he discovered it was gone. Feverishly he went through his other pockets, but the invitation had disappeared. A tall butler, looking like some celebrity himself in powdered wig, glittering epaulettes and knee breeches, answered the door. Lifting disdainful eyebrows, he gazed down at the young man.

'Yes?' he inquired.

'Is . . . er . . . is His Lordship at home?' Tom stammered.

'The Earl of Shaftesbury is engaged,' said the flunkey in a sepulchral tone.

'B-but . . . I have an appointment,' Tom protested as the butler was about to close the door.

'Indeed?' said the man sceptically. 'Have you an invitation?'

'I . . . I had one – but it's got lost.'

'Most unfortunate!' the butler replied. 'But my instructions are to admit no one personally unknown to me without an invitation.'

'Look here,' said Tom defiantly. 'Tell Lord Shaftesbury I've arrived.'

The butler looked at Tom quizzically, as if debating whether to accede to his request or throw him out. Fortunately he remembered that His Lordship had occasionally had even more unlikely visitors. Unbending slightly, he made a formal bow.

'Your card, sir?'

'I . . . I haven't one. Just say Mr Barnardo is here.'

'What was the name?' said the flunkey.

'Barnardo . . . Tom Barnardo.'

'Barnardo,' he repeated. 'Barnardo – excuse me one moment, please.'

The butler turned from the door and vanished down the hall into an off room, and was away for so long that Tom began to wonder whether the whole thing was not a mistake or an elaborate hoax, but just as he was thinking uneasily of how best to excuse himself, the pompous butler reappeared followed by the unmistakeable figure of the aged Earl of Shaftesbury. At the door the old man stepped in front of the flunkey, and with a hospitable gesture drew Barnardo into the hall.

'My dear young friend,' he apologized, 'you must pardon the discourtesy.'

With his own hands he helped Barnardo to remove his outer garments and handed them one by one to the butler, who accepted them in silence, but with an air which showed plainly that he still disapproved. Drawing his arm through the student's the Earl led him into the drawing-room and introduced him to the guests. This process Tom found extremely embarrassing, and blushed as each distinguished name was coupled with his own. 'What have I done,' he thought, 'a poor medical student, and not so outstanding at that, to be received amongst these lords and ladies on terms of equality, almost friendship?' At last the ordeal ended, and after engaging in some small talk with his host, Tom followed the guests into the dining-room. He sat very close to the Earl, on his right Shaftesbury's sister, Lady Harriet Cooper, and to his left Sir William Halley, the celebrated surgeon. What would his fellow-students say, he wondered, if they knew at this moment that the great Halley was chatting informally to one who was not yet competent to master the first half-dozen chapters of his classical text-book?

Halley and Lady Harriet quickly made him feel at home. As he had no social gossip, Tom found himself discussing the cholera epidemic with the doctor, and by her sympathetic questions Lady Harriet showed that she too was interested. The eight-course meal passed off without a hitch, and after grace the men repaired to the smoking-room for coffee and cigars. Standing forlornly by himself near the huge open fireplace, Tom sipped his coffee and watched the gestures of his fellow-guests as they animatedly discussed topics, the subjects of which he could only guess at. He began to feel that he had wasted his time in coming here. They were all charming people, no doubt, but it seemed that he would have to leave without advancing the cause of his children any further. He imagined that Splodger or the Black Doctor must have felt something like this when he had first approached them, regarding him as a stranger spying on their lives from without. Now he was in their position, and all these gentlemen, no matter how much they pried, could not probe to that kernel of misery that could only be understood from within.

'So you're the Barnardo we've been hearing so much about,' said a deep voice at his elbow.

Tom turned to face a tall, florid man, whose bushy grey side-whiskers reached down to his chin and gave him the appearance of a bluff country squire.

'Pardon me,' he apologized. 'I did not notice you.'

'Be peculiar if you had,' the other returned with a hearty chuckle. 'Damme! We're not made yet with eyes at the side of our heads – but with all these modern improvements, it may come still, one never knows.' He looked at the student critically. 'Strange, me lad, I don't know why, but I expected you to be a much older and a much bigger man.'

Tom flushed. He had never quite got over the sense of

inferiority produced by his shortness of stature. In his early youth it had been a sore point with him, but the best part of his sensitiveness on that subject had been overcome through contact with Hudson Taylor. He had the missionary to thank for more than directing his footsteps on the road to China. That day in Dublin when he and his friends had eagerly awaited the author of the famous pamphlet, and been rewarded by the appearance of a man smaller than Barnardo, had been a turning-point in the student's life. 'If such a man has carved a niche for himself in contemporary society,' the youngster had thought, 'then there is hope for me too,' and he had thereafter not felt his five-feet six as so severe a handicap, until this moment when all these brilliant people seemed to dwarf him with more than physical superiority.

'Sorry not to come up to your expectations,' Tom answered. 'But I am as God made me.'

His companion slapped a broad red hand jovially on the young man's shoulder.

'Very well put,' he said. 'Very well indeed. A nicely turned phrase, Mr Barnardo. Very nice indeed. It's easy to see why you are so popular in the East End. But tell me, speaking as man to man, do you really think your work in the slums is so important?'

'Obviously I think so,' retorted the student, 'or I should not spend so much of my time there.'

'Come – come, sir. Surely you realize that these poor people are necessarily poor. If it were not for the cheap labour they supply, our industries would not be able to span the world and add to the glory of our Empire – that includes the children. They are fit for nothing better. As a student of the Bible you must know that all these circumstances are divinely preordained. In the words of the hymn, "The rich man at his castle, the poor man at his gate" – eh, me lad? After all, Mr Barnardo, you don't set out to be the Messiah Himself!'

'I don't claim to be anything but an ordinary medical

student,' said Tom firmly. 'At the same time I refuse to believe God intended helpless children to starve in the gutters or sleep in the streets.'

'Nonsense!' his opponent insisted. 'In England nobody starves, and there is no need for anyone to sleep in the streets. In poor-law administration we lead the whole civilized world, and our Unions are there for whoever asks for the accommodation, apart from lodging-houses with beds available from tuppence a night. Damme! Because you happen to have found one or two misfits on the street, there is no need to shout to Heaven that something is rotten in the state of Denmark.'

'But something *is* rotten,' said Tom heatedly. 'And it isn't a question of one or two misfits, but hundreds and hundreds of children who have no homes but the streets.'

'Hundreds!' pooh-poohed his genial adversary. 'Pah! I wager you couldn't produce a dozen.'

Unnoticed by Barnardo he and the tall man had become the centre of a group of intent listeners. Before he could reply to the challenge, Shaftesbury appeared from the outskirts of the crowd to join issue with him.

'Hundreds!' the old man said gravely. 'That, if it were true, would be a blot on our civilization. Do you mean to infer that tonight, for example, on this bitterly cold evening, there are literally hundreds of homeless waifs asleep on our streets?'

'There are,' Tom asserted. 'I still say that is so.'

'Sir,' said his first questioner, 'if you were a betting man I would take you up on that.'

'My dear Barnardo,' Shaftesbury broke in soothingly, 'pay no attention to our friend Gannet. He is a cynic, but I assure you his heart is in the right place. Now you have made an extremely serious statement, and one that no person professing to be a Christian can afford to ignore. If these waifs are on the streets, can you prove your contention by leading us to them?'

'Your Lordship, I can!' said Tom confidently. 'I can, and I will.'

Soon after midnight the male guests set out from Grosvenor House, and Tom, with his host, Gannet and Halley in the first carriage led a line of cabs towards Billingsgate, where Barnardo knew there was a popular lay. At first not an urchin was visible, but the offer of a ha'penny for every arab that showed himself met with an immediate response, and from beneath the tarpaulins that covered the fish-boxes and barrels of Queens Shades seventy-three shabby youngsters emerged. Gannet could hardly believe his eyes as one tiny figure after another crawled from the lay, and was profuse in his apologies to Barnardo, who could not help noticing that his revelation had come as a terrific shock. Perhaps later Gannet's inner self-esteem would recover from this blow, but now it was apparent that the spectacle had severely shaken his comfortable feeling that everything was for the best in this best possible of all worlds. The bands of urchins crowded into Dick Fisher's, a nearby coffee shop, and were given as much to eat and drink as they could stomach, and Shaftesbury, changing half a sovereign into coppers, distributed the coins amongst them. It was obvious that the elderly statesman was more affected by this fresh evidence of juvenile distress than any of the company, and when at length the line of cabs set back westwards, leaving Tom to make his way home alone, the old man assured the student in a voice choking with emotion that the repercussions of this nocturnal visit would spread effectively far beyond the small circle of celebrities that had accompanied him.

CHAPTER 9

Tom knew that Shaftesbury would keep his word, but as he had learned from Comyns, legislation moved ponderously along sluggish channels, and meanwhile conditions remained the same with their accretions of outcasts and by-products of childish misery. Shaftesbury had said of his visit that all London would know of it. That was not enough. All England would have to know of it, the whole world would have to know of it to bring to an end once and for all this degrading situation, where children were treated as chattels, and could be discarded offhand to starve in the gutters with no responsible body to care for them, or to say that such a state of affairs could not be tolerated by any civilized nation. Haddock had it that these children were solely the government's responsibility, and that their plight could not be permanently improved unless the whole social system was altered. That was, or possibly was not, true, but Tom was not concerned with the wider aspects of the problem. The children were there, and he would do his utmost to save them now, and welcome whatever individuals would cooperate with him in this vital task.

Strange thoughts for a boy not yet twenty-two, ambitious and irrelevant programme for a youth who was studying medicine in preparation for China. Colossal conceit to think that he could make some impression, unknown and ignorant, where the finest brains of the nation had failed. If he had been an older and a more experienced man, he would have been appalled by the immensity of this problem, to which his earlier horizons were as a simple algebraical equation is to differential calculus.

His mind centred more and more on the children, oblivious

to everything else, and his heightened preoccupation did not pass by Comyns unnoticed. Phillip became afraid that his friend would have a relapse if he did not slacken the pace. The doctor had told him to laugh, to enjoy himself more, and here Tom kept pressing grimly towards half-known, hardly won objectives. Phillip determined to put his foot down. He had established himself as Tom's guardian, and he would see to it that his friend learned something of the lighter side of big city life as well.

When he first suggested a visit to a West End music-hall, Tom returned an uncompromising refusal. Phillip was not perturbed, but kept forcing his arguments on his friend, and after a while Tom's protests were silenced. It was not merely acquiescence, however, for Tom had decided to visit a music-hall, not as Phillip thought, to enjoy himself, but to study the audience, and discover a way to rope in even those men and women for the service of God. And he would not go to a West End haunt, but to one of the smaller halls with which Stepney was studded, the smaller and more disreputable the better. He had his mind on a 'penny gaff' which he had often passed on the Mile End Road, and which was much frequented by youngsters who could not afford the higher prices of the more popular halls. Comyns resisted stoutly, but he was no match for his stronger-willed friend, and though the penny gaff was ruled out, the two students decided on a visit to the Edinburgh Castle, the most notorious gin-palace in Limehouse.

The spacious façade of the public-house was brightly illuminated, and from the sound that came from the bars the interior was packed with an hilarious crowd. Tom and Phillip went in and squeezed past the customers crammed round the three long bars to the rear of the saloon that gave entrance to the music-hall. They made their way to a box past groups of nude statuary disposed prodigally about the large room, not from any artistic motives, but to whet the salacity of the patrons already inflamed by gin and the sly *double entendres* of the stage. A coarse-looking woman was singing a comic song in a loud hoarse voice, making up with winks and swirls of her petticoats for what little the writer had left unuttered. Waiters moved about the room, delivering drinks to the small marble-topped tables at the back of the hall and to the partitioned promenades at the sides. From the body of the room cheery voices accompanied the chorus on stage, and carelessly waved tankards beat through the air the rhythm of the song. Like a grey fog, clouds of tobacco shimmered round the large glass chandelier suspended from the centre of the ceiling, sour fumes of cheap shag mingling with the cloying colour of expensive cigars.

Tom found nothing to laugh at, the whole spectacle in fact disgusted him. But now he understood why these halls were so popular, and why the public-houses were always crowded. They were momentary, brightly lit avenues of escape from the dark reality of outside life. Here a man met his mates and forgot his troubles in a drink and a song. Haddock had been right. Apart from the taverns, nobody had any form of social life to offer these people in even spasmodic return for the monotonous grind of their daily existence, and the worst of them, surely, was entitled to some small respite from the grim struggles of the streets. Without the beer and the painted women on the stage, he could endorse such communal activity wholeheartedly; why *should* the publicans have the monopoly of these cheery meeting-places of the populace? Here, pushing China still farther away, was another problem to tack on to the homeless children. Possibly one went hand-in-hand with the other. Before his work in London was finished he would have a tilt at these sordid haunts too, and perhaps he would one day live to see the end of this Edinburgh Castle and another rise in its place to serve a nobler purpose – a public-house without beer.

With a loud blare of brass the turn ended. Wild applause

and a burst of 'Kentish Fire' rang down the curtain. The actress reappeared on the proscenium and blew her largesse of kisses to the whistling, stamping audience; then lifting her gaudily embroidered dress, she shook a thick leg at the men, and with a broad wink and a jerk of her huge befeathered hat, gathered the folds of the heavy plush curtain before her. When the tumult subsided, a cherry rubicund man dressed in the flash clothes of a 'sport' took the stage. Immediately he swept the audience into his confidence and launched into a description of his 'old woman', told with a thinly camouflaged string of swear-words. Every other phrase punctured with howls of laughter as each shaft of unmistakable obscenity struck home, and the loudest shrieks came from the women, who formed a small minority in the audience. Then the performer came to his favourite act that had earned him the soubriquet 'Gentleman Joe.' Exchanging his billycock for a high topper he stuck a pair of black beribboned pince-nez on his nose and started to imitate a swell on the drunk. Tom blushed uncomfortably as each exaggerated mannerism appeared to be directed solely at him. These people seemed to be born with a sense of hostility towards the upper classes, and their representatives on the stage showed their attitudes unmistakably. Sharing in the satiric drolleries of Gentleman Joe, they displayed their derision of and hatred for their enemies the 'toffs', transmuted vocally into raucous laughter.

A pretty soubrette followed the comedian, but Barnardo refused to stay any longer. He had seen enough. Every few moments a different woman had burst into their box as if by accident, and retired either discomfited because the two young men had ignored her advances, or angry and cursing as if Tom and his friend had no right to be seated there alone without women or alcohol. The waiter was more tenacious. His successive visits and wheedling requests for an order had irritated Comyns so much that he had given him a shilling and told him to leave them in peace. Phillip had also by this time found that the entertainment was beginning to pall. Without Tom he might have enjoyed it, with Brad and some of his cronies he certainly would have been as hilarious as the rest of the audience, but sitting next to his unsmiling companion, the pleasures he had once enjoyed seemed tawdry, vulgar triviality.

They rose from their seats and left the box, passing down the narrow gas-lit corridor to the body of the hall. At the exit a swaying figure, each arm round a woman's tightly laced waist, barred their passage. Tom tapped the man's shoulder gently.

'Pardon me, sir,' he said. 'Would you mind if we passed?'

'Not . . . hic! . . . not at all!' replied a cultured voice, slightly unsteady beneath its load of liquor. The hands – long, slim and well-tended – detached themselves from the corseted shapes, and the man turned. As soon as he looked down on Tom he burst into a roar of drunken laughter. For a moment Barnardo was nonplussed, the mist in the room had clouded his spectacles, and at first sight prevented him from recognizing Brad. The handsome youth doffed his hat and swept it before him with an exaggerated bow.

'Well! Well!' he exclaimed. 'The Reverend Barnardo! Fancy meeting *you* here!'

Tom without a word made another movement towards the door, but Brad lurched clumsily before him.

'Not so fast, your reverence, not so fast!'

'Brad – don't be a fool,' Tom protested. 'Let me pass.'

'Oh . . . no!' grinned Brad, swaying on his heels and shaking a slim remonstrative finger before his nose. 'Oh no, you don't! First you must meet my friends.'

'I don't want to meet your friends,' said Tom. 'I want to leave.'

'Nasty little squirt, ain't he, Bella?' remarked one of Brad's companions indignantly to the other woman. 'Snotty, an' no mistake!'

'That 'e is, Peg,' Bella returned in a shrill voice. 'Oo does 'e fink 'imself, anyways, the stuck-up froopenny bit. P'raps 'e finks we ain't good enough fer 'im.' She turned to Barnardo. 'I know yer sort, real gents when yer aout, but pigs when no one sees yer. I know wotcher like – an' believe me, I wouldn't let yer get close enough ter wipe me nose!'

Bella shook her tight black curls with a violent backward toss of her head, and to clinch the argument spat ostentatiously at Barnardo's feet. Brad roared again with laughter as Tom flinched before her outburst and looked round helplessly for some other way of escape.

'You know who this gentleman is?' said Brad, egging Bella on. 'He's a preacher. He preaches in the street!'

'I'll bet that ain't the only fing 'e does in the street,' Bella answered with a cackle.

'That's quite enough,' said Tom, addressing Brad. 'You've had your joke, now let me pass.'

'No jolly fear!' Brad replied. 'Not yet awhile. First let me tell you a thing or two, you slimy little hypocrite. Posing in the college as a plaster saint, and all the time you spend your evenings in places like the Edinburgh Castle. And we're not good enough for you! *Eh!* Well, let me tell you, what *we* do, we do in the open, and the whole world knows about it. As for you, you're not fit to lick our boots –'

''Ear – 'ear!' cried the blonde Peg raucously, clapping her hands in approbation, though her muddled brain could hardly grasp what it was all about.

Tom did not reply, but his contempt for Brad showed clearly on his face, which so angered the other student that he pinned Barnardo viciously by the shoulders as he made another move towards the door. This was more than Comyns could tolerate. He had remained silent in the hope that this encounter would end eventually with the passage of a few words, but now he pushed Tom aside and faced belligerently the drunken Brad.

'You leave him alone,' said Phillip grimly, 'or it will be the worse for you!'

'*Et tu*, Comyns!' Brad sneered. 'I thought at least *you* were a gentleman – one of us.'

'If being a gentleman means belonging to your crowd, then thank Heaven I'm no gentleman,' Phillip replied heatedly. 'Now get out of the way!'

He grabbed Brad by the arm and pulled him from the door, but immediately the two viragoes flung themselves on Phillip like wild-cats. Brad tried to pull Bella off; knowing her vicious nature he was afraid she might do Phillip an injury, but some malicious imp in his mind made his gesture a half-hearted pretence. Comyns defended himself as best as he could, Tom struggling with Peg, the noise by this time having attracted the attention of the audience, who infinitely preferred a brawl on the floor to any show on the stage. The orchestra played louder, the soubrette grinned as if her mouth would split and displayed her broadest antics, but the Edinburgh Castle audience had smelt blood, which was always a better entertainment than the make-believe behind footlights.

Several of the patrons recognized the women and hoarsely shouted them encouragement.

'Gorn, Bella!' 'Give it to 'im, Peg!' That was all the women needed. Their hair swept loosely over their faces as they struggled wildly with bursts of fierce language to get their fingers or teeth on Phillip, and he would have been left with some nasty scratches to remember them by if Nosher Bill Corum, the chucker-out, had not managed to elbow his path to them in time. The Nosher had a way with brawlers. Men he clumped unceremoniously over the head before he threw their inert bodies into the street; with women he had a gentler technique. Bending down, he curled one enormous arm round Bella and the other round Peg, and with an apparently effortless movement yanked them both off their feet. Their legs kicked futilely in the air to the huge enjoyment of the audience, as like a pair of captive piglets, they grunted and squealed their protests.

'Naow – wot's all this 'ere?' said Bill.

'Nothing,' Comyns answered. 'We just wanted to go – and these *ladies* stopped us.'

''E insulted me!' yelled Bella.

'Me too – the bloody ruffian!' Peg shrieked.

'You'd want a bit 'er insulting, the two of yer,' Nosher growled contemptuously. ''Oo's fault was it, guv'nor?' he inquired of Brad.

Brad's face turned a greenish tinge. He felt he was going to be sick. He knew Nosher Bill Corum and had seen examples of the chucker-out's brutality. Brad himself was only tolerated at the Castle because he was a prodigal spender, and he understood that Nosher was itching for the word to have a 'go' at the toffs. The small grey eyes in the gross bullet-head of the chucker-out were fixed on him meaningly. This had gone beyond a joke. Brad knew that if the Nosher started on the students, quite a number of the audience would not be loath to follow suit. He shook his head slowly.

'The men are all right,' Brad said. 'They're friends of mine.'

Nosher Bill turned towards Tom and his companion.

'Well,' he grunted. 'Yer wanted ter go – naow 'op it. Wot's stopping yer?'

He held the shrieking women under his arms until the two students disappeared, then with a scowl he dropped them to the floor. Immediately their indignation howled up at him, but he silenced them with a vicious kick apiece.

'Naow, you gels be'ave yerselves,' he said threateningly, 'or yer'll 'ave ter find another pub.'

Nosher Bill raised his arm towards the leader of the orchestra as a signal that the trouble was over, and without another glance at the grovelling women on the floor shoved his way back to the bar. Peg and Bella raised themselves, painfully rubbing the spots where the Nosher had impressed his gentle reminders, and as the brasses rose again the soubrette continued her interrupted performance. Slapping her swaying buttocks with her palms she strove to recapture the lascivious mood of the audience.

> 'Oosh – a – la – Ra
> Oosh a la la
> Lost the leg o' me drawers,
> If you find it
> Wash an' iron it
> An' give it to one of the boys.'

The attention of the audience became riveted once more on to the stage. The interruption had excited them, and the artiste, sensing their rising blood, twisted her sinuous body voluptuously as she sang, harnessing all their masculine vigour into bawdy appraisal of her performance.

Brad was left alone with his two companions.

''Ow about a drink?' Bella suggested, smiling up at him invitingly.

'Not me. I've had enough.' He pressed some silver into the woman's hand. 'You two go and have something; don't hurry, I'll wait till you come back.'

'Thanks, ducky!' Bella rose on her toes and kissed him heartily. ''At's wot I calls a *real* toff!'

Not to be outdone Peg repeated the performance and, with a wink, playfully pinched his cheek. Then linking arms with Bella, she flounced off with her to the bar, both women imperiously brushing aside the rough hands that stretched forward to fondle them. They had their own code of morals; while Brad paid for their drinks they belonged to him, and the promiscuous pawing that they normally encouraged with a laugh, they frowned on tonight, and either would have scratched out the eyes of anyone foolhardy enough to attempt to force on them his embraces.

Brad waited until they disappeared, then he quickly made his way through another exit to the street. Behind him Oosh-a-la-Ras whooped in fantastic abandon, but they only spurred him on to escape from those loud-mouthed harlots. He had no compunction in deserting them. When they discovered he had gone they would find someone else; if not, they were out of luck for the night. They would not hold it against him when they met again; to them each encounter was a separate chapter in their lives, no one could presume their slightest favours tomorrow even if they had sworn undying love all night.

CHAPTER 10

As soon as he reached the street, Brad felt thirsty again and completely sober. Damn that fellow Barnardo! He had been enjoying himself up till that little prig appeared, and now his whole evening was spoilt. He had intended to get mildly drunk, and then follow whichever path promised the maximum of pleasure, but now those simple, easily attainable delights appeared quite out of the question. He felt such a burning hatred for his colleague that it seemed he had to humiliate himself somehow and through his own person degrade Barnardo. In his present state of mind that thwarted bitter feeling engendered the thought that that was the only possible way to round off the evening with any satisfaction to himself.

He walked a little way down the road till he came to the Green Man. Botman, the owner, was a friend of Brad's, whose perverse humour encouraged the publican to treat him as an equal, not knowing that the student and the cronies who sometimes came with Brad mocked at every other word he spoke. Brad was that kind of person. People from all walks of life were attracted and won over by his charming manner and air of sincerity, until they crossed purposes with him at one time or another, and found to their cost the malignant spirit concealed beneath the suavity. He had plenty of money and was always ready to oblige with a loan, but those unfortunates who borrowed from him found themselves tied to Brad's cruellest whim, and as incapable of detaching themselves from those gilded cords as from the sharpest of money-lenders' clutches.

Botman's wife greeted him effusively as he entered. The publican apparently was out on some other business, and

Brad passed into one of the private bars. The Green Man, overshadowed by the more opulent Edinburgh Castle, attracted most of the younger people, and Brad found himself in a long, narrow room crowded with boys and girls, the oldest of whom did not appear more than twenty, the youngest roisterers perhaps below the age of thirteen. High-backed benches ran round the walls and in the centre was a large scarred brown table that stretched nearly the whole length of the room. The air was thick with tobacco smoke and noisy drunken shouts and snatches of ribald song. There was a sudden hush as the revellers took in Brad's presence, and one or two of the older boys made a threatening move towards him. The door opened and Mrs Botman appeared. Fixing her cold blue eyes on the surly youngsters, she halted them swaying in their tracks.

'It's all right, boys,' she said. 'Brad 'ere is a nice feller, a good sport.'

'Well, 'e'd better be a good sport some other plice,' said the taller boy. 'We don't want any toffs looking dahn our froats.'

Mrs Botman's red face turned a shade redder still. Her plump arms came to rest belligerently on her hips.

'Oh!' she replied. 'So this 'ere pub belongs ter you now, Jem Mason, does it?'

'Come orf it,' growled Jem. 'We're all reg'lar customers, Maggie, an' you knows it. Wot's more, we ain't gonner be no poppy show fer any bloody toff wot takes 'is fancy ter 'ave a squint at us!'

''Ear! 'Ear!' came shrill cries from the others. 'Chuck 'im auot! Bonnet 'im, Jem!'

'Just a moment, friends,' said Brad. 'This isn't the first time I've been here, and I hope it won't be the last.' His handsome face broke into one of its most winning smiles. 'Now, ladies and gentlemen, if you're not too proud to drink with me, call your orders to Mrs Botman, and I'll pay.'

'We don't want yer blooming drinks,' Jem growled obstinately.

'Speak fer yerself, Jem Mason,' one of the girls cried. 'I'll 'ave a tot er gin.'

'Me too.'

'Ale fer me.'

'Old an' mild, Maggie, an' not free-quarters frorth, neither!'

Mrs Botman nodded as she noted the orders, by merely counting the number of customers. She had no intention of pandering to any particular taste; they would have what they got, which was a pity, since as Brad was paying she would give them the best. Eventually she turned again to Jem who had retained a surly silence throughout the drunken clamour.

'An' you?' she asked.

'Orl right . . .' said Jem grudgingly at last. 'Make it a noggin er gin.'

'Doin' the gentleman 'andsome,' Mrs Botman replied sarcastically. 'Bit of er change from tuppenny ale, ain't it?'

'Oh! Give him what he wants,' Brad broke in impatiently. 'This is my party. Give him a gin. Give him a dozen if he can drink 'em!'

'Drink 'em!' cried Jem. 'I'll wager I kin drink any toff wot wor ever born under the table!'

'That's a bet!' said Brad. 'A drink for a drink, and may the better man win.'

One of the girls pushed her way up to Brad and pulled him with her to one of the benches. She was an attractive brunette of medium size, though her youthful figure had not yet developed, and the immature lines of her breast swelled delicately beneath her dark cotton frock that showed patches of dirty underwear almost as dark as her dress in between the frequent tears. Clutching Brad tightly by the arm, she sat beside him, and refused to let the other girls approach her prize, beating off with kicks and scratches any of those that came too near. As a consolation the other girls clustered round

Jem on the opposite side of the table, and he wallowed in their attentions, confident in his ability to hold his liquor and looking forward gloatingly to the tidy haul that not even Maggie Botman would be able to prevent his looting from the blotto toff's pockets.

Both men started to drink steadily. After several gins, Jem called for ale, and the barman replenished each tankard as soon as it was empty. Brad looked at the leering Jem through a thick mist of tobacco, and his rival's face seemed to have swelled to double its size. The girl's grip had tightened round his arm like an iron clamp and she rubbed her smooth face against his cheek and whispered endearments in his ears that cooed meaninglessly above the clangour of countless strident voices. What if Barnardo could see him now, swilling liquor at the same table as these gutter wretches in this rough house, lineal descendant of the old gin-shops that several generations earlier had signs boasting 'Drunk for a penny, dead drunk for tuppence' dangling invitingly over the door? How his Reverence would shudder! And yet that was not bad enough; if only Barnardo were here to watch him, he would devise some devilment to shake even that saint's belief in Man's immaculate soul.

Jem drank on. Brad envied his braggadocio, wondering how long he could keep it up, as each tankard swept into the air, tilted to his lips, and curved with a flourish to slither back empty on the brown puddles of the table. Damn it! . . . The fellow held his beer almost like a gentleman. He had evidently had plenty of practice. No wonder the dogs were starving. He began to feel indignant. A workman had no right to be able to stomach so much. Have pity on them! Huh! When all their wages went on drink!

Suddenly Jem looked at him, blinked owlishly, dropped his tankard with a clatter, and fell forward on the table, his tousled hair dripping in the foamy rivulets of beer. Immediately Brad rose, flushed with triumph and liquor, and making his way unsteadily round to Jem, grabbed his scalp and pulled his opponents head up to the light. His eyes were closed, the lower lip sagging downwards with an idiotic leer, trickles of beer coursing unheedingly down his face and neck. Brad smiled contemptuously. This plebeian clod dared challenge a gentleman to a drinking bout, a Wintringham whose forbears had spilled hogsheads of wine when the Masons had been feudal serfs and lucky to be able to slake their thirsts with water. His grip tightened on the dank hair, pulling it upwards viciously as if to tear it out by the roots. Giving a last triumphant grin at the bloated dirty face, he reversed the pressure, pushing downwards till Jem slid like a weighted sack beneath the table.

He remembered giving Mrs Botman some money and going to the door, but in the street he found to his surprise that the girl was still attached to his arm. The air seemed to have a remarkable recuperative effect on him, his head cleared as if he had just tossed down one or two drinks, and not enough to render several normal people insensible. Roughly he shook her off.

'What do you want?' he said.

The girl's eyes opened wide. 'But yer goin' 'ome wiv me, lovely! Yer said so inside.'

'With you?' Brad laughed uproariously. 'Why, I wouldn't be seen dead with a filthy little wench like you.'

''At's not wot yer said inside,' the girl repeated obstinately, moving closer to him with a slimy feline movement.

'Never mind what I said inside. I don't believe I said it anyway. Besides you're too young. Much too young!'

'I ain't!' the girl protested indignantly. 'I'm nearly fourteen.'

'Too young! Too young!' Brad pushed her aside and started down the street. 'Leave me alone, child, you're no more than a baby.'

She followed immediately behind him and before he had gone more than a few paces grabbed his coat-tails again.

'I ain't a kid – 'onest I ain't, lovey. Come 'ome wiv me an' I'll love yer like an old married woman.'

Brad stopped angrily, and faced her with a scowl. Eagerly she looked up at him, brazenly inviting, and clutched his arm, tightly pressing it against her breasts. Peg and Bella were bad enough, he thought, but this shabby drab was fit only for filthy hands like Jem's to fondle. Her rags stank of perspiration and beer, only her face shone with an attraction above her unprepossessing garments. Normally, Brad would have swept such solicitations into the gutter where they belonged, but the encounter with Tom and the enormous amount of liquor he had consumed had unleashed the conflicting desires that made up the hidden web of his character; the desire to hurt and be cruel and the desire to suffer as well, to make that cruelty greater. The girl noticed that his resistance was weakening, unaware that Brad was undergoing a species of mental flagellation. Thinking that all she had to do was increase his ardour, she pressed closer to him unashamedly in the street, and stroked his face and body with the practised lingering touch of the hardened prostitute.

'Come 'ome, lovey,' she whispered. 'Are yer comin'?'

'All right,' said Brad at last. 'All right. Where d'you live, far from here?'

'No,' she answered. 'Not very fer. Up at Ma Collins' plice.'

'Ma Collins, who's she?'

'She runs the doss-'ouse where I kips. An' I ain't like them low 'ussies wot sleeps in the common dormiteries. I gotter grand room of me own wiv only Lila ter share it.'

'And supposing Lila objects?' Brad said whimsically.

'She won't. 'At wor that ginger gel setting right next ter Jem. She won't bring no one else 'ome, nor 'erself tonight, neether.'

Passively Brad allowed himself to be led down the street, slouching along the pavement and leaning occasionally on the girl for support. Dark figures appeared in doorways, menacing shadows that disappeared as soon as it became obvious that the 'swell' was already in tow. Alone and befuddled with drink Brad would never have negotiated these apparently somnolent side-streets without accident, but the freemasonry of the underworld allowed him safe conduct so long as the girl was his companion; later the shadows would materialize like swooping jackals and yet find a little nourishing meat among the contemptuously discarded bones.

The alcohol still clouded a portion of Brad's brain and left him sublimely indifferent to the dangers he was facing. He felt a perverse satisfaction in the close presence of the girl that attracted him in its very repulsiveness . . . Well . . . Well . . . So now he was off to a common lodging-house, the last refuge of the lost. Might as well go the whole hog, do just those things that the sanctimonious hypocrites were scared to death about, and damn the consequences! A man wasn't a man till he'd had a couple of shots of the pox. Long live death – and decay – and putrefaction – and to Hell with lily-livered psalm-singing half-men!

At last the girl stopped outside a dirty-looking two-storied house. A naked gas-jet burned above the open door, and across the fanlight was daubed in whitewash, 'Good beds for women. Rooms to let by the day or week.'

'We're 'ere,' said the girl.

'So this is Ma Collins,' Brad commented. 'Why this fond maternal tag? Does she treat all her lodgers like a mother?'

'Dunno,' said the girl. 'She wor called Ma afore I kum 'ere an' I 'speck she'll still be Ma when I'm gorn. She ain't a bad sort, neether, though the gels says she's a terror when she's crossed.'

Brad laughed. 'I dare say she is. And I dare say you are too, my pet. Well, well – I don't expect I can ever get closer to the gutter – so lead on, my precious; lead on, my tattered little trollop of the streets.'

The girl clasped him firmly round the waist in order to help him on to the threshold, but with a jovial gesture Brad released her grip, and to show he was capable of mounting the stairs without assistance, climbed on to the first step and grinned down at her as though he had accomplished a meritorious feat. He turned, essaying unsteadily the next step, and would have fallen but for the girl's support from behind. Grinning with satisfaction as if her help were part of his own strength, Brad passed into a narrow, dark, evil-smelling corridor and towards some more stairs. Jauntily he picked his feet up, while they were still on the level floor-boards of the passage. One step . . . two steps . . . Oosh-a-la-la . . . Oosh-a-la-la – Lost the leg of me drawers . . .

The girl's room was on the first landing. She went in before Brad to put a light to the gas-jet, then welcomed her visitor in with obvious pride. The room was low-ceilinged, about ten feet square, and there was a small table in the centre and two iron bedsteads pushed against opposite walls. A straw palliasse covered each bed, and coarse tick-like sheets dangled to the floor like faded yellow sacking. So this was the grand room. Brad walked to the nearest bed and dropped on to it heavily, leaning his back against the wall for support.

'Lovely, ain't it?' said the girl eagerly. 'Fit fer any queen as ever wor!'

Brad smiled tolerantly. Through the smooth cloth of his trousers, the unaccustomed roughness of the palliasse irritated his buttocks. He was beginning to feel a bit ashamed of himself, the child was so obviously in earnest and so pathetically eager to please. The effect of the damned liquor came on and wore off in spasms; if only he felt himself, the devil of a fellow as he had been so surely a few minutes ago! Now he could feel no attraction in this dirty wretch, or foretaste the excruciatingly pleasureful pain of self-defilement.

The girl came across to him and nestled at Brad's feet, putting her head on his knees. She waited expectantly for his caresses to touch her hair, but Brad's hand felt irresolutely in his waistcoat instead. Suddenly the student's body stiffened, and the bed creaked as he sat up. His hand came down roughly on her shoulders, flinging her violently aside, and he jumped to his feet, standing angrily over the cowering girl.

'You thieving little whore,' he shouted. 'Where's my watch?'

She shrank back against the bed, drawing up her legs as if to minimize the effect of an expected kick. Piteously she looked up at Brad.

'Wot watch?' she said. 'I don't know nuffing about any watch.'

'You don't, eh?' Brad snorted grimly. He leaned over her and grabbed her roughly by the shoulders. 'Now let me have it, quickly, or you'll know a thing or two!'

'I ain't got it, 'onest I ain't. P'raps you left it at the Green Man.'

'If I did, you're the only one that took it!' said Brad. He pulled the girl to her feet and started to shake her violently as if he could thereby expel the watch from her rags. 'Now, come on! Out with it. Out with it!'

Nimbly the girl slipped from his grasp and ran to the door, but he was on her before she could open it. His hand caught her arm and twisted it viciously behind her back. He would teach this little gutter rat she was not trifling with an ordinary drunk. Her body twitched with pain as he forced her arm upwards and Brad felt a thrill of pleasure as a sharp twinge brought a shriek of anguish to her lips. Manœuvring her away from the door, he threw her roughly on to a bed.

'Now what about my watch?' he repeated menacingly.

The door opened silently behind him and a huge woman squeezed her way through the opening. It was the redoubtable Ma Collins herself. She wore dark clothes tightly laced, but her thirty stone of flesh could not be denied and ballooned in enormous sausages in the most unexpected places. Her faded blonde hair was piled high on her head and every other finger was indented by rings half-embedded beneath rosy pouches of fat.

'Wot's all this 'ere rumpus?' her throaty voice inquired.

Brad turned angrily on the intruder. When he had recovered from his momentary astonishment at her size he blurted out: 'What's that to you? What are you doing here, anyway?'

'I likes that!' said Ma Collins, with fluent self-possession. 'If it comes to that, wotcher doin' 'ere yerself? Arter all, I owns the plice, so I sorter gotter right ter be 'ere, but it's s'posed to be a lodging-'ouse fer women, an' *you* don't look like a woman ter me no'ow!'

'Oh! . . . She stole my watch,' said Brad.

'It's a lie!' the girl protested. ''E's drunk!'

'Orl right! Orl right!' said Ma Collins soothingly. 'We'll soon find out.'

She crossed over to the girl and ran expert hands over her clothes, as she did so catching a meaning wink in her eye, and a movement and a swift word that conveyed to Ma Collins that there was still money in that young man's pockets. Satisfied with her cursory examination, she returned to Brad.

'The gel ain't got no watch,' she said.

'She has,' replied Brad obstinately, 'and I don't budge from here till I get it.'

'Yer won't, eh?' said Ma Collins. 'Well, we gotter special way er dealing wiv drunks.'

She gave a shrill whistle, and a moment later a short, thick set, middle-aged man entered the room.

''E's cuttin' rough,' said Ma Collins laconically, jerking a fat arm in Brad's direction.

Without more ado she advanced her elephantine bulk on Brad, her arms outstretched like a wrestling bear. The student backed away from her, but the others were not idle and in a moment he found himself struggling furiously on the floor with the little man and the girl. Wrenching himself free, he rose to his feet, but Ma Collins blocked his escape and enveloped him in an overpowering embrace. He felt his strength being absorbed, beating unavailingly against the hideous soft cushions of her flesh that pressed against him like the nauseating odorous sliminess of an octopus. His coat was torn from his shoulders and he felt himself being lifted in the air. A fresh draught of wind blew against his face and he dropped, dropped with a thud on the pavement. A moment later his coat flew out of the same window and settled like a sack over his shoulders.

Fortunately Brad had fallen on his feet. Ma Collins had not troubled to have him thrown down the stairs, but had ejected the troublesome drunk through the window. If he had crashed on his head that would have been his own look-out and nobody would ever have come forward with any knowledge of the accident. Brad shakily pulled on his coat, leaning against the wall. He felt in his pockets and smiled wryly, his purse had gone to join his watch. Suddenly a 'bulls-eye' flashed on him, dazzling his vision as the light focused on his face.

'Now then, me lad,' said a gruff voice. 'Votcher doin' 'ere?'

Shading his eyes, Brad saw a burly policeman standing over him, and regarding him quizzically.

'Drunk, eh?'

'No,' Brad answered. 'Not very. But I'm glad you're here, constable – I've been robbed.'

'Robbed?' said the policeman. 'Vere?'

Brad jerked his thumb behind him.

'In here.'

'Vell,' commented the constable. 'You picked the werry splendidest 'ouse in London ter wisit – I shouldn't grumble if I was you – yer come off lucky!'

'Lucky!' said Brad ironically. 'Lucky to lose my watch and all my cash?'

''At's wot I said,' returned the policeman imperturbably. 'A bloke like you wot wisits Ma Collins is lucky ter come aout alive.'

'Lucky or not,' Brad replied, 'I've lost my watch and I want it back. Are you coming in with me? I could recognize the girl – and the man in there too.'

The policeman shook his head.

''Tain't no manner o' use. Yer won't find 'em now. Take me tip, son. Leave vell alone and go along 'ome, me lad.'

He caught Brad's arm and walked with him towards the door. At the entrance of the lodging-house the huge figure of Ma Collins appeared. She smiled jovially at the policeman.

''Evening, Mister Coates,' she said.

''Evening, Ma,' he replied. 'So yer bin up to some more o' yer tricks, eh?'

'Tricks?' Ma Collins's mouth widened in an expression of astonishment. 'Tricks? I'm surprised at yer, Mr Coates. Wotcher talkin' abaout?'

'You know right enough,' said the policeman. 'This 'ere young gent says as 'ow 'e's bin robbed in your 'ouse.'

''Ere?' Ma Collins shook her head in bewilderment. 'Yer know it's agin the rules fer men ter come in me 'ouse – an' I stick by the rules, Mr Coates, *I* does.'

'Oh!' said Brad. 'So I'm quite a stranger, I presume?'

Ma Collins stared at him blankly, then turned to the policeman.

'As true as Gawd I ain't seed 'im afore in me life – the young gent must be drunk!'

'Not drunk enough to be unable to recognize that girl,' said Brad heatedly, 'and that rogue of a man in there too.'

Ma Collins ignored him completely, and addressed her reply to the policeman.

''Onist,' she said plaintively, 'I don't know wot 'e's talkin' abaout. There ain't no man in 'ere at this time o' night. This is a respectable ken, this is, an' well yer knows it.'

'Then I don't suppose you'd object if we came in?' said Brad.

Ma Collins turned on him loftily. ''Course I objects,' she replied. 'Men wot comes in 'ere ter look raound 'as ter 'ave a permit from the Guvernment – an' seein' you ain't got one yer stays where you is, yer little nosey parker!'

'Never mind about the Government,' the policeman broke in. 'If yer really vant ter go inside,' he said to Brad, 'I'll take yer – only yer vesting yer time, me lad, believe me!'

Brad shrugged his shoulders. The outraged indignation of Ma Collins now struck him as extremely amusing. After all it was his own fault. He had asked for trouble and he had got it, and as the policeman observed, had been fortunate to be let down so lightly. He could write off the watch and the money as a temporary loss, but they would go on the debit account. It was really because of Barnardo. One day, he swore to himself, the saint would pay for this disastrous adventure, pay completely and with interest . . .

'Vell?' inquired the policeman impatiently.

'All right . . .' said Brad. 'Let's go.'

Ma Collins smiled at them from the doorstep.

''At's bein' sensible, young man. I know wot it's like when yer aout on er drunk. Fings get sorter mixed up.' She shook her huge head tolerantly. 'I bears yer no 'ard feelings, laddie – it 'appens when yer young – but yer didn't ought ter drink so much if it turns yer 'ead. 'Appy dreams, young feller, an' – Good night, Mr Coates.'

Majestically she turned and vanished down the corridor. Brad felt his knees beginning to sag, the excitement and the liquor were just starting to have some real effect. He flung his arm round the policeman, and waited for the dizzy, weak spell to wear off. At last, he straightened himself and grinned a trifle sheepishly.

'Orl right?' asked Mr Coates.

'Fine, constable,' said Brad. 'Just a little dizziness. It's gone off now. I'm feeling fit as a fiddle.'

'Good,' the constable replied. 'I'll see yer daown the road. An' take my tip, don't ever come near Ma Collins' agin. I seen drunks 'arf dead in this werry street an' no one knowed 'oo they vas, or vere they came from. Yer'd never 'ave found anyone in Ma Collins'; by this time the two of 'em must be 'arf a mile away. Vunce these thieves gets in the lodging-'ouses, they wanishes like ghostses. They got underground passages from one ken to another, and they burrows down 'em like rabbits ven the law's on their trail.'

Brad nodded. All this was very true and he had heard it before, but he was no longer interested in Ma Collins or the girl or the notorious thieves' kitchen into which he had blundered. He had suffered a loss, and he would never forget it, although it had brought him a vicarious sense of satisfaction, and now that he had a concrete grudge against Barnardo he would find an opportunity one day to more than level the score, even if that were to be the last thing he ever did.

At the Commercial Road his escort stopped.

''Ere ve are,' said Mr Coates. 'Stick ter the main road, keep in the middle er the pavement, an' you'll be orl right.'

'Thanks,' Brad replied. 'It was good of you to trouble yourself, but I'd be all right, anyhow. My watch and my purse are gone, I've got nothing else to lose.'

'I dunno so much,' answered the constable with a chuckle. ''At's a nice coat yer vearin', and ven that's lifted there's still some lads might take a fancy to yer trousis! Good night, young feller – look arter yerself.'

'Thanks,' said Brad. 'I'm obliged, and good night, Mr Coates, to you.'

CHAPTER 11

Tom stepped down from the box, and the good-humoured crowd that had been listening to him slowly dispersed. Knots gathered round the more persistent of his hecklers, a little way off, carrying on his arguments in more homely terms, more vigorously blunt expressions. The Mile End Waste always drew him like a magnet. Whenever he passed down that wide pavement and had half an hour or more to spare, Tom always took part in any discussion that was going, or started an impromptu meeting of his own. He had only two subjects, God and the homeless children, but he was sufficiently interesting always to draw a crowd that included a fair sprinkling of agnostics, atheists, and downright materialists – whose ingenuously shrewd Cockney witticisms kept the audience in high humour, and tested his powers of repartee to the full. Such jousting he felt almost to be a necessity, since even if he converted none of these hardened hecklers the thrust and parry of argument brought its own compensation in a sharpening of the inner vision, as if the corners were dusted off a familiar object long undisturbed, revealing anew its slumbering beauties.

He returned his platform to the adjacent coffee-stall whence he had borrowed the box, and, thanking the owner for its use, started off for home. Before he had gone more than a few yards he felt a tug at his sleeve, and turning, recognized his old friend Splodger, from Three Colt Street Market.

''Evening, guv,' said the labourer. 'Wot's the 'urry? Don't tell me yer gotter see a lidy!'

Tom laughed. 'I have no time for ladies. I haven't much time for anything except those things I've been talking about. Did you hear me, Splodger?' he asked.

'I 'eard yer,' said Splodger. 'But Gawd's got plenty o' time, an' if 'E kin wait, so kin you.'

'That's where you're mistaken,' Tom returned. 'God has countless ages in which to perform His works, and I've only got a little lifetime.'

'Aw! Come orf it!' Splodger chuckled. 'Yer talkin' as if yer was ninety, with one foot in the grave, and the other on yer death-bed. I'll tell yer wot, come in an' 'ave a pint, eh?'

'No, thank you, Splodger, I don't drink.'

'Don' drink, got no lady friends – well, I must say yer a rummy cove fer a young 'un.' Splodger shook his head with an air of mock gravity. 'I bin 'earin' a lot abaout you lately, an' I've listened ter you on the Waste once or twice. My! – but yer come on a bit since the old moke in Three Colt Street. It ain't above a couple er years. Then yer was a nobody, a furriner, a little green 'orn, now I dare say there ain't a bloke in the East End wot ain't 'eard of the young Doctor, an' ain't got something ter tell abaout yer, good, bad or indifferent.'

'It's very nice of you to say that,' said Tom. 'But I'm afraid you're hopelessly wrong – on all counts. I'm still a nobody, I'm not a doctor, and I've never been a foreigner.'

'Oh no!' Splodger returned, shaking his head again, gravely. 'I won't 'ave that. Oh no! I bin takin' all the credit with me mates fer 'avin' discovered yer, an' when I says yer famous in these parts I knows wot I'm talking abaout – maybe better'n you. It don't matter abaout not being a doctor neither, yer belongs ter the 'orspital, an' 'at's good enough. As fer being a furriner, yer looks like one, yer talks a bit like one, an' if that don't make yer a furriner, nuffing ever will.'

Tom smiled. 'All right, Splodger,' he conceded. 'I plead guilty, even to being a foreigner, although there are few places where I could really be one. I was born in Dublin, but there's Hebrew blood in me, and a bit of Spanish, and perhaps Moroccan and German, Yorkshire and Irish. A little bit of all sorts, and the whole lot at the service of my Maker.'

'Yer know,' said Splodger ruminatively, 'yer took on er big job when yer started with them arabs. Wot made yer do it?'

'What else *could* I do? I saw the way they live. That was more than enough. I don't think that in the whole world there can be a more piteous sight than the spectacle of children homeless on the streets.'

'Steady on, guv,' Splodger answered. 'Naow yer makin' a claim an' 'arf. When yer talks abaout wot yer knows yer in order, but there's still a lot abaout the East End yer don't know. There's some kids wot's got 'omes an' parents an' is a sight worse orf than them arabs on the streets. An' then there's the growin' boys, lads er sixteen an' seventeen, even them that's workin', 'as got no 'omes but the lousy doss-'ouses, an' I don't know as 'ow *they* wouldn't be better orf on the streets too!'

'You're right,' said Tom. 'It is an enormous problem, and I can assure you I know my limitations. That's why I'm tackling one thing at a time, and to the best of my ability, as the Lord leads me. So far as I know, the arabs are a virgin field, but for these young men there are several Christian bodies already interested in their welfare.'

'Carn't be very interested,' Splodger remarked dubiously, 'or they'd 'ave done somefing solid by this time.'

'I don't know,' said Tom. 'There's that fine woman, Annie McPherson, at Bethnal Green. She's doing the Lord's work in this vineyard too, and through her efforts close on eighty young men have already been trained for work on the land of Canada.'

'Canidy!' snorted Splodger. ''Oo the 'ell wants ter go ter Canidy? If I'm born 'ere I wants ter make a living 'ere, not be shipped orf like an 'ead of cattle ter Canidy!'

'But if you can't make a living here?'

'Then it ain't my fault. The conditions is ter blame. It ain't no solution ter send a shipload o' youngsters ter the wilderness, or even a dozen shiploads. The trouble's 'ere, an' them emigrants don' matter a fleabite, one way or t'other. It don' make things better ter send em aout of it. No, guv, the solution ter the problem of these unemployed youngsters is ter find 'em work 'ere, where they belongs, an' fer as long as yer can't do that yer won't make things better by sendin' a few on 'em away.'

'I'm not disposed to argue with you on that score,' said Tom slowly. 'Obviously the only real remedy is to find them work in England.'

''At's it, matey!' Splodger nodded approvingly. ''At's it. 'At's jest wot I says – 'at's jest wot I says.'

'Then we're in complete agreement. That is the ideal solution, but conditions being what they are, they haven't got work, and don't seem likely to have any in the near future, and even you as a materialist must admit they're better off, healthy and working on the land in Canada, than starving and unemployed at home.'

'Orl right,' said Splodger grudgingly. ''At's true, but it's a bad reflection on the state er affairs in our country when she's got ter send 'er young blood auot of it. 'At still don' even begin ter touch the problem,' he answered doggedly.

The labourer took a tiny stump of cigarette from behind his ear and lit it carefully. Holding it gingerly between thumb and forefinger he gave one or two puffs with every evidence of enjoyment, and as the burning rice-paper encroached on his very fingertips he reluctantly threw the soggy, smouldering pellet away.

'Naow I fink we'll 'ave a drink,' he grunted.

'By way of a change, eh?' said Barnardo.

'Change is right. Berlieve me, I wisht I didn't 'ave ter drink – only the more I finks of wots goin' on in the world araound me, the more I 'as ter drink ter make me fergit.'

'That's only an excuse,' Tom answered. 'Perhaps you have to drink at your work, but I don't believe you drink to forget. Why should you forget, anyway? Just the reverse, you should keep those evils on your mind all the time, then perhaps you'd try your best to do something about them.'

'Wot's the use?' said Splodger resignedly. 'I 'ave tried. I bin talkin' on this same Mile End Waste afore yer was pupped, but all I gets is a sore froat. I'm done wiv talkin', naow all I'm goin' ter do is drinkin' until somefing really 'appens – then I'll be there, guv, yer kin bet on me; old Splodger ain't dead, 'e's only arf asleep.'

He turned away from Tom and made as if to leave him, but the student detained him with a quick gesture.

'Where are you going?' he asked.

'Ter the boozer,' said Splodger in a matter-of-fact tone.

'Don't go,' Tom pleaded earnestly. 'I want to talk to you. I feel there's something fine about you. Don't throw it away on the pub. Honest, Splodger, I believe you can still be saved.'

Splodger loosed a hoarse guffaw. 'I'm parst savin',' he replied. ''Oo wants ter be saved, anyways? The only fing kin save me naow is a couple er pints er old an' mild. Don't bother wiv me, guv, I'm parst that stage, I tells yer. I knows too much – I ain't no good any more.'

'Everybody has *some* good in them all the time,' said Tom.

'Even a 'ardened repobrite the like o' me?' Splodger chuckled. 'No, guv, I've 'ad me fill o' Gawd, an' savin' – but if yer wants ter do a real bit er good, why don't yer go dahn the doss-'ouses an' try yer 'and at some o' the young 'uns? I'll tell yer wot, there's a kid at the ken where I lives. 'E needs savin' mighty bad, in fact 'e looks ter me like 'e's goin' ter 'eaven any day naow, saved er not saved. Whyn't yer 'ave a shot at aour young Terrence?'

'Is he ill?' Tom asked.

'That 'e is,' said Splodger, 'or I ain't seed an ailing person afore in me life. 'E ain't left 'is bed fer four days – an' 'e couldn't, even if 'e was minded.'

'Why not?'

''Cause the deputy's got 'is clobber, an' won't give it back till 'e pays 'is rent. If us blokes dahn there didn't give Terrence a bite o' grub naow an' agen the pore kid'd starve.'

'That's enough,' said Tom. 'I'll be down to see him. Where d'you live?'

'Coppock's. Flahr An' Dean Street. Yer carn't miss the plice. It's right in the middle er the street, an' painted white like a bloody great tombstone. When yer comin' – soon?'

'In an hour or so,' Tom replied. 'I can't say definitely because I have several things to see to at home, but I'll be there tonight, without fail.'

Splodger patted him commendatorily on the shoulder. ''At's the ticket, guv,' he said. 'I'll tell 'im yer comin'. Well, naow I'll be orf meself, an' as yer won't jine me I'll swaller an extra couple er pints an' say "'At's fer the little doctor."'

Tom watched the tall labourer slouch off with a slightly unsteady gait, his long legs bending with an exaggerated movement at the knees until he disappeared into the nearest pub. Splodger was past redeeming, yet he felt no antipathy to the coalie in spite of his drunken habits. They seemed as much a part of the man as his dirty deerstalker cap or his grease-loaded knee-belted corduroys. Tom always seemed to come across him at some crisis in his life. On that memorable Saturday he had brought him to the Black Doctor, now Splodger was leading him to a lad in a doss-house. He wondered if this fresh adventure would be as pregnant of revelations as the event that led to his meeting with little Jimmy in the whitewashed donkey-stable. Whatever happened, it seemed that God was calling on him again, and moving in this peculiar way through an avowed and drunken disbeliever.

CHAPTER 12

The packages were opened, the pamphlets sorted out, done up again in parcels and neatly ticketed. Tom felt a thrill of satisfaction as he surveyed his handiwork. He always worked to a system; if the Lord sent him first into a merchant's office he understood now that it had been done for a reason, to teach him to be methodical for the greater glory of God. Now everything was ready for distribution, but that would have to wait for another night.

If he had one weakness, they were these religious pamphlets. A pamphlet had brought him to the Saviour, and most of his father's allowance went towards the purchase of these tracts. He had paper-cover Bibles, quotations from the prophets and apostles, the messianic revelations and modern evangelical brochures. He distributed them in the streets and public-houses, but like a keen psychologist placed a small charge upon the more expensive productions, so that having some monetary equivalent, they would not be discarded unread. Leaflets were free, but for Bibles and bulkier pamphlets he charged exactly half of what they cost. He was becoming a familiar figure in the East End, and equally familiar was the brown-paper parcel stiff with literature that he usually carried under his arm.

Tonight, however, was an exception. It was late, and he was going out for a specific purpose; if he dawdled on the road he might be refused admittance to the lodging-house, and that would be an evening wasted where every hour, every minute was important and dedicated to his self-imposed tasks.

Leaving his lodgings he crossed Whitechapel Road, and passed down the Waste. Even at this late hour there were still groups of men dotted about, arguing fiercely, as serious in their vocal efforts to hit on next day's big winner as in their attacks on the standpoint of orthodox theology or Tory politics. Several of the disputants acknowledged him as he passed by, lifting their hands to their caps, but Tom was too engrossed in this new adventure to notice them or hear their greetings.

He walked nearly as far as the Hay Market, then turned right, down Brick Lane, and crossing the road found Flower And Dean Street a little way up on the left. Whitechapel Road and Brick Lane, being main thoroughfares, were fairly well illuminated, but this side turning was practically without lighting. A single lamp shed its faint yellow rays in a nebulous circle on the pavement midway down the street and there was another at the far end. That seemed the sole illumination except for a red glow that shone above the doorway of one of the houses, and being a sign of the best 'kens' was probably the tinted lantern that marked Coppock's palace of rest. At this distance and in the poor light, Tom could not distinguish the 'White Tombstone' of Splodger's picturesque description, but to make perfectly certain he scrutinized each house carefully on both sides of the road as he made his way towards the red glow.

He had not gone more than a dozen paces when, passing a narrow alley, hands shot out behind the student, and dragged him into the darkness before he could utter a sound. Three or four shadows surrounded him, and with dexterous movements his coat was yanked off his shoulders, his pockets deftly rifled, his watch and chain extracted, and his hat whisked from his head. The whole operation was carried through practically in silence; Tom was too surprised to shout, and his assailants, apart from the pressure of their hands, and the rapid shuffling of their boots, uttered only sharp little grunts mingled with their heavy breathing to show they were anything more substantial then shadows themselves.

A violent push that jolted his glasses from his nose sent

him staggering out of the alley again, and quick footsteps like a soft rush of wind faded down the street. Tom turned and dropping on his hands and knees groped for his spectacles. He did not mind so much losing his money and his other belongings, but he was blind without his glasses, and if they were broken or he could not retrieve them he would have to forgo his promised visit, and far less important, the thought struck him, be lucky to make his way home alone.

His anxious fingers combed the cold stones as he moved with infinitesimal gradations in the direction of the alley until, after what seemed an age, the smooth surface of a lens brushed against his knuckles. Eagerly his fingertips moved round the steel rims, and to his huge relief found the glasses intact. He rose to his feet breathing a little prayer of deliverance, and setting his spectacles more firmly on his nose resumed his interrupted journey.

As he came closer to the red light, the outlines of a grey building merged from the uniform darkness of the contiguous houses. This was Coppock's without a doubt, so one part of his journey was ended, and that the least difficult; the remainder, whatever happened, could certainly not prove so disastrous. Before he quite reached the lodging-house he heard again rapid footsteps behind him, but he walked straight ahead without flinching or turning. 'What have I to fear from man,' he thought, 'if God is with me?' It had been proved to him again and again abundantly to his own satisfaction that he was never completely alone. 'Yea, though I walk through the valley of the shadow of death I fear no evil . . . I fear no evil . . .'

In spite of his firm beliefs, he gave a little jump when a tentative hand touched his shoulder. The recent events had shaken him up somewhat and he had not yet recovered his equilibrium. It showed that there were still chinks in his armour that the devil could pierce. His faith was not yet complete if it could be so instantaneously abrogated by what was after all only a minor mishap. These things were merely sent to try him. The student pulled himself together, stopped and turned. He saw facing him a shabby youth of heavy build with a bundle in his arms, surmounted by a top-hat, which gave him the appearance of an itinerant dealer in the old-clothes exchange. With a hang-dog look the youth held the bundle towards Barnardo.

''Ere y'are, guv,' he said shamefacedly. 'Take 'em. They're yours.'

Mystified, Tom took back his garments, and became even more surprised when his watch, chain and purse were thrust into his hands.

'There y'are, guv,' said the youth. ''At's the lot.'

'Th-thanks,' Tom could only stammer. 'But . . . b-but why snatch them in the first place?'

'We're sorry, guv, the lot on us. We didn't recognize yer or we'd never 'ave done it. Yer see we're a bit 'ard up, h'ain't even got the price of a kip an' some grub, so when we sees a toff comin' dahn the street, we finks 'ere comes somefing good ter eat – that's only nacheral, but when we sees it's you – well . . . it ain't like a stranger, we couldn't do er fing like that ter you naow – could we?'

Tom laughed. 'I'm extremely glad you couldn't, but if you wanted some money, why didn't you ask?'

'Well,' replied the Cockney, a little more cheerfully, 'first, we ain't the arstin' sort, second, arstin ain't never much good, h'an' third, a swell wot comes dahn 'ere is arstin fer trouble 'isself – an' 'e knows it, h'an' if *we* didn't lighten 'im some uvver blokes would, as might not be so gentle neither.'

'Then I'm extremely fortunate not to have met those "other blokes" as you call them. And I must say, much as I disapprove of it, that you did the "lightening" with efficiency and dispatch.'

Tom put on his hat and coat and restrung his chain across his waistcoat. He weighed his purse in his hands, there were only a few shillings in it. He could get more tomorrow, while this boy was one of three or four who needed the money for food and shelter. Impulsively he stretched forward for the youth's hand, and emptied the purse on to his open palm.

'There you are,' he said. 'Share it between you.'

The Cockney stared at the money with bewilderment. He held his hand in front of him and looked first at the coins and then at Barnardo, then, seeming to come to a decision, he closed his fist and thrust his hand towards the student. Determinedly, he shook his head.

'No, guv,' he muttered, 'we didn't ought ter take it.'

Tom patted the Cockney's outstretched fist and pushed it firmly away from him.

'Nonsense,' he insisted. 'Keep it, with my compliments!'

'But we h'ain't done nuffing ter derserve givin' us all yer money,' the youth protested.

'Oh yes, you have,' Tom chuckled. 'Someone stole my clothes, and you found them. That's the reward.'

Raising his hat, he bade the astonished Cockney 'Good night,' and passed through the open door of the lodging-house. There was a gas-light burning in the passage, illuminating a staircase that led upwards to the dormitories, and another short flight of steps that descended to the communal kitchen.

Tom pushed open the kitchen door and found himself in a large room lit by two hissing gas-jets and a huge coke fire that was kept burning day and night, being the only facilities available for cooking or obtaining hot water. A large table stood in the centre of the room, flanked by two long benches, but only one man sat by himself at the far end, a man who appeared rather better dressed than the other lodgers – a rough, dirty crowd, who were grouped on chairs and low stools before the fire, engaged either in playing cards or as spectators, or squatting on the floor rolling dice. A bearded, dishevelled man raised his hand in the air, holding an incredibly dirty trump card, and, grinning broadly, was about to slap it triumphantly on his opponent's ace with the vigorous, blasphemous chaff that such play demanded when he caught sight of Tom standing by the door. The language froze on his lips, and his hand became arrested in the air as if it had suddenly become paralysed.

'Well! Well!' he exclaimed.

'Come on, Curly,' grunted the man behind him. 'Wot's up wiv yer? Clap it on an' git it over!'

'Well!' Curly repeated, dropping his arm limply. 'Look 'oo's 'ere. Boys, we got er wisiter!'

At once all eyes turned on the student, who felt himself blushing uneasily before the massed battery of stares. As soon as they recognized him, the hostility instantaneously evoked by the mere sight of his neat clothes dropped, and he was accosted by cheery greetings.

''Evening, guv, wotcher doin' 'ere?' bawled Curly. He shook his head comically. 'If yer lookin' fer a bed yer aout o' luck – the Lord Mayor o' London booked it 'isself this mornin'.'

A chorus of guffaws greeted this sally. Curly, who amongst other things earned a few shillings as a sandwich-board man, was the accepted comedian of Coppock's, and always expected to be funny; if his remarks were not invariably humorous, the way he uttered them usually was. This time even Tom had to join in the laughter at his expense as he advanced into the room.

'Good evening,' he said.

'Wotcher arter, guv?' said a perky little fellow from the floor. 'Lookin' fer orphans?'

Before the student could reply, Curly broke in, his face suddenly grown very serious, as if this were no laughing matter at all.

'If it's orphans yer arter,' he commented with a wide sweep of his arm, 'wot price me? I bin a norphan fer nigh on fifty year!'

His seriousness became dissolved into an appreciative roar of laughter, and when the harsh cackles subsided Tom spoke again.

'Is Splodger here?' he asked.

'Splodger?' said Curly, with a blank stare. ''Oo's Splodger? There ain't no Splodger livin' 'ere.'

The student looked around him in bewilderment.

'But surely this is Coppock's?'

'It's Coppock's orl right,' said Curly, 'but Splodger don't live 'ere. 'E only kips 'ere – 'e lives in the pub at the top er Brick Lane.'

'Oh! . . .' Tom smiled wryly. 'Will he be back soon, do you think?'

Curly scratched the top of his unruly mop of hair.

'Dunno,' he answered ruminatively. 'Wot day is it terday? – Fursday, ain't it? Well, 'e should be back soon. 'E ain't got much o' the browns left, they'll soon be chuckin' 'im aout.'

'Thanks,' said Tom. 'Would you mind if I waited a while?'

'Me?' Curly replied. 'T'aint got nuffing ter do wiv me, mate. It's the deputy wot says all the fings as 'as ter be said raound this 'ere doss. 'E'll be dahn from upstairs in a minit. Set yerself daown, guv, take a 'and at cribbage.'

'No, thanks,' said the student. 'I'll sit at the table, if there are no objections.'

'None wotsummevver,' Curly answered airily. 'An' if yer wants some beer or a drop er gin jest say the word an' it's on the 'ouse.'

Tom seated himself at the table, and the scruffy crowd resumed their interrupted pursuits. They were a motley group, dressed in the shabbiest clothes imaginable, with tattered coats, torn trousers suspended by string round the waist, fantastically indented billycocks and deerstalker caps trailing streamers of cloth as if they had been the sport of playful dogs.

A man, too intent on preparing his meal to join the badinage, was stooped over the fire cooking a herring on a gridiron. Around the fireplace were suspended huge black frying-pans, and on the broad mantelshelf was the crockery, a few old jam-pots and some dully glinting bashed-in tin teapots. Having cooked the herring to his satisfaction, the man speared it with a clasp-knife and carefully brought it across to the table where a folded newspaper served as a plate. Seating himself opposite Barnardo, the man fished a hunk of bread from his pocket, and breaking off a piece tossed it in his mouth, then turning his attention to the herring, tore at it voraciously with his fingers, peeling off the skin to join the bread in his mouth, and chewing at them both with an air of ineffable contentment.

At the far end of the table the other man still sat in lofty isolation, busy scribbling with a long quill pen. He had partitioned off his corner of the table with a block of wood and in front of him were a mass of envelopes, a pile of printed leaflets, and at his left hand a long list to which he constantly kept referring. His clothes, now that Tom looked at him more closely, were old but quite clean, and at one time must have been, from the cut, fairly expensive. A delicate thin face with a long nose, cadaverous cheeks and bloodless lips peered out from beneath a high-domed top-hat, almost devoid, from frequent brushings, of pile. Long shapely hands and thin wrists stretched from the sleeves, which had been turned back a little and were protected by paper cuffs. The air of industry and respectability about this strange figure seemed entirely out of keeping with the atmosphere in this den of rough, uneducated, shiftless labourers.

Tom was intrigued, he rose, and passing the table seated himself opposite the scribe. He waited until the man had finished addressing an envelope, then as he looked up smiled at him. The writer at close quarters seemed still to be in early middle-age; first sizing up what was visible of Tom's body, he grinned in a friendly fashion as he met his eyes, and returned his pen to the inkwell.

'Good evening,' said Tom.

'Good evening,' the other replied in a well-modulated voice, with an extremely cultured accent. 'I suppose you must be surprised to see me here?'

'I am,' Tom admitted. 'And I expect you must be surprised to see me.'

'Not so much,' said the man. 'I know who you are, but I don't imagine that you can know me.'

'That's true,' Tom answered. 'You have the advantage of me there. My name is Barnardo.'

'Barnardo, eh?' the man mused. 'Well, I suppose you had to have some name, but I have always heard you referred to as the "guv'ner" or the young doctor. Mine is Charteris, Lancelot Charteris.'

Tom leaned across the table and shook his hand.

'I'm pleased to meet you, Mr Charteris.'

'I can assure you the pleasure is entirely my own,' the other returned courteously.

'Charteris . . . Lancelot Charteris. That sounds a very aristocratic name.'

'I can assure you, sire, that it is,' said Charteris proudly. 'I come from a most distinguished family. I have one brother who is a judge, another a Lord-lieutenant, and a third holds a very high command in India. As for me, I am the black sheep of the flock, which fact has perhaps not eluded you by this time.' He sighed reminiscently. 'I have squandered thousands of pounds in my day – my own, and I must admit, other people's money as well, and now you see *me*, a Charteris, addressing envelopes at one-and-ninepence a thousand to keep body and soul together.'

'But surely your family could help you?'

'They have done. But now they have washed their hands of me, and not entirely without justification. I must admit, sir, that I have not behaved as a Charteris should have done. Gambling, and wine, and expensive women – a surfeit of them can quickly bring even wealthier men than I was to the gutter.'

'If you can speak so dispassionately of your faults surely that is a sign that you are repentant?'

'Repentant!' scoffed Charteris. 'Not a bit of it. I have

enjoyed myself in my day without stinting, now it is equitable that I pay the penalty.'

Tom fished in his coat-tails for a pamphlet that he knew must be there. Drawing it from his pocket he passed it across to Charteris.

'Read this,' he said. 'It will interest you, and I sincerely hope point the way out.'

Charteris glanced at the title, looked at the first page, and with a tolerant, amused smile passed the pamphlet back to the student.

'I'm afraid that would not interest me in the slightest,' he remarked. 'I may live amongst these ignorant unintelligent savages, but I don't live *with* them. I hope you don't think I forget for a moment that I am a gentleman even though my nearest neighbours have no manners, no morals and no aspirates.'

Tom was mystified as he reluctantly pocketed the pamphlet.

'Tell me, pray,' he said tenaciously, 'what has all this to do with religion?'

'Just this,' replied Charteris. 'Those others may know no better, but I have had an education. Religion, you must admit, sir, in the face of modern discoveries and critical knowledge is completely out of date. Why, the whole spirit of our age is materialist, and people in our station of life are agnostic almost to a man. This is the era of enlightenment, we are the spiritual descendants of Tom Paine and Rousseau and Voltaire – surely, sir, you have read them?'

'I have,' said Tom. 'I knew all about them when I was sixteen.'

'Tut! Tut!' Charteris pursed his lips in an exclamation of disparagement. 'Then you should know better. Between me and you, my dear sir, religion should be left to the poor, the scum, the rag-tag and bob-tail of humanity.'

'Mr Charteris,' said the student, 'if your materialism has taught you anything, it should have taught you that the "scum" are not very materially different from us. Some of the finest men I have ever met are part of your rag-tag and bob-tail.'

'Humm!' grunted Charteris sceptically. 'That's all you know. The lower classes may fawn on you while they can use you to advantage, but they'd as lief cut your throat for a shilling. The working man is getting out of hand, I know this from personal observation, and it only needs us to assure them, as you seem to be doing, that they are our equals for them to turn the whole country topsy-turvy, and end in a night all that our forebears have laboured for generations to build. Remember what happened at Sheffield? The hooligans go on strike and want to assert their right to stay outside the union and work – and what happens? They are rewarded with the franchise. Votes for workmen indeed! – though I must admit, sir, a large register is an asset to me at election times – but in the interests of the country I would sooner forgo the few shillings I get from addressing election circulars rather than give our families over to the domination of the riff-raff.'

Tom smiled. 'You seem to be taking a very pessimistic view of our workmen,' he said, 'though I seem to recall that these same Sheffield hooligans elected a very respectable mill-owner to represent them in parliament.'

'That may be so,' Charteris replied. 'They are a cunning lot, and you can be sure they have done it for a purpose. It is, my dear sir, the thin end of the wedge, and one of these days, ere long, I assure you, our statesmen will have cause to rue their short-sightedness.'

That seemed to end the argument, for Tom remained silent. He saw it was useless to continue this conversation further with this derelict. He was an anomaly, a pauper with the view-point of a patrician, and acceptable neither to one nor the other. If Tom had imagined Splodger was beyond redemption, here was another well past praying for, and if he were St Peter, he knew very well which of the two he would sooner welcome through the pearly gates.

'If it is not an impertinence,' the suave voice of Charteris percolated into his thoughts, 'may I ask why you came here?'

'Indeed you may,' said Tom. 'It was in the first place to see Splodger!'

'That drunken sot!' exclaimed Charteris disapprovingly. 'I don't know why you want to see him, but I can assure you, Mr Barnardo, that whatever it is, you are wasting your time. There is nothing sober or decent about the fellow. All he does is drink.'

That was hardly news to the student, but, Tom reflected, decency went beyond a clean coat or mellifluous accent; Splodger, he was convinced, was fundamentally quite a decent sort. If he drank, there were a variety of reasons for his drinking, among which not the least potent were his birth and early environment, neither of which could serve as an excuse for Charteris. He felt suddenly angry at the insolence of the man. If ever a person had been ruined by drink that man was Lancelot Charteris, euphemistically named aristocrat, and yet he, chock-full of those very sins, dare cast a stone!

'And do *you* not drink?' he asked sharply.

Charteris smiled. 'But of course. In moderation, however, and like a gentleman. Nobody has ever seen me in a common tap-room. I detest beer. When I have money I go to a reputable wine-house, where I can drink with my equals – and that, as you must admit, is not the same as indulging in one continuous guzzle. Er . . . er . . .' he paused a little uncertainly, and then continued with an ingratiating smile, 'Addressing envelopes is extremely thirsty work, I can assure you, Mr Barnardo, and since our conversation has robbed me of a portion of my very meagre pittance perhaps you would care to compensate me with some trifle, which you may be certain will not be spent on beer?'

Tom rose to his feet. 'I am sorry,' he said. 'I haven't a single penny-piece in my pocket, and if I had, it wouldn't go for wine for you or beer for Splodger. That is not what I came for. Splodger told me of a lad named Terrence who might be needing my assistance.'

'Terrence! Oh, he's nothing but a lazy lout. He refuses to work and expects us and the deputy to keep him.'

'But I understood he was very ill,' Tom protested.

'Ill! – Fiddlesticks!' Charteris dismissed the lad with a callous toss of his slim white hand. 'And if he were ill, what of it? Even if he were to die that would be no great loss to the world either!'

Tom moved away from the table. If he spoke to Charteris much longer he was afraid he would lose his temper. In his early days in the East End slums he had walked about with a stick, but very quickly took to leaving it at home so that he could not be tempted to strike out at the bands of cheeky urchins that sorely tempted him. He felt that same terrific irritation now with Charteris, and though he would not have struck him he might have scolded him severely, and he was not the one to judge or to reprove. He had a long way yet to go himself in the path of wisdom, and Charteris was probably being punished all the time he lived here, tortured by unquiet thoughts, by the oppressively dingy, smelly kitchen, by the very people he rubbed shoulders with daily in this *milieu* that he so manifestly detested.

At this moment the door opened and the deputy lumbered into the room. He was a tall, heavy man with a huge paunch, dressed only in a shirt, a dirty sweat-rag round his neck, and trousers. His head was shaped like a swollen egg and completely bald, with a bulbous nose, like a crudely fashioned turnip of porous red clay, stuck over a loose thick-lipped mouth and a brutal bristly chin.

'Hey, you! – Wotcher doin' 'ere?' he said to Barnardo suspiciously.

Before Tom could reply the irrepressible Curly broke in. 'It's orl right, Baldy, keep yer 'air on! 'E's only come ter wisit Splodger. Sorter social call like they allus does in the 'ighest circles.'

The deputy thrust his hands angrily in his pockets.

''E did, did 'e?' he growled. 'Well, I'd like ter know 'oo give that drunken dock-walloper permission ter invite strangers ter this 'ouse?'

'Aw, cut the cackle,' Curly answered. 'Yer knows the doctor ain't no stringer. I s'pose 'e's got some bisness wiv Splodger, mebbe mighty important.'

'Bisness!' grunted the deputy. 'Splodger ain't got no bisness aoutside the pub. If 'e wants visiters 'e kin invite 'em there. Wait till 'e comes in. 'E won't 'arf get a tousin' from me!'

'One moment,' said Tom. 'Don't put all the blame on Splodger. It's entirely my fault. I wanted to come here.'

'Fer wot?' asked the deputy. 'This is the 'ighest class lodgin'-'ouse in Stepney, good beds, lily-white sheets, an' no monkey bisness wiv women or sich-like; we got a certifikit er good character from 'arf a dozen respectable 'ouse-'olders. We ain't never 'ad no trouble in Coppock's – wotcher come 'ere fer?'

'I understand one of your lodgers, a lad by the name of Terrence, is ill.'

'Oh – 'im!' said Baldy contemptuously. ''E ain't ill. 'E's bloody lazy. Won't go aout ter work an' specks ter be waited on 'and an' foot like 'e was Mister Gladstone 'isself.'

'But it's possible that he *is* ill,' Tom insisted. 'Would you mind if I had a look at him?'

The deputy shook his head. 'Carn't be did. Unauthorized persons ain't allowed up in the dormitery wivout a permit.'

'Aw, let 'im up,' interjected Curly. 'Wotcher 'fraid of – fink 'e'll eat yer lousy beds?'

'I ain't afraid er nuffing,' Baldy retorted angrily. 'An' the beds ain't lousy – an' if they ain't good enough fer yer Lordship, yer kin sling yer blooming 'ook right naow!'

'Orl right,' said Curly, calmly scratching his tangled beard. 'I'll 'op it, but yer may as well know yer'll lose a lot more custom aside o' me.'

Several of the men seated near him shook their heads

gravely. They meant it too. Coppock's wouldn't be Coppock's without Curly, and if he shifted they would certainly go with him. The deputy realized he had made a mistake. The men needed him, but he needed them just as much. He nodded his head with an ill-concealed scowl and pointed a dirty thumb towards the ceiling.

'Up on the first floor,' he said grudgingly. 'Bed number 17. An' go quiet so's yer don't wake up them as is asleep.'

Tom tiptoed up the stairs till he came to the dormitory on the first floor. Opening the door silently, he entered a large room where two rows of low iron bedsteads were ranged against opposite walls. The single gas-jet was turned low and a thin yellow-blue fan of flame wavered with a soothing hum, casting changing fantastic shadows over the sagging bulges of the low ceiling. As soon as Tom's eyes became accustomed to the lapping gloom he saw a middle-aged man near the door, lying face upwards on the palliasse. His head rested upon his arms, the coverlet drawn above his chest, and in spite of several large 'No Smoking' notices pasted on the walls, he lay contentedly puffing at an old clay pipe. He turned his face towards the student, and as he recognized him, nodded in a friendly fashion without changing his position.

'Which is Number 17?' Tom whispered.

The man indicated the position of Terrence's bed with a thrust of his neck, and speaking out of the corner of his mouth, amplified his direction.

'The uvver side, guv. Right under the gas.'

'Thanks,' said Tom.

He made his way quietly towards the gas-jet, accompanied by a chorus of snores and lethargic grunts, and an occasionally whispered ''Ullo, guv!' Stooping down over Bed 17, he saw a thin face, tossing uneasily to and fro above the pillow. Straightening himself he turned the gas full on, and resting sideways on the edge of the bed resumed his examination. The boy opened his eyes at the student's touch and smiled faintly, his pupils were glazed and his pulse raced feverishly, but before Tom could reach any sort of diagnosis, the deputy appeared in the room, and moving down the narrow gangway with surprising grace for a man of his bulk, loomed over the student and with a rapid movement turned down the light.

''At's enough,' he whispered hoarsely. 'Naow yer seen 'im yer can 'op it. I don't want yer ter wake the 'ole bloomin' plice.'

Tom rose to his feet. Around him the occupants of the other beds were stirring. Light sleepers, they reacted instantaneously to the slightest movement, for the exigencies of their economic position oppressed them even in their slumbers, and in the doss-house no item of personal property was safe, even of the meanest description, unless its owner had it constantly under guard.

''Ere!' said Baldy disgustedly, pointing at the semi-recumbent, stirring shadows. 'Look wotcher done!'

'I'm sorry,' Tom answered. 'They can get all the sleep they need later. I must get the boy out and into hospital at once!'

'Take 'im, an' welcome,' said the deputy. 'Only afore yer goes 'ere's a little matter er some rent ter settle.'

Tom felt in his pockets, and suddenly remembered that he had given all his money away. 'I . . . I . . . haven't any cash with me,' he apologized, 'but I'll see that you get it in the morning.'

'Oh no, yer don't!' replied the deputy sarcastically. ''At ain't good enough. I 'as me money naow, or Terrence stays 'ere.'

'But you can't keep him, man – he's seriously ill!'

'Carn't I!' said Baldy. 'I knows me rights. 'E stays 'ere till I gits me rent.'

'Very well,' Tom answered. 'I didn't want to be too hard on you. But this is very likely a contagious disease. If you don't let him go I shall come back with a policeman, and before you know anything more the whole place will probably be in quarantine.'

The deputy thought rapidly. It was more than he dared do to allow such a thing to happen. That would put the kybosh on it proper! He realized that he was defeated, but he was not disposed to submit without a struggle, and he would make it as difficult for the meddlesome nosey parker as he possibly could. The trouble was that this cocksure little interloper held most of the trumps, and there seemed no way at the moment of venting his mounting spleen.

'Well?' Tom repeated sternly.

'Orl right,' came the reluctant reply. ''E's yours. Yer kin 'ave 'im.'

'Good! I thought you'd see reason. Now let me have his clothes and I'll rush him to the hospital.'

The deputy shook his head obstinately.

'Carn't do that,' he asserted. ''At's agin the rules o' the 'ouse. I ain't the guv'nor, I only works 'ere. Yer gits no clobber till I 'as me rent.'

'But I can't take him through the street in his underclothes!' Tom protested.

The deputy shrugged his shoulders maliciously.

''Tain't nuffing ter do wiv me. Rules is rules. I didn't make 'em, and I got ter bide by 'em, same as everyone else. 'E goes as 'e is, or yer pays up the rent!'

Tom stared at the brutal, unsmiling bully in baffled bewilderment. He had thought that his bluff about a contagious disease had succeeded, overlooking any other obstacles that the surly deputy might place in his path. He could be forced to release the lad, but for all Tom knew he was probably within his rights with regard to the clothes. It was too late now to start arguing or rushing round for legal advice. Terrence was obviously in bad shape, and by hook or by crook had to be shifted to hospital. The irony was that the hospital lay but a few hundred yards distant, yet with succour almost within grasp it might be miles and miles away. It was difficult to believe that a man could lose so much of his humanity, but he had seen it in genteeler form below in the person of Lancelot Charteris, and if one of aristocratic birth and education could be so callous it was no wonder that the deputy remained unflinching in his bestiality.

Very well. If there was no other way he would take Terrence in his underclothes and chance getting a conveyance *en route*, or better still, the thought struck him, he could go out and hunt up a stray hansom. On mature consideration he dismissed the idea. Terrence could not be left alone for a moment longer. Now that his plight had precipitated an open rupture with the deputy, there was no telling to what unscrupulous lengths the ruffian might go to defeat the ends of justice and common humanity.

He flung back the coverlet and revealed the lad's lean form covered by a long tattered shirt, quivering with cold in spite of his high temperature. Placing his arm behind his back Tom helped the youth up to a sitting position.

'Do you think you could walk just a little way?' the student inquired.

'In course, guv!' Terrence answered with a weak smile.

'Hay! – wait a minit,' came a drawling voice from the next bed. 'Yer ain't takin' 'im like that, is yer, guv?'

'Looks like I must,' said Tom grimly.

''Ang on, 'ang on,' the voice insisted. 'Wait till I gits outer bed.'

Terrence's neighbour sleepily pushed his dirty feet on the floorboards and sat for a moment scratching his grey head with loud yawns. Then he reached over to his pillow, and throwing it aside produced a bundle of clothing complete even to boots. Curling his arm round the clothes, he lifted them and with one movement tipped them at Barnardo's feet.

''Ere y'are, guv. Yer kin 'ave a lend o' mine – only I got

ter git 'em back ternight,' he explained in a melancholy sing-song, ''cause all me uvver suits as been borrered by pals wot's been invited ter stay at Buckin'am Pallis – an' fer the time bein' I ain' got nuffing else ter wear.'

'Thank you,' Tom answered gratefully. 'Rest assured you shall have them back tonight – and may God bless you, my friend, for what you have done,' he added.

The man crawled back into his bed.

''At's orl right, guv,' he said sleepily. 'I ain't done it fer Gawd, I done it fer Terrence, an' 'cause I knows I kin trust yer wiv me clobber. 'Sides, it'll do 'em good, they needs a bit 'er airin'. Naow fer 'Evin's sake get the kid aout of it an' lets 'ave anuvver bit er kip.'

He covered himself with the sheet and settled drowsily on his side, his head sinking in the unaccustomed resilience of the pillow.

''Urry up wiv me fings, guv,' his nasal drawl emerged. 'I ain't used ter sleepin' so low . . . Goo' night.'

'Good night,' Tom whispered softly. 'Sleep well, my friend, sleep well.'

CHAPTER 13

Splodger had done it again. Somehow a psychic intimation had possessed Tom immediately after their meeting on the Mile End Waste that the coalie was destined to lead him yet a stage farther towards the real meaning of his presence in the slums, and a stage farther away from his original intention of embarking at once upon his missionary work in China. This East End was just another bit of a big city when apprehended from a distance, but living in it and getting more and more closely in contact with those indigenous to it, revealed the district round the dockside as a gigantic Pandora's Box whence all the evils had not fled but were waiting to be uncovered one by one by diligent searchers who knew where to look for them.

Terrence was in hospital and, probably for the only time in his life, in good hands, sleeping in a clean bed and eating wholesome food. There must be countless thousands of Terrences, Tom thought, who lived just as that lad had been accustomed to do, working at some blind-alley occupation all day, and spending the nights at 'kens' of which Coppock's was a superior example, subject to all the bad influences of the unsavoury characters that haunted all the common lodging-houses. For a brief space of time the ragged schools and his arabs were dwarfed into insignificance by this new discovery, but as Tom pondered the matter closer, he saw that these three problems were interrelated and a solution applicable to one would be relevant to them all. A grandiose scheme was formulating in his head. Why not a large mission with commodious premises embracing a school, a chapel, and a lodging-house? The school and church were the logical extension of his first donkey-stable venture, and the lodging-house would have to be a bright, sanitary building, capable of accommodating a large number of boys who would fall into three categories. First, good steady respectable lads, in work, but needing a home, for which they would pay a small fee, where the influences around them would be of the highest order. Second, boys who desired work, but having no immediate opening could be provided with something useful to do in the house to keep them out of mischief, and third, the wholly destitute who would be fed, clothed, housed and taught trades.

His brain caught fire with the idea. Such a scheme was eminently desirable at once, and it would not end with just one lodging-house, but if God willed, a whole string of them stretching the length and breadth of the country, gathering up those Terrences that were falling by the wayside in the streets of big cities, and giving them a fresh start and a new impetus to adjust themselves to life. He felt like shouting Hosanna! as if the idea were a divine revelation, and the more he thought it over the more he became convinced that it was. In everything, even though hidden behind the scenes, Tom detected the hand of God, not vaguely so, but guiding him to some definite plan. His coming to London had detached him from home and family ties, the ragged schools had kept alive the missionary zeal that might have been lost entirely if he had concentrated on medicine, and the cholera had made him accepted as a friend into houses where people of his class were regarded as implacable foes. He was still young, in his twenty-fifth year. China would have to wait a while longer. Now the immediate problem was to start the homes and get them going, and as soon as that work was progressing satisfactorily he would be able to return to his books, obtain his degree and set sail joyously for the 'Land of Sinim!'

When Phillip came home that evening from the hospital, he found Tom waiting for him in his room. They had not been seeing each other so much of late, for Phillip was absorbed in his work, and only accompanied Tom on Sundays. He threw his books on the table after greeting his friend, and wearily stretched himself on a low chair. He was tired and needed a rest, but he felt Tom's presence meant something extremely important was on hand, and a half-smile flitted across his face as his volatile friend jumped from his seat and started to pace excitedly about the room without a word. Comyns recognized the symptoms. Tom had another ambitious experiment in mind, and was about to try it first on the dog. Changing the East Enders had become a passion with him, but Phillip had other things to do. He was not cut out to be a reformer, and had no deep inclinations that way. If he had helped Tom in the past, it was because that seemed the only decent thing to do, and he felt he had outlived his usefulness as an evangelist. That was a childish complaint like measles, and he had grown out of it, but although he was still extremely sympathetic, not even Tom's persuasiveness would be able to make him drop his all-important work and gird his loins like a very miniature David against the repulsive Goliath of the slums.

'Well . . . ?' Phillip asked at last.

Tom stopped in his nervous pacing. He had hoped to rope in Phillip for this work, but as he looked at him he realized that his friend was not the enthusiastic young man of four years ago. Comyns had dropped his Wednesday evening classes, and it was becoming increasingly difficult to pull him away from his books even on Sunday. However, this was something entirely different, perhaps the very ambitiousness of the new project would revitalize the spark in his friend that was rapidly becoming extinguished. He told him about Terrence and sketched out his overwhelming idea of an all-embracing mission, where the lads would be theirs not for a fleeting few hours, the benefit of which was speedily dissipated in the doss-houses, but all the time to mould in the ways of righteousness. Tom warmed to his task, and addressed Phillip vehemently, talking to him as though he were an audience on the Mile End Waste, and gradually Comyns felt himself stirred in spite of his rigid control, for Tom had in abundance the power to move people, and combined fanatical religious zeal with a winning Irish way of persuasion.

He stopped at last. His eyes were shining as he stooped over Comyns expectantly.

'That's it, my dear fellow,' he exulted. 'What do you think of it?'

Phillip pulled himself together, trying to escape into normality now Tom's feverish flow of words had ceased. It was a near thing. Another five minutes and he would have volunteered to follow Tom on this fresh adventure, even if it meant throwing four years' work on the dust-heap. He had control of himself again, though a reluctant admiration for the stupendous sweep of the idea still lingered.

'It's a grand scheme,' he admitted. 'More power to your elbow, Tom.'

'Then you'll help me?' said Tom eagerly.

'I didn't say that,' Phillip replied. 'I'm with you, but from a distance. Now let's be sensible about it, Tom,' he argued soberly. 'None of us can do two things at once. Medicine and this new Mission are both full-time jobs. I want to become a doctor, another year or so at the clinic and I shall get my degree. You started at the same time as me, yet you haven't passed your second MB. You've got brains, only you've spread them all around Whitechapel; you're a success as a missionary, but as a student you're a failure. It's a matter of choice, Tom. I've chosen to be a doctor. Now it's up to you. It's either the college, or giving up most of your time to this . . . this wild scheme,' he concluded after a moment's hesitation.

'Wild? But you assured me it was grand.'

Phillip grinned sheepishly.

'I was intoxicated for the moment – anyone's liable to be when you're jawing at them – but now I can think it over rationally it's more than wild, it's hysterical – scatterbrained.' He leaned forward on his chair.

'Let's get down to brass tacks. Have you got any money towards it?' he asked.

'Not a shilling,' Tom confessed.

'I thought so,' said Phillip. 'And where are you going to get it from? You surely don't believe like old parson Müller at Bristol that all you have to do is pray to have the shekels rolling in?'

'Müller is not wrong,' Tom replied. 'Most things are answered by prayer. Of course I shall pray, but I shall also go into the highways and byways and make known the need to the stewards of that Lord.'

'How, Tom? – How? By publishing letters in *The Revival*? Be reasonable for Heaven's sake!' Phillip cried emphatically. 'When you started the King's Arms ragged school you asked for two hundred pounds and you only got ninety, and your letters should have got blood out of a stone, let alone the devout Christian readers of *The Revival.*'

'But the money came in,' said Tom obstinately. 'It dribbled slowly, but it came. This will come also, in the same way.'

'I thought it was one of your evangelical principles,' Phillip retorted quizzically, 'never to beg for the Lord's work?'

'It isn't begging,' said Tom. 'I make known the need to the stewards of God, and they contribute voluntarily of their own free will. That will be one of the foundation stones of my mission, the second will be never to get into debt, and the third not to publish the names and addresses of the donors.'

Phillip laughed. The whole thing was so manifestly absurd. If the idea itself was wild, these three provisos placed it entirely beyond any hopes of realization.

'I'm sorry to dash all your dreams,' he said, 'but if you had a job raising money for the ragged school, you can't possibly manage to find the sum you require for this new project. I don't see how you can avoid getting into debt, and as for not publishing the names and addresses of the donors, that finishes the scheme altogether. You surely don't suppose that Lord Slash and Lady Clare and the Honourable Chirpetty-Plank are going to give you money without the whole world knowing the extent of their munificence; come now, do you?'

'I do,' Tom replied slowly. 'That is a principle from which I shall never depart. If Lord X and Lady Y can't contribute to a good, a sacred cause without any thought of self or any material consideration, then they can keep their money, I shall do without them.'

'Brave words,' Phillip answered. 'But I can't see how you can get support any other way. Besides, on what authority do you base your departure from the accepted methods of receiving charity?'

'On the very highest authority,' said Tom. 'On the Gospel itself. The sixth chapter of Matthew, the third verse, the fourth paragraph. "But when thou doest alms, let not thy left hand know what thy right hand doeth: that thine alms may be in *secret*: and thy Father which seeth in secret Himself shall reward thee openly."'

Phillip brushed the quotation aside.

'All right. I believe you,' he commented. 'But Bible or no Bible you can say goodbye to the money on those terms. What lunatics are going to contribute thousands of pounds to a mission run by a youngster of twenty-five, who is practically unknown outside the East End? I wouldn't consider such a proposition myself, and I know you and can trust you. The responsibility's too big to rest on such young shoulders. Drop the idea, Tom,' he pleaded. 'You'll only make yourself a laughing-stock – if nothing more serious happens to you.'

'No.' Tom shook his head. 'My mind is made up. I'm prepared to take the risk, any risk, to do something that I feel should and must be done. And it *will* be done, Phillip,' he reiterated determinedly. 'I ask you again, are you with me, old fellow?'

'No,' Comyns said. Somehow he had the uneasy feeling that his headstrong friend would triumph over even these apparently insurmountable difficulties. Uneasy because he knew Tom needed his help and he could not give it to him. But it was quite final. To Comyns his career came first. 'No,' he repeated slowly. 'You'll have to count me out. You're going too far for me, Tom. Too far and too fast.'

Barnardo turned reluctantly towards the door.

'I'm sorry,' he said. 'I thought I could have convinced you.'

'You have,' Phillip answered. 'A couple of years ago, I'd have thrown in my weight like a shot, but it's too late now. I've seen what's happened to your studies, and I'm too near my finals to take any chances. I'm sorry too, believe me, but I've made the decision to become a doctor as soon as possible, and I won't let anything or anybody sidetrack me now. There it is, Tom. You have my sympathy and my moral support, if that's worth anything to you. That's all I have to offer for at least another year, and as I shall probably start a practice somewhere in the country when I'm through, it means that for practical purposes you can eliminate me entirely.'

'All right,' said Tom slowly. 'So be it.'

He closed the door behind him and climbed the stairs to his room. When he had first thought of approaching Phillip he had a suspicion that his friend would fight shy of the venture, and his reception at the outset had made the suspicion almost a certainty. But he had seen him weakening beneath his arguments, and the certainty of refusal had given way to a new hope that his words might yet prevail, only to be dashed by Phillip's rationally posed objections. On the face of it, it did appear a wild scheme, but something of the sort was absolutely necessary, yet if he could not convince his old and intimate friend Phillip, how could he ever hope to harness the vast amount of support that was essential for his cause from the outside world – particularly when donors would have to be anonymous? How to overcome the suspicions and head-shakings that a new project of this description must inevitably occasion? That was the problem. He had to sell himself and all those unfortunate God-forsaken children to a sceptical public already overburdened with appeals from old-established charities, and prove that his and their claims were at least as worthy of consideration as any of those countless others. A problem indeed, but God had pointed the way before, and would do so again, and Tom's momentary depression gave way to a feeling of confidence. If it were the Lord's will it would happen. With God all things were possible.

His epistolary messengers sped over the country, to the Press; *The Revival*, the local *Tower Hamlets Independent*, to private individuals, to the Earl of Shaftesbury and his friends. He was determined not to beg, but his letters were couched in such a tone that he made it quite obvious that money was very urgently needed. Here there was a fusion in him of the peculiar qualities of the Quaker and the distant Jewish strain that poured forth with Irish naïveté into print. In obedience to his first principle he was simply making known the need to the stewards of God, but he knew very well what acceptance of that message betokened. He was not begging, but through the publication of the facts he felt certain that the necessary donations would come rolling in.

As he had expected, money came. It came very slowly, and not in great amounts, but the response was sufficient to give him confidence in proceeding further. Again the Black Doctor came to his assistance and recommended him some commodious premises that were to let in Stepney Causeway. Tom saw the building, and in his imagination it overflowed, already engulfing the surrounding cottages. The visionary in him gave, as always, the impulse to the springs of attraction. Looking over the building, he speedily envisaged its possibilities, and leased the property with the smallest delay, although the money he had in hand was not sufficient to defray the cost of renovation, let alone furnishing it with all the necessities and sanitary requirements of an up-to-date hostel.

He flung himself enthusiastically into the task, supervising personally every detail of construction and decoration. This by the grace of God was his own creation. Out of his brain and the crying need of neglected children around him was growing the East End Juvenile Mission. China had receded so far that it was now like a distant dream, but he treasured the memory still in the background of his brain, half-convinced that one day his work in the slums would be completed, and he would be left free to take up his original vocation. This was his new dream, the living enlargement of himself, and by this, in spite of scoffers and detractors, he hoped one day to be remembered in the children's cause . . . Grow! . . . Grow! . . . He could hardly wait to see the rooms taking shape. If only he had the power of the Almighty to say, 'Let this be! Let the water run. Let the gas flow. Let there be light and warmth and cleanliness and loving hearts and healthy bodies praising the Lord!'

But Tom was not God, he was not even a man with unlimited funds. He was simply a young student of twenty-five who had conceived an ambitious scheme and was crazy enough to imagine he could carry it through in his own way to fruition. He had expected to open the homes in the summer, but weeks passed before he had sufficient cash to pay the builders at least part of what they demanded. Then after the builders had been paid off, the plumbers and gas-fitters also demanded their due, and his cash gave out before they had half-completed their tasks.

True to his first principle still, as he conceived it, of not begging, he invited a friend to visit the unfinished building, and took him round the tenantless chambers, the lead pipes, paint pots and benches of workmen lying by idly, as mute reminders that everything was not well. Tom knew that his friend was in touch with Shaftesbury's circle; he did not ask for assistance, simply mentioning, as if in passing, that the workmen were idle because there were no longer any funds, and when the visitor left, Tom felt certain that his Irish method of begging without solicitation would have the required result. Parson Müller, that unflinching believer in the omnipotence of prayer, would have frowned on his deviation from the path of the steadfast believer, but Müller was the provincial in Bristol, and not faced with the thousandfold difficulties of the London slums, and while the stolid Teutonic strain was uppermost in Müller, in Tom there coursed a comparatively recent admixture of bloods, each adding their extra talent to the combination that was this strange, headstrong dreamer and doer.

The money came. The East End Juvenile Mission was completed, a fine up-to-date building with, apart from living quarters and common-room, five dormitories capable of accommodating sixty boys, but it was not until the winter that it was able to open its doors. Tom immersed himself completely in his work – living, teaching and sleeping at the mission. He was determined to make it a success, but obstacles cropped up on all sides. Those respectable lads who were in work preferred the freedom of doss-houses rather than what appeared to them the regimentation of a Christian institution, and the workless lads fought shy of the mission for the same reason. They had an ingrained dislike for charity in any form, associating it with the melancholy faces and starchy manners of most of the evangelists who tried to woo them from their impecunious but sturdy independence. For the homeless waifs, however, there was never enough room. Tom saw his mission developing inevitably into an asylum for lost children. Its functions were being turned upside down, the waifs and strays, the third item on his charter, were becoming the first, overwhelmingly the first and his most important consideration.

The problem became not gathering in the arabs, but

selecting the most necessitous cases, and providing for them in the homes. As soon as a few beds became vacant Tom made one of his visits to the regular lays, and chose the lads with the direst appearance of destitution to fill them. It was a heart-breaking business and Tom had to curb his emotions rigidly not to overtax the capacity of the mission and the funds. There was never enough money, never enough beds, for every child he admitted he had to leave half a dozen equally sad cases to the mercy of the streets. He was beginning to think that Haddock was right in apportioning the responsibility of the care of these children to the State, but so long as the State did not accept the responsibility, he felt it his bounden duty to salvage as many waifs as was within his power from the gutter.

He worked eighteen hours a day, teaching at the ragged school, superintending the physical welfare of his charges, occasionally looking over some of his long-neglected medical books, and in the early hours of the morning combing the lays for arabs. A few years ago the inevitable parcel of litera-ture had marked him out, now he gained in the East End the additional soubriquet of the 'young 'un with a lantern.'

One day, there happened to be five beds vacant at the mission. At three o'clock in the morning Tom filled his lamp with oil and set out for Billingsgate; although early in May it was bitterly cold, and in spite of his heavy top-coat and woollen scarf, the wind penetrated through him as if he had no outer protection whatsoever. Grimly he made his way to Queens Shades, knowing that, cold as he was, there must be scores of urchins beneath the tarpaulins and empty fish-boxes. On his arrival he quickly ferreted out a dozen youngsters, and from the dozen picked out five of the smallest and most tattered. Tom knew that there were probably above six times that number scattered around the leaky sheds in the vicinity, and his heart ached for them all, but it was as much as he could do to cope with the handful he had selected. These trips invariably had a depressing effect on him, because each fresh visit to one or other of the lays only revealed how hopelessly inadequate were his resources for battling against the seemingly increasing number of derelicts. He felt like a modern Perseus unavailingly slicing at the Gorgon's head, or like a fisherman embroiled in the tentacles of a nightmare octopus, hacking off one feeler only to be enmeshed in a dozen others.

Having given the children cards that would gain them entrance to the mission, he set back homewards, but was accosted by a small boy who had materialized from a dirty barrel. He was a frail lad, barefoot and covered with a few filthy rags like most of the others, but he had a bright, perky carriage, and a mop of red hair that distinguished him from his companions in misfortune. Tom knew that the child had recognized him, since the arabs usually fought shy of any strangers at night in case they were given away to the police, their arch-enemies. The waif smiled up at him and raised his forefinger shyly in salute to his forehead.

''Evening, guv,' he said.

'Good evening, my little man,' Tom replied. 'I see you know who I am.'

'In course I does, guv,' said the urchin. He paused and looked at Tom expectantly, without another word, his mouth half-open as if waiting for something important that the student had to say.

'Well,' said Tom. 'You know who I am – and I've a surprise for you – I know who you are, too.'

'Garn!' the urchin's mouth widened into a broad incredulous grin. 'Garn!' he chuckled. 'Yer only jokin', guv.'

'Oh no, I'm not,' said Tom, keeping up the pretence. 'I do know who you are. I'll tell you your name – it's "Ginger!"'

The waif shook his head disappointedly.

'I fought there wor somefing wrong. 'At ain't me name. It's "Carrots," leastways, 'at's wot the boys calls me. Me real name is Johnny Somers, though it's a tidy while since anyone called me Johnny.'

'Very well, Johnny,' said Tom. 'Now we really know each other. What can I do for you, young man?'

'I wants yer ter tike me inter the mission. Please, guv, please let me go wiv yer,' the lad pleaded.

Tom shook his head.

'I'm sorry,' he replied. 'We're full right up.'

The urchin's bright smile faded from his face, and a look of distress took its place.

'Oh! . . . oh! . . .' he stammered.

Tom put his hand on the child's shoulder and patted it gently, then placing his palm beneath the lad's chin, lifted his face towards him. In the lantern's dim light he saw tears in the corners of his eyes, and two fugitive, glazed channels passing down the freckles into his wide half-open mouth. These urchins were usually a hardened lot, so inured to the discomforts of the streets that most of them had to be cajoled into entering the homes, but apparently Carrots was hypersensitive or had suffered so much that he was prepared to accept anything other than the evils he knew.

'Come, come, Johnny! Cheer up,' he said. 'We're quite full up just now, but I promise I'll find a place for you today week.'

A glad smile chased away the unshed tears in an instant from the urchin's face. He clasped Tom's hand and hugged it with delight. Pathetically eager, he looked up again at the student.

'Yer ain't jest sayin' it, is yer, guv?' he demanded. 'Yer really means it, don't yer?'

'Of course I mean it, Carrots,' said Tom cordially. 'Come next week and you'll find us ready and waiting for you.'

A few moments later the urchin bade him good night and darted away like a shadow into the darkness of Queens Shades, leaving Tom to make his way slowly homewards. It was not fair, he decided, and utterly unjust for him to have to turn a lad like Carrots away. From a few brief words he had gleaned the lad's history. Eleven years old and fatherless, he made a living on the streets, running errands, blacking shoes, helping costers, or selling matches. His mother was alive, but it would have been better for Carrots if she had been dead as well, since she often waylaid the child and spread-eagling him on the ground went through his pockets with maternal thoroughness and spent every copper she found on gin. When he had no money, she boxed his ears viciously as an additional penalty for daring to be penniless. Eleven years of age! Surely Carrots had gone through enough in his short life to have earned the comparatively princely comfort and security of the mission?

All the way home, Tom thought of the child, and reproached himself for having turned him away, although under the circumstances there was nothing else he could have done. He hoped devoutly that the child would call before the appointed time. He looked round, there was no sign of the boy following him, and it was useless to return now to Queens Shades. Carrots would come soon, he was certain the boy would call before his time, and Tom made a vow that the moment he came he should be admitted at once.

Several days later, Thornton, one of Tom's voluntary assistants, was seated in the common-room when the caretaker brought in a shabby youngster who refused to go away until he had seen the 'guv'nor'. Thornton dismissed the old man and drew the boy in friendly fashion against his knees.

'Now, young man, what is it?' he inquired.

'I wanter see the guv'nor,' said the urchin.

'I'm afraid the "guv'nor" is very busy,' Thornton replied. 'But perhaps I can help you. If you want to come in, you must know that new boys are not admitted except on Fridays.'

'I ain't comin' in, I want ter see the guv'nor,' the urchin repeated obstinately. 'I must see 'im. It's terrible 'portant. I got 'er messige. It's abaout Carrots.'

Thornton rose at once. Tom had told him about Johnny,

and for a moment he had thought that this lad was Carrots until he had noticed the colour of his hair. Asking the boy to wait, he went into the office and returned a moment later with Tom.

'Where's Carrots?' asked Tom at once.

'Dead,' said the boy unemotionally.

'What!' Tom exclaimed. 'Dead! – are you sure?'

'Sure as I'm standin' 'ere. I seed 'im meself. I was kippin' wiv 'im in a 'ogs'ead up by Rawlinsons when some blokes shifted us in the mornin'. In course I runned away, but Carrots didn't stir, an' I seed the chaps bend over 'im and call a peeler, an' they carried 'im in a pub. Then I arst one of the chaps an' they said as 'e was dead, an' I knowed 'e was comin' 'ere so I runned to fetch yer.'

'Thank you,' said Tom. He felt crushed and numbed, as though someone had struck him a paralysing blow. 'Thank you,' he repeated dully. He had no real sort of responsibility with regard to Carrots, yet he felt that somehow he was to blame. The child had begged to be admitted. If he had just said 'Yes,' and how easy that little word was to say; if only he had mouthed that simple monosyllable, Carrots might have been at this moment playing happily in the yard, instead of lying dead in some hidden corner of a tavern.

'Kin yer take me in 'is place?' importuned the urchin boldly.

Tom looked at the boy. Necessity knew no sentiment. The tragedy of his companion had passed him by and left him untouched. He had hurried to bring the news and at the same time to assure himself of taking Carrots' place. Tom felt too broken by the shock to say very much. Turning his face from the boy, he looked out of the window at the bright May sunshine. Truly little Carrots had been called before his time.

'Very well,' he agreed at last, as if talking to himself. 'Very well, you can come in.'

'On Friday, my boy,' Thornton reminded the urchin. 'Come on Friday.'

'In course!' said the lad delightedly. 'Friday.'

At that moment Tom came to a momentous decision. He turned to the shabby urchin and took hold of his grubby little hand.

'Are you really destitute?' he asked. 'Have you no home? No friends?'

'That I ain't – I'll tike me oath,' averred the boy.

'All right. You stay.'

'Naow, guv?'

'This very moment, if you want to.'

'But Tom,' Thornton interjected. 'You know there's no room.'

'There will have to be room,' said Tom. 'One Carrots is enough.'

Leaving the boy in Thornton's care, Tom took a hansom and drove at full speed to Billingsgate. In an off-room of the Piebald Mare he found Carrots laid out on a table surrounded by a group of urchins snivelling and wiping their noses in unrestrained grief. The student had sufficient medical experience to forecast the coroner's verdict. From the blue, pinched finger, it would be 'Death of exhaustion, the result of exposure and malnutrition.' There could be no other verdict. Carrots. Dead at eleven. His only home the streets, his only beds boxes and barrels, his father dead, his mother a drunkard, and now Carrots dead too.

This must never happen again. Tom swore that no truly destitute child would ever again be turned away from his door at any hour of the day or night. It meant that he would get heavily into debt, and if he had to he would beg without compunction from door to door like a mendicant to save any more unhappy children from going the way of Carrots. Tomorrow he would hoist a sign over his mission door, 'No Destitute Child Ever Refused Admission.' In future those six words would be his motto, his flaming beacon, and worth more to him than the rest of his principles put together.

CHAPTER 14

There began for Tom an age of miracles. The expenses of the mission always outran his funds, and it seemed to him a miracle that he was able to keep the homes going from day to day. Buying blankets for the boys one bitterly cold evening, without a penny in the bank, and the next morning finding a cheque in the post for the exact amount from an anonymous clergyman. Another miracle to receive £7,000 in donations the year following the opening of the homes. But the £7,000 became insignificant when he started a new branch ragged school in Salmon Lane, and soon he had a hundred persons helping him, twenty-four of whom were paid, and seventy-six giving their services voluntarily, some of them old enough to be his father. Miracles . . . Miracles . . .

He started a wood chopping brigade to sell firewood, and had an arrangement with the boot-polish firms to use as shoe-blacks in the locality lads he recommended. Within three years the annual income of the mission touched the £20,000 mark, surely a miracle of miracles that that immense sum should be placed at the sole disposal of a young man of twenty-eight who refused to publish names and addresses of donors, but merely sent receipts of donations with only initials to identify the charitable in his annual reports. Tom began to take them as a matter of course, as a sign that his work was divinely allotted, so that when the miracles were slow in coming he chafed at their dilatoriness, as if he expected that mankind and the supernatural were together harnessed to his children's cause.

The student, for officially he was still on the roster of the London Hospital, had a single-track mind. From his early teens he had always thrown himself completely into any activity he undertook. At fifteen he was an iconoclast, an agnostic, at seventeen a Bible student, at twenty-one a candidate for China, and at twenty-five he was a juvenile mission. The Orient had now completely vanished from his plans. As his work in the East End broadened he saw that he would have enough to do in that particular sphere to last him a lifetime, and yet leave a host of unfinished tasks to occupy those that were to come after him. Almost single-handed, this unknown youth from Dublin had undertaken the redemption of the outcasts of the slums, a problem that successive Governments had either neglected or not deemed worthy of their consideration. Nothing else mattered to Tom. God was his ally, and if he had the divine approval, what was Man to say him 'Nay'?

All those miracles in the early days of the mission he took in his stride, but then came the perennial miracle that disturbed the tempestuous rush of the human little dynamo. Tom fell deeply in love. A year after the opening of the homes, when his work was achieving recognition outside the narrow sphere of East London, he had been invited to address a ragged school gathering at Richmond. After talking to the lads he had been introduced to a pretty young lady, Miss Elmslie, who had organized the tea-party, and sent him the invitation to attend. Tom had taken in her attractions with half an eye, and on his return to London and his mission had promptly forgotten about her. On the following day, however, he ran into her again at the railway station, where she and her father were waiting for his train, but bound for a more distant destination. Hurriedly changing his third-class ticket for a first, he joined them, and they spent the journey together as far as he went.

Again Syrie Louise passed out of his life, but this time she had left a lasting impression. In his dreams her image constantly appeared, and for her part, Miss Elmslie admitted to her bosom friends that the 'little rascal' had disturbed her equanimity. Still Tom made no further approach, so engrossed in the mounting work of his homes that he barely had sufficient time to sleep, let alone think of courting, until, again accidentally, he bumped into her at the funeral of the Reverend Pennefather, a mutual friend.

After this meeting matters came to a head. It was too bad. Tom found that his work was suffering. Not only did he dream of Miss Elmslie, but her imagined presence was intruding into his tasks. In the middle of a conference with his helpers he would find his mind wandering off to the vision of fresh beauty he had encountered first at Richmond, then at the railway station, and again at the Reverend Pennefather's funeral. Instead of drawing up plans for future activity he found his pen involuntarily scrawling her name. She began to monopolize more and more of his time, she was constantly in his thoughts. Like the refrain of a song, her name murmured tantalizingly in his head. She was so serene, her unstudied poise breathing the essence of repose. He realized now that his life was incomplete. Syrie Louise was his perfect complement, and absolutely necessary to him if he were to emerge to full stature either in his work or in himself. His restless nature, volatile like mercury, needed the calm soothing influence of someone like Syrie Louise, who seemed to carry about her an air of serene contentment. Always that word cropped up when he thought of her. Serene. As a goddess above turmoil. Serene. Like the words of the jingle that were now so familiar that it would not have surprised him in the slightest to hear someone sing out loud:

'Syrie Louise,
Syrie Louise.
Serena . . . Serena.'

There was a practical aspect too. Pragmatic as ever, even though head over heels in love, he thought of the enlargement of his work that would inevitably blossom from this association. Hitherto his work had been entirely amongst the boys; with Syrie Louise, Serena, by his side, he could extend his mission to embrace the girls too, for both sexes endured alike the hardships of the streets. Serena would co-operate with him in rescue work, he was almost certain; he felt she must have a bent in that direction, or she would not have undertaken teaching at the ragged school. Yes, it was decided. Apparently it was impossible to get her out of his life – not that he wanted to expel such a sweet pleasure – so she would have to become part of him, and both of them together a centripetal force in his mission.

Yes. It was decided, but only Tom had reached a decision; he had not yet asked Syrie Louise, but his mind brushed every hint of a refusal aside. It had to be. Tom was so used to major miracles, that this seemed quite a minor revelation. It had taken eighteen months for the idea to germinate in his mind, but now he acted quickly, impatient of any further delay.

It was early in spring when he went down to Richmond, but so phenomenally hot that the day might have been cut from a scorching summer. Tom had had a struggle to decide what to wear, but with innate masculine conservativeness attired himself in his usual dark business clothes. True he was going into the country, and on a sentimental journey, but if it turned chilly, or started to rain, he would appear still more ridiculous in a gaily striped blazer and boater. Serena met him at the station. She had no such sartorial qualms, and had dressed according to the weather. With feminine logic, her clothes reflected the sunshine, and not the date on the calendar. So she greeted him on the platform dressed in spotted white muslin, puffed at the shoulders, cut low, but not too low at the neck, and cascading in frills like an artificial waterfall over the fashionable bustle of her hips. Tom, remembering Serena in the dark clothes of the ragged school and her subdued appearance at the funeral, had at first some difficulty in recognizing this gorgeous creature, twirling a smart parasol above her shapely head, but as she approached him, smiling, he realized that this was indeed that same Syrie Louise.

For the first time he had misgivings about the result of his visit. Serena in this unexpected flowering seemed utterly beyond his reach. She had all the virtues, was young, beautiful, intelligent, kind-hearted, and fairly well-endowed with worldly goods, while he, nominally still a medical student subsisting on his father's bounty, had brazenly imagined he had but to call at Richmond to collect this handsome booty as his prize. Yet really, he was not the wooer, it was his work, his mission; if Serena was unmoved by his physical attraction, and it was hardly possible that she should not be, perhaps the thought of those helpless children might conceivably tilt the scales in his favour. That, however, would be his second line of attack. First, to be honest, he had to offer himself for himself alone, then to explain how much she would mean to him, and beyond him, his mission. He had no independent existence now outside of that, and to be honest again, even if she accepted him as he was, he would have to warn her what that acceptance would mean, that she would be marrying not a man, but a mission.

Those, however, were merely theoretical meanderings. He had not yet asked Serena to marry him, and looking at her, every moment discovering some new facet of beauty, the small straight nose, the hair worn low Grecian style, curving in a bun on the white graceful neck, he wondered whether he would be able to pluck up the courage to do so. But he had come here for that reason, stolen the time from his children, and in all fairness to them he had to press his suit, whatever his fears of the outcome.

An open carriage was waiting for them outside the station, a small, handsome, neatly dressed boy perched on the driving-seat beside the coachman. As soon as they climbed into the carriage and it began to move off, Tom felt again that unaccountable air of serenity flowing over him. To come home to such a haven of peace every evening after the turmoil of the mission, to know that after the heartaches and difficulties of the day he would have Serena . . . Syrie Louise . . . Syrie Louise . . . Serena . . . Serena!

He found himself murmuring conventional replies. Yes. The weather was very fine indeed. – Yes . . . Exceptionally so for the time of year. – Yes. He had had a very pleasant journey. – He was very well, he hoped she was well too. – Yes. The view from this hillock was extremely pretty . . . He felt uncomfortable, Serena was making all the conversation, it was up to him to say something too. Glancing towards the coachman he noticed the boy. Serena had said something about him at the station, but he had forgotten just what.

'A fine lad,' he commented.

'Yes,' she said.

'Very refined and gentlemanly for a coachman's son.'

'My father has never been a coachman,' she replied with a smile.

'Your father?' he asked, puzzled.

'Yes,' she said. 'I told you at the station. I told you the lad was my brother.'

Tom relapsed into silence. His brain seemed unable to function. All he appeared to be able to do was just sit back and breathe in the tranquillity of his companion and answer whatever came easiest to his mind. Yes. The coachman was a fine driver. – Yes indeed. Both horses moved like a single animal. – Yes. – Yes indeed . . . And so on and so on and so on until the narrow wheels of the carriage crunched startlingly down the gravel of the drive, warning him that the miraculous journey was almost at an end.

Tom was introduced to her parents and family, but still entranced by Serena's presence, he barely managed through the halting brusqueness of his replies to avoid the appearance of rudeness. He got through lunch somehow, his sociable self functioning independently, as though it were a separate entity and had become divorced from the corporate body that was Tom; he seemed to be sitting at the table listening in amazement to his own talk as if a stranger were speaking in a voice remarkably like, but not quite his own. He was certain that if tomorrow he met these, his prospective in-laws in the street, he would pass them by without further recognition. The part of his brain that recorded impressions, faces and conversations seemed to have suspended its duties, and all these things that were happening seemed to be occurring in a vacuum, were unreal, dreamlike. Everything was a fantasy, an illusion of voices and people without unity of time or place, everything was tantalizingly fugitive except that almost tangible charm of Serena's presence.

After lunch Tom and Serena found themselves in the garden walking down one of the paths that led to the river. Behind a clump of rose bushes the path dipped sharply, and stopped at a steep, grassy bank that was the boundary between the garden and the glittering Thames. Tom climbed the bank, and leaning downwards helped up Serena to his verdant perch. Almost unconsciously his hand slipped round her waist and they stood together gazing idly at the softly lapping water. Rivers had always fascinated Tom, at home it was the Liffey, and where he was now living the Thames. This was that very same Thames that flowed past the warehouses a stone's throw from his mission, yet the river had quite a different aspect here at Richmond from its sluggish, muddy, Limehouse face. He found a ready parallel in his uppermost thoughts. That was what he wanted to do with his slum children, to sift the mud of a big city from their lives and allow the clear drift of adolescence to sparkle freely and unpolluted along its natural course.

'Shall we sit?' broke in Serena's soft voice.

'Why yes,' he said, awakening from his reverie. 'Of course!

One moment . . .' Tom interjected as she was about to lower herself on the bank. 'Your dress. I don't want you to spoil it.'

'Really?' she smiled. 'I didn't think you'd noticed it.'

'Oh, but I have!' he protested. 'And I think it's perfectly delightful.'

'I'm glad you like it,' she said. 'I made it myself, with Mother's help, of course. A simple little thing, really, the grass won't hurt.'

'But it may be wet –'

'Nonsense! – It hasn't rained for days.' She stooped and touched the grass with finely tapered fingertips. 'See for yourself. It's brittle as tinder.'

Without more ado she lowered herself on the bank as though dropping a graceful curtsey, and Tom, slightly abashed, seated himself beside her. For a while they sat contentedly without speaking, watching sticks of driftwood curvetting with the delicate eddies of the current.

'I suppose you can guess why I have come here?' he said at last.

She answered without looking at Tom, her eyes still fixed on the dancing flotsam.

'Was it to see me?' she murmured.

'You know it was, Syrie – may I call you Syrie?'

'Of course you may, Tom – I am Syrie to all my friends.'

'Syrie' – he caught her hand – 'Syrie,' he whispered ardently, 'I want to be much more than a friend. Syrie, I want you to marry me!' There! He had got it out at last. Now a curious mixture of relief and anxiety seemed to sweep over him, and almost as soon as he had uttered the words a full sense of their rashness overwhelmed his earlier emotions. 'I . . . I don't suppose you expected this as well,' he brought out lamely as if in apology.

A faint flush suffused her cheeks. She nodded, still without looking at him.

'It is rather sudden,' she said slowly, 'but not entirely unexpected.'

His grip closed more tightly on her hand.

'I want you to understand that this is not a sudden whim or a momentary infatuation. You have been on my mind and in my thoughts for a long time. For eighteen months I have dreamed of you. Let that answer as courtship. I have loved you all that time . . . and perhaps you have sometimes thought tenderly of me? . . .'

'I have, Tom,' she admitted. 'I have for a long time, too.'

'Then . . . then you'll marry me?' he blurted out.

For the first time she lifted her face to meet his eyes, her lips parted in a gentle smile. A barely perceptible nod gave him his answer. For a moment he could hardly believe that this treasure had fallen so easily into his lap, that Serena would soon live with him, not only in his dreams. He lifted her hand to his lips and pressed a burning kiss to the delicate skin. Then they returned to silence and immobility again, looking at the water as if the river knew everything, understood everything, and gently applauded, taking to its smooth bosom their separate emotions and returning them to common dreams.

The moments of unruffled happiness sped quickly for Tom and soon his mind began weaving plans for the future. His children were never very far from his thoughts, and as soon as the first bewildering ecstasy of conquest faded he started to fit in Serena to his work.

'I'm glad you said "yes,"' he murmured at last.

'Are you?' with a deliciously intimate squeeze of the hand.

'I am indeed,' he said. 'It means a very great deal to me. Let me tell you a little story. Not so long ago I was walking home from Billingsgate rather late at night, and passing through Shadwell a group of shabby girls recognized me. As soon as I got close to them one of the girls raised the cry, "'Ere comes the feller wot took away our pals," and without more ado they set about me.'

'You mean they actually assaulted you?' asked Serena incredulously.

'I mean precisely that,' said Tom. 'And assaulted me with such good effect that they left me black and blue and unable to move in comfort for days.'

'Oh, I am sorry,' Serena commented. 'But I fail to see where I come into all this.'

'I'll tell you,' said Tom. 'For a long time I have wanted to extend my mission. Those same lads that come to me have sisters or girl friends in exactly the same unfortunate position, female arabs, possibly more to be pitied than the boys. As a single man I have had to confine my work to rescuing lads, but married, I shall be able legitimately to extend the mission to embrace the girls. Now do you see how much you mean to me, Serena?'

'I see,' she whispered quizzically, turning her head away so that he should not notice the mischievous sparkle in her eyes. 'I understand now. You want to marry me in such a hurry, not because you love me, but because I would be a welcome addition to your mission. Is that it, Tom?'

The student sat up as if stung.

'Oh no,' he protested. 'Let me assure you, my dear, that you have been the only woman in my life, and there will never be another. I have never loved anyone in the same way before, and I never will again. My love is real, Syrie, very real and very deep, but I will be unable to show you those many tokens of affection you ought to expect from any man. I have so many calls upon my energies, Syrie, that mostly you will have to take my love for granted.'

'Yes . . .' she answered. 'I can see I shall have to.'

'I want you to go into this with your eyes open, my dear. My whole life is the mission. I work eighteen hours a day, in the six that are left I shall have to be husband, friend and lover. And I have no job and no money. What little I receive from my father is just about enough to keep me . . . You understand?'

'I understand,' she said. 'But I have a small income of my own too.'

'I wouldn't dream of living on your money,' Tom answered. 'For myself I can exist on very little, in fact most of my allowance goes on the homes. But it seems very unfair to drag you into this hand-to-mouth existence. After all, you have been used to everything of the best, while all I can offer is very little at present, and an even more problematic future.'

'I see,' she murmured. 'But you should have told me all this before. It's too late now. I have accepted you. Are you trying to wriggle out of your obligations, Mr Barnardo?'

Suddenly she burst into a merry laugh. Tom knew that the dream Serena and Syrie Louise were one and the same. He knew that they were in perfect accord, and that the journey to Richmond had not been in vain. Again the whole scene, the riverbank, the perpetually sliding, sun-splashed water became changed into a Parnassian half-world with Serena as the presiding goddess. Somehow beside her, all those difficulties he lived with from day to day dissolved in the comforting spell of her presence. As if she understood, and to prevent his uttering any further objections, Syrie drew his head down on her lap, and stroked his hair tenderly like a mother fondling an inarticulate child.

'Serena,' Tom breathed softly. 'Serena . . .'

'Serena? . . . And what is that?'

'It's a name I have for you . . . Serena . . . you like it?'

'It's charming . . . Charming, Tom . . . Charming.'

The student closed his eyes. This was very heaven. He was at peace with himself and the world, and a soft hand stroked his head with a silken caress and a soft voice crooned his name through half-opened lips. He purred like a satiated kitten, and as she bent over him she heard again and again her name like an oft-repeated sigh . . . 'Serena . . . Serena . . .'

CHAPTER 15

Sitting back in his easy chair in the lounge of Seeley's Club in Piccadilly, Bradley Wintringham reflected that, after all, his life had not dealt too harshly with him. His father had died before he had even managed to pass his first MB; if only he had had the patience to wait for his son to achieve that honour he might have been alive yet. Of course Brad had jumped at the opportunity of leaving the hospital, for he had inherited all his father's money, a tidy fortune; in 1867 he had been a rich young man, now, ten years later, he was still young, but no longer rich, in fact he was completely penniless beneath the façade of prosperity that was the armour of every man about town. Anyhow, he had enjoyed himself, and did not regret a guinea of that enormous sum he had squandered through the years. His credit was still good with tradesmen, and his gambling debts were balanced by gratefully accepted IOUs. He was *persona grata* in all the fashionable West End clubs, but he knew that as soon as his subscriptions ended with the current year he would be unable to renew them, not even here, at Seeley's, where a Wintringham had been represented for generations.

It was no use worrying. In for a penny, in for a pound. He could manage to live in precisely his old style for at least another year, then, when he could no longer conceal his position, the vultures would gather for the kill, but that was twelve months ahead. He would circumvent them yet. He had an uncle who was on his last legs, but the moneylenders refused to loan him a penny on that expectation, and the uncle himself was as tight as a clam. Well, well, if worst came to the worst he would sell himself to a rich young lady, who under those circumstances would probably be neither young nor a lady. He had no particular family in mind, but when the time came he would lead a bride to the altar, even if her blushes were only rouge, and she had to be led in the real sense of the word. Brad sighed contentedly. He had nothing whatever to grumble about.

He leaned forward, and tapped a bell on the table. Silently a tall, stooping, grey-haired waiter appeared before him.

'Yes, Mr Brad?' he said.

'A bottle of sherry,' Brad ordered nonchalantly. 'The best, Hawkins. I want to celebrate.'

'Very good, Mr Brad,' said Hawkins.

Silently the waiter disappeared. Brad sat back in his chair and regarded approvingly his image in the tall mirror on the opposite wall. Although he looked a little more than his age, his thirty-two years sat comfortably on him. At this distance the crows feet at the corners of his eyes were invisible and the deep purple pouches beneath his bottom lids only set off to better advantage the smouldering dark eyes in the pale, handsome face. Looking at him one saw this man had lived, while the prematurely greying hair at the temples added a touch of dignity to the dark, fiercely military moustache whose spread cut almost in two an altogether distinguished countenance.

Brad frowned when a stocky torso and long legs interposed themselves before his admired image. He waited for the body to move, but it remained stationary as if for the purpose. He looked up to see the reason for its presence, and as soon as he recognized bluff Richard Gannet, the disagreeable expression vanished from his face and a welcoming smile took its place. Brad had a great deal of respect for the old man who had been a friend of his father's, a respect that never diminished since the elder Wintringham, a doughty drinker, had admitted that Gannet had once drunk him under the table without turning a hair. He always thought of him in his father's words. 'A blasted Whig – but damme, son, a jolly fine fellow!'

Brad rose to his feet.

'Good evening, sir,' he said.

'Good evening, Brad,' the old man answered, shaking his hand. 'All alone, a youngster your age? Why, bless my soul, when I was thirty –'

'Thirty-two,' Brad interjected with a smile.

'Thirty-two – pah! Why, when I was your age you wouldn't find me seated in this – this damned mausoleum all by myself.'

'Not quite by myself,' Brad answered as Hawkins arrived with the wine. 'You see, I have company, some of Seeley's special – won't you join me, sir?'

'Don't mind if I do,' said Gannet, seating himself opposite Brad. 'I've nothing much to do for a moment, and if I have to talk to these other old fogies I shall either wind up in an apoplectic fit myself or start a resurrection in this crypt of lost souls.'

Brad laughed.

'I shouldn't do anything as drastic as that. Our friend Hawkins might object.'

'Hawkins!' growled Gannet. 'He's as dead as the rest. 'Pon me soul, I believe he was born dead, made to measure for Seeley's. I remember him thirty years ago, and except for the colour of his hair he hasn't changed a scrap.' He turned to the imperturbable waiter. 'Tell me, Hawkins, were you ever a baby? Did you ever go to school? Did you ever busk a pretty wench, man?'

'I probably was a baby, sir,' Hawkins returned soberly, his grave demeanour unruffled. 'But I never went to school, and as for busking wenches I might remind you, sir, that I have nine children and five grandchildren, and as you probably remember one of my sons is named after you.'

'Splendid,' said Brad. 'We'll drink the health of his godfather. Another bottle of sherry, Hawkins, and another glass.'

Gannet shook his head.

'No sherry for me. Vile stuff – vile. You young men seem to be getting effeminate – I don't know what's come over you all. Either you drink wine, or ghastly mixtures like punch-cup, or even, Lord save us, Spa water! Pah!' he exploded disgustedly. 'The country's going to the dogs. Hawkins, fetch me a bottle of Napoleon brandy.'

'Napoleon it is,' said Brad.

'No – no,' Gannet protested. 'I won't allow you to pay, me lad.'

'Nonsense,' Brad insisted with his suave smile. 'You've paid often enough for me, sir.'

He waved his hand and Hawkins disappeared. Only Gannet had suggested he would pay; the old man could have ordered a dozen bottles, for Brad knew very well something Gannet couldn't know, that Seeley's would never receive another guinea from him, salving his conscience with the thought that they had taken sufficient of his guineas already. It was all very pleasant while it lasted. Just to make a motion with the hand, drop a few syllables, and with the greatest deference the best of Seeley's was wafted to the table. While it lasted . . . Brad looked at Gannet. His face was still ruddy pink as if he had just emerged from a broiling bath, his grey mutton-chop whiskers still stiff and bristling, his appearance in the generously cut dark whipcord more than ever resembling a country squire up in London for the weekend. Must be getting on for seventy, and looked good for another seventy more. He would never reach that ripe old age, Brad reflected, for already he was beginning to feel his vital energies flagging. But soon he would settle down, this was his last fling. In another twenty years he could almost imagine a portly version of himself saying, 'Pah! The country's going to the dogs . . . You young fellows! . . . Why, when I was your age . . . When I was your age . . .'

'But why have you entered this mausoleum, as you term it?' he found himself asking.

'Not because I wanted to,' said Gannet. 'Oh no. The moment I come amongst these mummies I find myself reaching for the shroud.' His face turned suddenly serious. 'Have you seen anything of my nephew lately – young Anthony Crawford?'

'Tony Crawford? . . . Tony? . . . Well, come to think of it I haven't seen him for months and I often used to bump into him here.'

'That's just it,' said Gannet. 'Nobody's seen him and he's not at his lodgings, either. I had a letter from his mother, my sister, last week; she can't understand why he doesn't write. Why, the damned woman is almost off her head with worry. That's why I've come here. I tried it as a last resource, and the doorman told me he'd been here a while ago and was calling tonight for his letters. So I'm here, and if that young puppy hasn't got a good reason for keeping us all in the dark as to his whereabouts, I'll shake the wits out of him, old as I am.'

Only the gurgle of the brandy decanter into a large tumbler mollified the old man. He lifted the liquor to his nose and savoured its bouquet, then, clinking his glass against Brad's, tossed it down in a few gulps as though it were nothing more potent than the Spa water he detested, his large Adam's apple jerking beneath the wrinkled skin of his neck, almost the only concession of his physique to old age. Brad watched him with an amused smile. He hoped the errant nephew would not show up in a hurry, for he would dearly love to test the old man's capacity for Napoleon's at the expense of Seeley's Club, wondering what capers the septuagenarian would cut; would he gradually become bawdy or maudlin, or more and more subdued until he lost complete control of his senses?

Brad's experiment did not go beyond three-quarters of the first bottle. It had had not the slightest effect on the old man so far, in fact his eyes were still unclouded and his speech without the slightest slur. Brad was disappointed; although he liked Gannet he would have enjoyed the spectacle of the old man disgracing himself in this temple of propriety, but

Hawkins suddenly appeared and behind him was Tony Crawford.

'Thanks, Hawkins,' said Tony, dropping into a seat. ''Lo, uncle. How are you, Brad?'

'I'm very well,' said Brad.

'I'm fine too, damme!' growled the old man. 'But where in blazes have you been?'

'Where?' said Tony. His face looked tired and finely drawn. 'Where? Why, I've been here in London all the time.'

'Don't give me all that poppy-cock,' retorted Gannet. 'I've scoured the West End, every rabbit-hutch and burrow, and not a smell of you anywhere, and not a soul has seen you.'

'I said London,' Tony replied. 'London doesn't begin at the West End, and doesn't end there. In fact I've learnt lately that it isn't London at all.'

'It isn't, eh?' said Gannet. 'Well, before another brandy turns your head completely, tell me what is?'

'No, thanks.' Tony pushed the brandy aside. 'I don't feel like drinking. I've been living in Stepney, and what I've seen there makes me feel like a cur every time I eat a decent meal, every time I go to sleep beneath a raintight roof on a soft feather bed.'

'So that's it,' said the old man. 'So that's where you've been. Snooping round the East End like Haroun El Raschid or Santa Claus. Poking your nose in where you're not wanted. Frightening the life out of your mother, and all the while you're safe and sound playing at reformers.'

'It hasn't been a game, believe me,' Tony answered wearily. 'It's been a tragedy, or rather a series of tragedies. I must have been drunk when I landed there first, but I haven't been drunk since. I've been going round with someone who picked me up, visiting houses for a Health Commission. The things I've seen – appalling! A woman and four children, all of them working at making matchboxes, a task involving the pasting together of seven strips of wood, seven distinct operations, and the remuneration three-ha'pence per gross of boxes, so that all of them working twelve to fourteen hours a day earned together the princely sum of one and fourpence! I asked a tiny tot of six about her work and she answered, "I likes it, guv, only I feels so tired!" In another house a mother with three children, the oldest nine and the youngest five, made paper violets, and roses at half a crown per gross, working from six till school-time in the morning, and after school till past midnight, to earn less than two shillings for their combined labours. Now I ask you, uncle, with all this fresh in my mind, can you expect me to sit here in comfort drinking Napoleon brandy, well knowing that these things I have witnessed are but samples of a thousandfold misery – can you now?'

Gannet twirled his glass thoughtfully between his thumb and cupped fingers.

'I don't see why not,' he said calmly at last. He raised his hand as his nephew was about to burst into a fiery protest. 'The trouble with you young people is precisely that you are young – and hot-headed. What are to us the facts of life, sordid, unhappy if you like, come as a revelation to you as though you were explorers discovering repulsive man-eaters in an uncharted jungle. We know all about it, me lad, we know all about these unfortunates in the East End, but there is nothing whatever can be done.'

'Why not?' demanded Tony. 'Surely it is up to us, the legislative class, to put an end to such conditions before the workers as a whole rise in protest and upset society and us with them?'

'You take our workers too seriously,' said Gannet. 'They most of them prefer to stew in their own juice. I am an old politician, me lad; if they had wanted to alter their conditions of life they would have done so long ago. They are getting no better deal than they deserve. Pah! The workers haven't enough guts between them to furnish bow-strings for a quartet. I remember when they earned the right to be treated as men.

I remember my father standing at the gates of his mill and whipping operatives who came late. They hated him for it, and he knew that well, and when those firebrands Feargus O'Connor and Julian Harney and Bronterre O'Brien spread their Chartist gospel it fell on eager soil, and as soon as they got the chance they burned my father's mill about his ears. My father understood that sort of argument because it was the same form of reasoning that he employed himself, and the men got what they wanted. Nowadays if there's a dispute, the workers send their leaders to us, and after a glass of brandy and a pat on the back they are ready to lick our boots. Trade Unionists – pah! They're not the same breed as those Chartists of forty years ago. They were men, these are worms, and only too happy if we leave them alone. And you ask reform for that rabble! Reform when they want it, reform when they are ready for it, but not when everything we do for them is flung in our faces!'

'I don't know what they've flung in our faces,' Tony argued. 'But if we pass any measures that will benefit them, those poor wretches certainly won't kick, because you know and I know that that legislation only became statutory a long time after they forced us into it.'

'Nonsense!' Gannet replied vehemently. 'Stuff and nonsense, me lad! Facts speak for themselves. The Lancashire textile workers have always been the stoutest opponents of legal restrictions on child labour, and the spectacle of children working seems the thing that has got most up your nose in the East End. Time and again their spokesmen at their congresses have pleaded for the right of parents to supplement insufficient earnings by those of their children. As a matter of fact, since the celebrated Ten Hour Act of 1847, not one legislative measure for the limitation of child labour passed upon the demand of workers; such reforms, every one of them, and I defy contradiction, being invariably sponsored by bourgeois reformers, philanthropists and educationists.'

'I can hardly believe that,' said Tony. 'I feel sure that this acquiescence to child exploitation is confined solely to the lowest stratum of the labouring classes, and when the workmen become sufficiently politically conscious to organize themselves into trade unions for the betterment of their conditions, when they not only understand what they really should have but also know how to get it, then the first plank in their platform must be the abolition of child slavery.'

'Pah!' growled the old man, raising his voice exasperatedly. 'You're an incorrigible optimist, Tony, and if you were not so young I'm damned if I'd be bothered to talk to you. I've said it before and I'm saying it again, only louder, so that you'll take notice, that the sole responsibility for the exploitation of children and juveniles can be laid entirely at the door of those same trade unions which seek to increase the wages of their members not by having a show-down and fighting openly for it, but by enslaving the children. That's gospel, me lad, and I can produce chapter and verse to prove it. Those Chartists forty years ago refused to hide behind women and children's petticoats, they came into the open and fought like men. Workers! Trade Unionists! – pah! If you want to look for the genuine reformers, the real friends of the working class, you need search no further than our party, the Whigs!'

'I wonder if I may interject my mite into this weighty consanguineous discussion?' asked Brad suavely.

'Of course you may,' said Gannet, 'providing you have something to say on the subject, and,' cocking his thumb at his nephew, 'unlike this sentimentalist here, know what you are talking about.'

'Well . . .' Brad answered. 'Perhaps it isn't important, but as an hereditary Tory, I rather resent you claiming all the reforming credit for the Whigs; from what I've heard and read, the Chartists were never very enamoured of them, in fact they got along much better with the old Tory landowners. My own grandfather was a champion of the Chartists. He was that Wintringham who stood up in Parliament with his friend Oastler to defend the rights of workers. Can you deny that, sir?'

'Deny it?' said Gannet. 'Why should I deny it? Facts are facts, and I have built my life on the recognition of facts. Of course the Tory landowners spoke up for the Chartists, but why? Because they loved them? Not a bit of it, me lad – merely out of hatred for us, the "Base, Bloody, Treacherous Whigs." Because they were afraid of the industrial developments we were inaugurating, that were sweeping their old still half-feudal mode of life on to the dust heap. That's the explanation, my boy,' he concluded unctuously.

'Well . . .' Brad hesitated. 'I don't know sufficient to argue. But perhaps you're right.'

'No perhaps about it, me lad,' Gannet asseverated. 'I have half a century of political experience to back me up.' He turned to his nephew. 'Now *you've* been living in the East End. Are the workers doing anything up there to help themselves? Of course not! They are a drunken, depraved, vicious lot, the hoi-polloi. Have they inaugurated any schemes for bettering their conditions? Of course not! Who are agitating for better houses, less drunkenness, more morality? I'll tell you – people of our class, and Whigs, almost to a man! Take the case of the homeless children for example, the waifs and strays of the streets, whose parents would gladly have bartered them for a keg of gin, who's lifting them out of the gutters? I'll tell you, me lad. That fellow Barnardo. And is he a workman? Of course not! I don't know about his politics, whether he has any or not, but he's one of us, a bourgeois bred and born, and I defy you to show me a member of the labouring classes in that same East End who's doing work of equivalent importance! Well?' he demanded triumphantly, as his nephew remained silent. 'Well, me lad, what have you to say for yourself?'

'I've nothing to say about Barnardo,' said Tony quietly, 'but for the rest of your arguments I've got quite a bit in reply. You mustn't forget that I'm grown up, uncle, and have learnt more in the past few weeks than in the previous ten years of my life put together. Of course I have something to say, and it's this, that in apportioning the blame for their vile conditions on the workers themselves you are doing them a grave injustice. Certainly they seem indifferent to their misery, but after we clamped down their protests so ruthlessly a few generations back the fires of revolt were stamped out, yet I can tell you that they are still smouldering beneath the surface.

At present they still have memories of Peterloo and Tolpuddle to restrain them, and until they feel themselves strong enough they dare not risk a further dose of repression. It's all right your bringing up grandfather's mill as an example of militancy, but if he had been at the fire and you too, neither would have hesitated to call out the militia and slaughter as many operatives as you could in cold blood, in spite of your appreciation of their robust spirit. Their spirit is still pretty good now too, although you may want to see less drunkenness and more morality. That's what *you* want, but they want food first and the morality can look after itself, and if they want to drink, why not? We've left them precious little else to get from life. If, instead of worrying about drink, our legislators saw to it that the adults got higher wages and better conditions of labour, the children wouldn't be forced to work; I can assure you, uncle, that the parents only countenance it because they have no option if they are to keep body and soul together. I've been living down the East End and know what I'm talking about, and I tell you, uncle, in spite of your casuistry it's wrong – all wrong!'

'Maybe it is all wrong,' said Gannet, 'or maybe it's all right. Depends on which side of the fence you're sitting on. Depends on your viewpoint, on which side your bread's buttered. Of course, if you feel you must do some useful work in the slums nobody will stop you, provided you let the family know where you are. In fact, if you want to, you can go down to Barnardo's mission one or two evenings a week. I'll give you a letter of introduction if you like. A gradual dose of reforming is the best antidote to that missionary zeal that gets some of us when we're young. When you get to know the labouring classes better you'll realize that not all of them are suffering angels and we're not all of us monstrous tyrants. Well, Tony, what d'you say?'

'I . . . I'll think about it,' Tony answered. 'It certainly sounds interesting. I would like to meet Barnardo. I didn't while I was there, but it seems that everybody else in the East End has.'

'I met him once, too,' said Gannet. 'That was before he started his homes. He showed me a sight then that I shall never forget as long as I live . . . Why, damme! I never dreamed ten years ago that that little student would become the famous Doctor Barnardo. Think of it. Hundreds of boys and girls under his care, dozens of paid and voluntary helpers, and money rolling into his coffers from every corner of the world, almost to the tune of thirty thousand a year. That terrific sum at the sole disposal of a youngster not much older than you, Tony, and certainly not as old as Brad. Think of it, thirty thousand pounds a year – damme, it takes my breath away. It's amazing for a boy of thirty.'

'Not so amazing,' suggested Tony, 'when you remember what other youngsters have done. After all, Napoleon conquered half Europe before he was thirty, and was an Emperor at thirty-five.'

'But then,' Brad interpolated dryly, 'you're forgetting Napoleon was a genius.'

'And how d'you know Barnardo isn't?' demanded Gannet abruptly. 'I don't like admitting it, but he's pulled some tidy sums out of my own pocket, and if anyone can do that to me with only a few chits and some anonymous initials on a donations-list for return, then, damme, lad, that fellow's a genius, and deserves to rank with Napoleon.'

'Perhaps initials are all *you* get in return,' said Brad. 'Very nice too for the Napoleon of the waifs and strays. How do you know *he* doesn't make something more substantial out of it than initials?'

'How do I know? Why – damme, man! I told you I met him!'

'So have I,' said Brad. 'Probably before you. I knew Tom Barnardo very well. He was in my year at medical college, and went to some questionable places and kept very strange company for an evangelist.'

'What's that?' asked Gannet suspiciously. 'How do you know, anyway?'

'Because, my dear sir, I went to those places myself. However, if you like Barnardo, it's your money you're giving away, and your initials you'll get back. You're welcome to them.'

Brad smiled quizzically and signalled to Hawkins, hovering in the background, for his bill. Deferentially the waiter stooped over the young man, and Brad, taking a slim gold-cased pencil from his pocket, scrawled some hieroglyphics at the bottom of the extended sheet.

'Here, Hawkins,' he said. '*You* can have a couple of initials too.'

Brad rose to his feet. 'It's been very pleasant to have met you, sir. Good night. And good night, Tony, to you.'

With a formal bow he retired from the table, noting in their uneasy expressions how his words had affected his companions. Without definitely accusing Barnardo he had suggested that the missionary's conduct was not entirely above suspicion, and there was more than a hint in his words that such charges, whatever they were, could easily be substantiated. Brad knew Gannet, and was sure that those apparently spontaneous, careless words would act as a challenge to the old man's conviction that he was an infallible judge of character, and represent him to be as gullible as those sentimentalists at whom he scoffed.

What Brad had to gain by his quite unwarranted remarks he had no idea, but he was certain that in the building up of a gigantic charity such as Barnardo's there were bound to have occurred one or two questionable episodes to convince prejudiced inquirers who set out to look for them.

Brad very rarely read the papers except to skim through the sporting news, but on the few occasions he had lately glanced at items of social interest, he had been disturbed by the frequency with which Barnardo's name was featured. He still held against him the affair at Ma Collins' that had cost him his watch and purse, but on top of that had been grafted a senseless jealousy that increased with Barnardo's ever-growing prestige. After all, they had been to college together, and Brad had had advantages denied the youth from Dublin. When the elder Wintringham died, Brad departed from the Hospital in a blaze of opulence, leaving his colleagues earthbound like indistinguishable grubs, while he, jumping the chrysalis stage, flew off on iridescent wings, a full-fledged butterfly. That was the normal working of Nature for a Wintringham, but with the passage of years, Brad was forced to recognize his own insignificance, while every fresh triumph of the contemptuously dubbed 'plaster saint' seemed to him an added slight, a direct personal insult.

He collected his hat, coat and gloves, and twirling his gold-mounted cane thoughtfully before him passed through the lounge into the narrow hall that led to the street. Automatically he drew a cigar from his pocket and thrust it between his lips, biting the end till the crisp leaves moistened by his saliva had the taste and texture of soaked cardboard. Descending five stone steps from the porch to the pavement, he looked around as though in search of a conveyance, then tilting his handsome head in the air, he brushed his moustache upwards with the knuckle of his hogskin glove, and turned towards a side-street, his coat-tails spread like a frigate in full sail.

'Pardon me, guv,' said a voice behind him. Brad turned to

see a shabby individual holding towards him a tray of matches. Emphatically, without a second glance, he shook his head.

'Buy a box of matches, guv?' urged the man.

'No, thanks,' Brad replied.

''A'penny a box – 'at's all.'

'No, thanks,' Brad repeated frigidly.

He turned on his heel, annoyed by the man's brusque invasion of that mental self-immolation that tormented him, yet was part of his attitude to and enjoyment of life. Barnardo made him feel depressed and miserable, yet he derived a certain amount of pleasure from his misery, and thinking of Tom roused his vengeful nature and titillated his sense of martyrdom as though he, Bradley Wintringham, were rightfully entitled by birth and accomplishment to enjoy the praises showered on the Irish interloper.

'Fusees? – Cigar-light?' the wheedling voice followed him down the street.

Brad shook his head without turning and increased his pace, yet a moment later the same cringing whine was at his elbow.

'Fusee? – Cigar-light?'

Brad turned angrily on his heel, his right fist closing tightly round the knob of his cane. Damn the fellow! Couldn't he understand English? He raised his stick, and thrust it under the nose of the cowering tramp in the gutter.

'Confound you, man!' he ejaculated fiercely. 'Can't you take "no" for an answer?'

'Yes, Mr Brad,' the shabby figure replied, tipping a shaky finger to his forehead.

Brad half-turned, then, as it dawned on him that he had been addressed by name, he wheeled to face the shrinking scarecrow in the road.

'What did you say?' he demanded.

'Matches – fusees – cigar-light?' the other returned hopefully, extending his tray.

'No. No! – What you said just now – this very moment.'

'I only said "Yes, Mr Brad."'

'I thought so,' said Brad. 'Who told you my name?'

'No one told me, guv, I knowed it.'

'Know it? How did you know it, man? I suppose you'll say next that I know your name too.'

'Aye,' said the stranger. 'Yer knows me right well, guv.'

He removed his shabby cap, revealing a large bald head fringed with wisps of dirty flock, and thrust his face upwards, parting the thick lips in a querulous half-smile that showed strong, sharp-pointed canine teeth, the enamel stained by plug-juice, and dulled from long neglect.

'Reckernize me naow?' he croaked.

'Good Heavens!' Brad exclaimed. 'Surely . . . surely it isn't Botman?'

'Aye. It is. It's me. Sam Botman.'

'But what's the meaning of this masquerade?' Brad asked in bewilderment. 'What is all this, a joke?'

'I wisht it wor, guv,' the other answered glumly.

'Now let me get this clear,' said Brad. 'You're Botman all right, the Sam Botman I knew. But what's happened to the Green Man?'

'Shut,' Botman replied.

'And Maggie?'

'Runned away,' he answered dolefully. 'When I gets on me uppers, she ups an' all an' runs away ter Manchester. I did 'ear she was 'angin' raound with a racing man for a while, but someone else brung me tidings she's charrin' an' doin' odd jobs for a publican up north somewheres.'

'Poor Maggie!' said Brad. 'I'm sorry for her.'

'I ain't,' Botman replied shortly. 'Serves 'er jolly well right. She did ought ter stick by 'er old man like she promised in 'er wedding vaows, in fair weather or foul, in 'ealth or in sickness. Wimmin's all alike, guv, believe me, when things is going good they're that sorft butter couldn't melt in their mouths, but when yer real dahn on your luck an' wants a bit er 'elp orf 'em, or even sympathy, wot don't corst nuffing, then yer finds aout their 'earts is 'ard as the knockers 'er Newgit.'

'Well . . . Well . . .' Brad nodded commiseratingly. 'The Green Man closed, Maggie in Manchester. The world's full of surprises, and not the least of them is the Green Man going phut. Isn't the East End like it was ten years ago? Have the people changed so enormously? I can't believe it. Why, I remember when you were crammed to the door every night. It must be your own fault. There can be no other explanation. Tell me now, Sam, as man to man. What have you been doing? Women? Gambling?'

Botman shook his head.

'Yer wrong, guv. Dead wrong. 'Tain't wot I done, it's wot's bin done ter me. I speckt yer don't believe wot I'm tellin' yer, but it ain't my fault at all, narry a scrap. If the Edinburgh Castle was forced aout o' business, it ain't no wonder the Green Man 'ad ter close the doors.'

'The Edinburgh Castle?' said Brad incredulously. 'That shut down too?'

'Not exackly,' Botman replied. 'Only in a manner o' speaking. It's still open, only they don't sell beer or spirrets any more.'

'Open and no liquor? What are you talking about man?'

Botman grinned. 'It's true. I'll take me oath on it, guv, an' if yer'll go dahn ter Lime'ouse yer'll find aout fer yerself. Them long bars wot was the pride of East London, they're still there, but the pretty barmaids is gorn, an' the beer's gorn. They've turned it into a corfee palace!'

'A coffee palace – save the mark!'

'Aye,' Botman answered. 'A corfee palace, an' packed out every night wiv men wot calls 'emselves men – yet they carn't get a drink there er enyfing stronger nor tea!' he said contemptuously.

'And the music-hall at the back?' asked Brad. 'Don't tell me that's closed too!'

'Aye,' said Botman. 'Aye. That music-'all's gorn, but the place is still open. They're using it fer a church.'

'A church!' Brad burst into a roar of laughter. 'A church! Next thing you'll tell me Ma Collins is in the choir! . . . Seriously now, Botman, tell me what's happened to you all?'

'You oughter know,' said Sam, 'seein' as 'aow one er your mates done it.'

'One of my mates? Whatever are you talking about? My mates? . . . Whoever do you mean?'

'Barnardo . . . Tom Barnardo . . .'

Brad suddenly became serious. That man again!

'Yes,' he replied half-apologetically. 'He was a colleague of mine at the London Hospital, but never a friend. In fact, he was quite the opposite, I assure you.'

'I'm glad o' that,' said Botman. 'I allus did like you. Yer allus was a real toff, a reg'lar swell – but 'im, the cunnin' snake, 'e used ter come inter the bar with 'is baby smile an' 'is "Gawd bless yer, me good man," an' sellin' 'is books an' pamphlets abaout Jesus an' the evils er drink right under me very nose. I should 'a' run 'im aout on 'is ear as soon as look at 'im, 'sted o' which I lets 'im get on wiv it, an' 'e gits on so well 'e runs *me* aout. Fust fing I know 'e's pitched a big tent on the waste ground aoutside the Edinburgh Castle an' fillin' it up wiv people night arter night preachin' the Gorspel. Well they carn't be in two places at once, so if they're in the tent they carn't be in the pub, and once they come aout o' the tent they don't feel like pubs any more. Next, arf me customers signs the pleadge, the Edinburgh Castle goes bust, Barnardo takes it over, an' afore yer kin say Jack Robinson, Maggie's in Manchester an' I'm in the gutter.'

'Well, well,' Brad interpolated, 'here today and gone tomorrow. Nothing like being philosophical about it, my friend. The world doesn't stay still, Sam, it revolves round and round. Rich last year, a beggar this, perhaps next year it will revolve full circle again. There's comfort in that, Botman, old fellow.'

The derelict shrugged his shoulders.

'Mebbe it is fer you,' he commented bitterly. 'Yer don't need comfortin', but it's pretty cold comfort fer me. Sam Botman drove in the gutter, an' likely ter stay there, an' all the while that Paddy waxing rich on the fat end er the land, wivout stirring a finger. Me, beggin' in the streets fer a crust, wot was born 'ere, while that furriner tucks aour good guineas in 'is own breeks.'

'Come! Come!' Brad protested. 'I'm sure Tom Barnardo isn't that sort.' In spite of himself, Brad felt driven to defend him. It was all right Barnardo's being attacked by one of his own class, but such denunciation coming from the Cockney's mouth seemed to leave an ugly aroma in the air. Dash it all! It just wasn't done. Scratch any Cockney, and enmity towards his superiors showed itself immediately, no matter how seemingly well intentioned his usual behaviour.

'After all,' he elaborated, 'all his work is done quite voluntarily. He doesn't get paid for it.'

'Hummm!' grunted Botman sceptically. ''E don't 'ave ter. The money comes in – 'e jest 'elps 'isself – an' not arf 'e don't!'

'Is he as well off then as all that?' asked Brad.

'Well orf! Wot der *you* fink? I ain't wishin' yer no 'arm, guv, nor meself neether when I ses we'd both be satisfied wiv a quarter o' what 'e makes. Don't get no wages, got no reg'lar job, yet 'e manages ter live in the country like a bloomin' Lord. Got a mansion, wiv servants an' gardeners and carriages like any haristocrat wot ever wor.'

'A mansion, eh?' said Brad dubiously. His defences were tottering. This was what he would have liked to believe, what he had maliciously hinted at in Seeley's without the faintest shadow of proof to substantiate his innuendos. And yet Botman seemed to bear it all out. And Botman should know, a native East Ender, and unlike himself, not cut off from Barnardo's activities for nearly a decade.

'When I knew him,' Brad admitted, 'he rented an upstairs room in a cottage in Dempsey Street.'

'Aye!' Botman nodded. 'There y'are, guv, speaks fer itself. An' that ain't the arf of it, neether.'

'No?' said Brad. 'What else do you know?'

'Plenty.' Botman grimaced. 'I knows plenty, an' wot I ses, I kin prove, every word.' He glanced up slyly . . . 'Yer allus was a generous sorter feller . . .' he brought out at last.

Brad glanced down at the dirty outstretched hand and fished in his pockets for a large piece of silver. He was nearly as broke as Botman, but this information was worth his very last copper, and if it proved correct he would see to it that it reached a wider circle than Seeley's club. He dropped a crown into the cupped palm.

'There you are, Sam,' he said magnanimously. The coin, propelled by force of habit to Botman's mouth, gleamed for a moment between his strong yellow teeth. Undamaged, it dropped back into Botman's hand, and spitting on it for luck, the match-seller thrust it into his tattered jacket.

'Thankee kindly, guv,' he whined.

'That's quite all right, Sam. Forget it.'

'I'll never fergit it,' said Botman. 'I wisht they was all like you. Straight as er die, and 'onist as they makes 'em. Yer allus was the same, yer liked yer fun like everyone else, but yer wasn't ashamed ter drink when yer fancied, or chase a petticoat when yer 'ad a mind ter. It's fellers like Barnardo I carn't abide. Posin' as a man o' Gawd, an' I seed 'im wiv me own eyes walkin' dahn the street wiv drunken trollops, an' goin' 'ome wiv 'em to their own 'ouses!'

'Really?' Brad commented dryly. This seemed very ordinary tittle-tattle, and extremely poor value for his last piece of silver. 'I suppose he drinks as well?'

'Aye – that 'e does. I'll take me oath on it.'

'I thought so,' said Brad.

'An' the 'omes is terrible,' Botman continued eagerly. 'They works the kids ter death, an' arf starves 'em on top of it – strite, guv!'

'How do you know?' asked Brad sharply.

''Ow'd I know? 'Cause some of me own customers 'ad their kids there, an' they'd swear their oaths on it.'

'Oh! . . . Go on, Botman.'

'An' when the kids is bad, an' wot kids ain't at times? – arter all, it's only natcheral – when the kids kicks over the trices, they shoves 'em in dark underground cellars, with nuffing ter eat only bread an' water, so damp dahn there that mud oozes through the floor, an' the rats bites lumps aout o' their toes.'

'Toes? – Why then, are their feet naked?'

'Aye, they takes their boots away ter punish 'em, an' the pore kids lives there fer weeks on end. I did even 'ear a case where one youngster was shut up in a cell and the door nailed fer nigh on a week.'

'Botman,' said Brad sternly. 'You are being ridiculous. I gave you some money, it's true, but I didn't expect a cock-and-bull yarn in return. If you imagine I've swallowed all this twaddle you're mistaken.'

He turned disgustedly on his heel, but Botman's dirty hand gripped his arm detainingly.

''Old on, guv, 'old on,' he pleaded earnestly, his face deadly serious. 'I ain't tellin' yer no stories, guv, 'onist I ain't. I sed I could prove wot I ses, an' I kin. I kin even take yer where these folks lives and yer ain't got fer ter go ter meet a fellow wot used ter work in the 'omes 'isself. 'E kips up at my ken in Drury Lane, an' 'e told me abaout the kid bein' nailed up in 'is cell, an' that's somefing 'e seed wiv 'is own eyes!'

Brad swayed irresolutely. After all, this had nothing whatever to do with him. Then he remembered his purse and Ma Collins.

And Barnardo . . . Napoleon Barnardo. It would indeed, if this proved true, please him immensely to unmask the plaster saint, and by now Brad was convinced that his motives were entirely disinterested, that as a good citizen this was merely a matter of public duty. He made up his mind, he would go to Drury Lane with Botman, but God help the shifty scarecrow if he dragged him all that way for nothing!

CHAPTER 16

Near Whitechapel Church, in Church Lane, Brad found the Heaven's Way mission. It was housed in a shabby two-storied building, a few illustrated texts in the dirty window, and a large board over the door revealing its purpose as distinct from the uniformly dull aspect of the anonymous dwelling-houses that lurched like crumbling, black headstones on both sides of the tiny narrow street. Entering, Brad passed through a short passage into a large room that was decorated with a frieze of scriptural quotations, coloured pictures of the last temple in Jerusalem, a Hebrew priest sacrificing the Paschal lamb, and in the place of honour in the centre of the wall above a raised dais, Jesus surrounded by a multitude of infants, with beneath the legend, 'Suffer little children to come unto me.'

Several rows of benches were grouped before the dais facing a table and a high throne-like chair, the chair unoccupied, the table bare save for a massive leather-bound Bible and a glass of water. The room was empty except for an old man lethargically sweeping a corner of the floor with a long-bristled broom. Brad walked up to the stooping figure, and halting him waited for the man to speak. The hunched shoulders swayed on in a slumbering adagio, but no sound issued to show that Brad's entrance had been noted. At last the young man gently tapped the sweeper's back. The unhurried movement ceased, but the man remained stooping and stationary, as though undecided whether to turn or not.

'Pardon me,' said Brad.

The man swung round ponderously like a rusty door, and resting his hand on the broomstick looked up at the newcomer with pale watery eyes.

'Yus?' he said. 'Wotcher want?'

'I was told I could find a gentleman here by the name of Quelch.'

A knotted unsteady hand reached up behind the long-lobed ear.

'Eh?' said the old man unblinkingly.

'Quelch . . . Zachariah Quelch . . .' Brad's voice, trying to stir some comprehension into the expressionless face, rose in an exasperated crescendo. 'I want to see the Reverend Zachariah Quelch!' he shouted.

'Oh,' said the old man thoughtfully. 'Yer wanter see parson.'

'That's it. Thank Heaven you've got it at last.'

'Eh?' he inquired, puzzled. 'Wot's that yer just said?'

'Nothing . . . Nothing, man . . . Where is he? – Quelch. Zachariah Quelch?'

The old man's bleary eyes gazed at Brad unwaveringly, until the young man felt discomfited as though he had in his impatience done something to be ashamed of, then the broom made a shaky arc in the air and pointed to a door behind the dais.

'If it's parson yer wants, yer'll find 'im froo there.'

Brad nodded, relieved, and hurried to the door. Turning, he looked back and saw the old man gazing after him immobilely, passively, as though he were quite aloof from Brad and his surroundings, the broom tucked under his arm, his shrunken attitude petrified in the drooping make-believe stance of a music-hall comedian, yet in that chill authenticity not evocative of laughter. Behind the door he found another passage and a short flight of stairs. Mounting the stairs he came to a second door, slightly ajar. Brad listened for a moment. There seemed no sounds of an occupant, but unless the old man was dull-witted as well as being deaf and half-blind, he should find the Reverend Quelch in this room. Gently he tapped at the door and waited.

'Come in,' boomed a sonorous voice.

Brad pushed the door open and entered. He found himself in a small, dingy room. Theological books were ranged on shelves round the walls, and pamphlets lay piled on the floor in precariously balanced top-heavy stacks. Behind a large table littered with papers and impressively bound tomes, the torso of a man faced him, whose left arm rested on the table, his right hand holding a long quill pen in the air pointing straight at Brad. For a moment Brad looked at the man in silence. Zachariah Quelch seemed very small and slim, the wrist that stuck out from his dark clerical sleeve was bony and blotched with large freckles, the big head and jutting chin appearing disproportionately developed in relation to his narrow shoulders. A thin patch of hair, the indeterminate colour of dead straw that a sandy growth achieves when grey, spread over the skull from the high-domed forehead, too innocuous looking for the intense, bony, cadaverous face with the deep-set burning blue eyes framed by bushy scimitars of brows that swooped like the wings of a gull hovering athwart the bridge of his sharp nose.

'Mr Quelch?' said Brad at last.

'Praise God!' the seated man replied unctuously. 'That is my name.'

'I'm Bradley Wintringham. You knew my father at Oxford.'

The missionary laid down his pen, and stroked his aggressive chin thoughtfully.

'Ah!' . . . he said. 'Bradley Wintringham. I knew him well . . . And you are his son.' He rose to his feet, thrusting his head forward, a curious light springing to the deep-set eyes, his whole attitude like that of a man transformed, a hypnotist with a message.

'Tell me, brother,' he boomed earnestly, as though this were the chief concern of his life, 'are you saved?'

'Saved?' said Brad.

'Saved,' Quelch repeated. 'Are you washed in the blood of the Lamb?'

'Oh!' Brad understood. 'I suppose so,' he replied unconcernedly.

For some reason the mildness of this assertion displeased the Reverend Quelch. 'There is no suppose about it,' he burst argumentatively. 'There is no supposing about God. With the Lord, it's either Yes or No. there are no two ways about it. What is it with you, friend?'

'Yes,' said Brad.

The victory seemed too easily won for Quelch.

'So many people say they are saved,' he commented wistfully, his burning eyes still fixed on Brad's face. 'So many people call themselves Christians, but it is the Devil they serve, not Christ. That is why I ask you, brother, in all earnestness, have you got the personal Jesus in your soul?'

'Yes . . . I have,' Brad answered.

'Then Praise God, brother,' Quelch said, obviously a little disappointed. 'Praise the Lord.'

Brad nodded impatiently. He had met several of Quelch's type before during his student days in the East End, fanatics who knew the Bible backwards, swamping every conversation with a flood of sacerdotal allusions, and especially enjoying a tussle with the Devil, whom they recognized immediately lurking in the bosoms of anyone who disagreed with them.

'Look here, sir,' Brad pointed out firmly. 'I have come to talk about something very important.'

Again the flame leapt to Quelch's eyes. He moved from behind the table and approached Brad with a curious stilted step. In his fanaticism, from an excess of religious zeal, he had developed a secret ritual of walking mainly on his heels since even the word sole had a holy connotation in his mind. Because of the pious association of the sound, he avoided treading on his soles, but, being an educated man, and something of a philologist, he told no one of this extraordinary devoutness which, beginning as a temporary penance to discipline his body, had developed into an obsession that he felt brought him nearer than most men to God. He stopped an arm's length from Brad, and resting one hand against a bookshelf near the door, braced himself for yet another encounter with the Evil One.

'There is nothing more important than God,' Zachariah asserted dogmatically. 'And nothing I would rather talk about. Brother, I could talk about Him and praise Him all my waking moments. Everything that hath breath shall praise the Lord. Yea, even with harps and cymbals.'

Brad stroked his dark moustache cynically and looked down at his queer companion. He nodded as if to humour him.

'All right,' he said. 'You please yourself. But at the moment I want to talk about something else.'

Quelch shot out his hand till the skinny, freckled wrist was almost beneath Brad's nose. 'Take heed, brother,' he warned him, his sonorous voice quivering with agitation. 'Take heed. The Lord slumbereth not, neither does He sleep. He is listening and your own words shall condemn ye, for words are sharp, brother, like unto a two-edged sword.'

Brad began to feel annoyed. If it were not that he could use this man, he would have left the mission there and then. He knew Zachariah Quelch hated Barnardo and all his works, and coming into contact with the man, he understood why the Heaven's Way mission was a failure, while Barnardo's thrived on public acclaim. Quelch antagonized people right from the outset, as if every fresh person came to him steeped in sin and the onus was on him to browbeat them into salvation. If that was the way he treated a perfect stranger, how did he behave towards those unfortunate slum children that came under his care? With difficulty Brad controlled himself, and ignored Quelch's last outburst.

'I have called to talk to you about Doctor Barnardo,' he remarked as evenly as he could.

The name had a remarkable effect on Quelch. He looked

at Brad suspiciously for a moment, then his temper got the better of him, and he let fly viciously.

'Doctor Barnardo?' he snorted. 'There is no such person, brother. There is a Barnardo, but he has no right to masquerade under an academic distinction to which he has no title. Humph! A doctor without a medical degree, a parson without ever having taken Holy Orders! Don't talk to me about Barnardo, brother, he is the Devil's own spawn, and belongs to purgatory with all his works!'

'That's just what I'm getting at,' said Brad.

Quelch moved away from him with his stiff peculiar gait. He only needed an audience to work himself into a fury about Barnardo. He forgot Brad's existence, and shuffled round the room booming denunciations that he had repeated scores of times before. It irked him that he who had been labouring in this vineyard before Barnardo was born should have attained so small a measure of success, while the East End Juvenile Mission went from strength to strength under the ægis of a comparative newcomer.

'I can tell you some things about Barnardo, brother, things that you probably don't know, things you never heard of – that charlatan who preys on an unsuspecting public and lives himself on the fat of the land! And those poor children who have fallen into his clutches raised as pagans without the fear of the Lord, with no training in morals or religion. Do you know what he squeezes every year from misguided servants of God? Do you?' he demanded fiercely.

'No,' said Brad. 'But I have heard it is a vast sum.'

'Vast!' shouted Quelch. 'It's enormous. A fortune! Do you realize, brother, that he takes upwards of thirty thousand pounds a year from the public?'

'Really!' Brad seemed shocked. 'It's incredible!'

'Incredible, but true. That's something you didn't know, brother. Thirty thousand pounds a year! Why, for half that sum I could spread the light of God amongst these forsaken children and bring them to Jesus through Heaven's Way, as it is writ in the Holy Scriptures. And what does *he* do? He sends them out selling firewood, and polishing boots! But if these brigades are self-supporting as he claims them to be, what need has he of thirty thousand pounds a year? And even that is not enough, he clamours constantly for more. What does he do with all that money? How does he spend it? He was a poor student, yet now he lives in a style to which I who was born with a silver spoon am not accustomed. If he carries on his charity without fear, or hire, whence comes his livelihood, for he does nothing else? I am a charitable man, brother, a God-fearing man, yet even to me there occurs but one explanation, much as I detest the very thought of it.'

'I can guess what that is,' said Brad. 'And that is why I have come to you. I can prove that all those stories told about the Homes are true.'

Quelch stopped short.

'Stories? These are no stories, brother.'

'I know, I know,' Brad assured him soothingly. 'But I have lately come in contact with a friend who knew Barnardo well, and he led me to one of Barnardo's old employees. For several weeks I have been checking up on what he told me, how Barnardo fakes photographs, stripping the children's clothing as they come to him, and daubing their bodies with soot to make a piteous picture for a gullible public. And I have spoken to people whose children are with him, who utilizes their labour while their parents are cut off from the help their able-bodied lads would bring. I have all that and much more in black and white, with names and addresses of people ready to substantiate their stories before the highest tribunal in the land.' He drew a slim notebook from his pocket, and held it towards Quelch. 'I give this into your safe keeping, sir. I am sure you will know how to make the best use of it.'

All semblance of a Christian mask dropped from Quelch's face as he pounced on the book. Looking hastily through the pages, he seemed the personification of harsh eager vindictiveness, with not a jot of the Christian humility and meekness of spirit that his own calling glorified. Brad watched the long fingers curl lovingly round the crisp edges of the paper, and poke at haphazard places, while the deep voice rumbled an accompaniment of half-incomprehensible comments. The young man smiled at Quelch's mounting excitement and his hand rose to his moustache, twirling the soaring tips to a tighter, more impeccable curl.

'Well!' sighed Quelch at last with oily satisfaction. 'Well! . . . Ah, brother, I have long had my suspicions about that wolf in sheep's clothing. Now I have evidence of his cruelty, hypocrisy, chicanery and general knavery. Rest assured I shall bruit it throughout the land. You have this day done the Lord's work, brother. The battle is joined and the sword shall not rust in my hand till I have routed this whited sepulchre before the whole world!'

'Excellent,' Brad replied. 'I'm glad I called, and in truth something impelled me to come to you.'

Quelch nodded.

'Aye! Aye!' he answered gravely. 'It was the Lord's doing, even though He led you to me, who am the humblest of His servants.'

His demeanour changed to mirror his sentiments, the look of triumphant vindictiveness was expunged, giving place to a melancholy gravity lit up only by the feverish sparkle of his eyes. Suddenly he sank to his knees, and without looking at Brad, bowed his head reverently.

'Let us pray, brother!' he said in a loud voice.

Brad glanced at the kneeling missionary. His work here was finished, for the rest he could safely leave what else was to be done in this fanatic's hands. He tiptoed to the door and passed down the stairs, while behind him the unctuous tones bellowed through the room as though the Reverend Zachariah Quelch were leading a mighty audience in a devout psalm of thankfulness.

CHAPTER 17

Zachariah Quelch only needed Brad's evidence to let himself go completely about Barnardo. He had been fulminating about him so violently and for so long, that very few people took Zachariah seriously. Now his pronouncements had a new authority and he erupted into the local Press, the *Tower Hamlets Independent* and the *East London Observer*, but when his letter received no indignant refutation from Barnardo, the East End began to think that perhaps there was, after all, some germ of truth in the Reverend Zachariah's wild statements.

Haddock in particular was very much perturbed. He had watched Tom since his arrival in Stepney, and had seen him grow up with his beloved mission. He disagreed with much of what Tom did, with the student's ideas he was in direct antipathy, but he knew Tom well enough to be certain that such stories had not the slightest foundation. All round him Haddock heard gossip – malicious, ignorant and so pervasive that even those who should have known better were also beginning to repeat embellishments of Zachariah's charges. Haddock was a blunt man. He felt he had a right to know the truth for himself, and to find out there was only one way, to approach Barnardo directly.

His surgery was only a little way from Stepney Causeway, Barnardo's headquarters, so, warning Ernest to have Rachel ready saddled on his return, he set out on his first visit to the East End Juvenile Mission. Haddock waited good-humouredly in an ante-room while he was announced to Barnardo. Tom was a busy man. No longer was it possible for callers to see him immediately without an appointment, but like a very efficient business chief, he had a staff of assistants acting as intermediaries to keep him from spending his valuable time on any matter but those in which his personal intervention was absolutely necessary. Haddock had no appointment, but as he expected Tom asked to see him at once. The Black Doctor often had, except of late, met him in the East End streets, but neither had found the time to pass more than a few impersonal words, so engrossed were each of them in their own tasks. Today Haddock meant to see to it that Tom would unburden himself before him as he had so often done in those early days.

Haddock was glad to see his friend so bright and energetic, his brow unclouded and serene as though no dark shadows were jostling at his elbow to engulf him. Here was a cheery young man, a successful business executive, with the world at his feet, rather than a slum missionary whose name and reputation were being daily assailed by countless tongues and flayed in the open Press. Tom looked extremely well; sitting behind the table he seemed a massive specimen of manhood with his well-developed torso and the large, powerful head on a short thick neck. Rising to greet Haddock, he dispelled the illusion of great stature, yet with his firmly knit frame diminishing downwards to the hips like an athlete, he lost, in standing, little of his commanding presence.

'My dear fellow!' said Tom. 'I *am* glad to see you. Take a seat and tell me why I am so honoured by this visit.'

'Mah friend,' Haddock replied gravely, 'the honour is all on mah side. Ah hope you are keeping well.'

'Never felt better in all my life,' Tom assured him briskly. 'Thank God, my health never lets me down. It had better not,' he chuckled. 'I can't manage to get through all my work as it is. I can't even afford to sleep very much, so I certainly can't afford to be ill.'

For a moment Haddock's professional curiosity overcame his desire to probe the origin of the rumours. He leaned forward and held his friend with his soft eyes. 'Are you sure you're not over-working, Tom?' he asked.

'Of course not, my dear fellow! After all, I am a medical man too. I know of how much my body is capable. Why, I never arrive here before half-past two.'

'And when do you leave?'

'In time to catch the midnight train.'

'And then you go straight to bed?'

'Sometimes.'

'Often?'

'Well . . . Not very often.'

'You mean hardly ever,' said Haddock severely.

Tom smiled. 'Perhaps you're right.'

'And you get up early?' Haddock continued relentlessly.

'Usually about half-past six.'

'And what do you do all morning?'

'Work until half-past twelve or so.'

'And after that?'

'After that it's practically time to go to the office.'

'And then more work!' Haddock threw up his sensitive hands protestingly. 'It's too much for you, Tom, it's too much for any man. Luckily for you, you have an iron constitution, or you would have cracked up before now. As it is, you can't go on for ever. You must remember that even if the rest of your body won't wear out, your heart is not too strong, and sooner or later will revolt at the liberties you are taking with it. You're still young, and provided you look after yourself, there's no reason you shouldn't live to be eighty. You've got the physique. But if you carry on this way, Ah don't give you above twenty-five years more.'

'Twenty-five years,' said Tom thoughtfully. 'By that time, if God spares me, I shall be nearly sixty. I wonder, Haddock, will my work be done?'

The Black Doctor shook his head. 'Ah'm afraid not, Tom. Ah've told you before now that it's too big a job for one man. It is a social problem, and only a complete transformation of society can finally solve it.'

Tom picked up a pencil and rapped it on his table.

'Now you're speaking not as my colleague, the Black Doctor,' he said, 'not as Haddock, my practical friend, but as Haddock the idealist, Haddock the revolutionary.'

Haddock smiled. 'Me a revolutionary? And how about you, mah friend? – Are you not a revolutionary too?'

'Me?' Tom's keen eyes gazed through his pince-nez at the negro in surprise. 'Me?' he repeated. 'I don't meddle in politics, how in heaven's name can you call me a revolutionary?'

'Of course you are a revolutionary,' Haddock asserted. 'You could hardly be otherwise. You come from the land of revolutionaries. You are the countryman of Bronterre O'Brien and Feargus O'Connor and you follow a master who was the earliest of revolutionaries, He who whipped the money-changers from the Temple. That was an act just as revolutionary as your determination to save the outcast children from the streets.'

'If you call founding my mission a revolutionary act,' said Tom, 'then perhaps I might agree with you.'

'That's the whole point, mah friend,' Haddock replied. 'Ah don't! Your determination to save the children was revolutionary, but your mission in actual practice has precisely the opposite effect.'

'But I have never tried to be revolutionary or non-revolutionary,' Tom protested. 'These things have never concerned me. I have seen children homeless, and starving on the streets, and my one aim in all those years has been to save them. All right, I agree with you that it may be a revolutionary idea, something that has never been attempted before in an organized fashion, but why should it be other than revolutionary in practice?'

'It shouldn't be,' said the Black Doctor, 'but it is. And the proof of it is that even members of the Cabinet are interested in your homes. Ah have lived among the labouring classes long enough to know that they mistrust their rulers. They are naturally "agin the government" whoever they are, and Ah have caught the habit from them, mah friend.'

'But surely it is possible for philanthropists like the Earl of Shaftesbury or Lord Cairns to be interested in my homes merely because they hate to see innocent children starving, and not to make political profit?'

'Possible,' said Haddock, 'but to mah way of thinking, not probable, mah friend. Ah do not deny that Shaftesbury and Cairns may be well-meaning, charitable old gentlemen in their private lives, acting out of the goodness of their hearts so far as they know it, but Ah believe too that they may be motivated by forces beyond them, of which they are only imperfectly aware.'

'My dear fellow!' Tom replied. 'With all due respects, I think you're talking perfect nonsense. Surely there are and have been instances where statesmen have espoused humanitarian causes merely because of their sense of justice and fair play?'

'Ah can't think of any,' said Haddock, 'not in the last century at least. Can you, mah friend?' he challenged. 'Can you?'

Tom thought for a moment and suddenly an apposite illustration flashed to his mind.

'There's the emancipation of the slaves,' he brought out triumphantly. '*You* should understand that, Haddock. If it had not been for Bishop Wilberforce, Buxton, and their colleagues, your people would still be slaves.'

'Maybe,' said Haddock, a wry smile playing about his thick lips. 'But perhaps they would be better off to have remained slaves. Ah prefer to think that Wilberforce and Buxton were not so much concerned with helping the slaves as with assisting the plantation owners for whom their friends in parliament voted a compensation of thirty million pounds to save them from bankruptcy.'

'Really, Haddock!' It seemed to Tom that his friend was flippantly evading the issue. 'Come now, my dear fellow, without cynicism, tell me, don't you honestly think that slaves are better off as free men?'

'Hardly,' said Haddock obstinately. 'Hardly. Ah stick to my guns. In the words of O'Brien, "By emancipating the slaves they lose nothing, for when the slave is free they employ and feed him only when they want him, but the slave in bondage has to be supported whether they have work for him or not. Emancipation enables the masters to get more work done and pay less for it. Emancipation emancipates the slave from his whip, but also emancipates him from his dinner!" That hardly seems like progress to me, and very little like pure disinterestedness.'

'Tuh chuch!' Tom pursed his lips. 'You are a funny fellow, Haddock. And you have the advantage of me in that you appear to know our history better than I do. You may or may not be right. Personally I am sure you're not, and at the moment I don't want to argue, but your objections hardly seem to apply to my mission. What can any member of the Government gain by assisting me to rescue the children?'

'Well, what happens to those unfortunates left on the streets?' Haddock countered.

'What *can* happen?' said Tom. 'They grow up thieves, rogues and vagabonds, enemies of society.'

'Exactly,' Haddock concurred. 'Enemies of society. But what constitutes society? Who makes society as we know it, and all its laws? People like Shaftesbury and Cairns, and of course they don't like children to grow up as adults in conflict with that society. But what happens to your boys when they grow up? You send selected lads to Canada, and that raises another problem, the question of emigration.'

'Surely no person in his right senses can question the benefits and efficacy of emigration!' Tom insisted vehemently.

'Maybe,' said Haddock gently. 'Maybe Ah am not in mah right mind, but there always seems to me two sides to every problem, and emigration is no exception. Tens of thousands of the most vigorous young men in the country emigrate annually of their own volition, because they can't find work in England. Left here, they would also no doubt develop into enemies of a society that keeps them unemployed, so it is in the best interests of the Government to encourage emigration. Then again, of course, you have to consider whether by sending your boys overseas you will not be displacing the indigenous labour there.'

'Nonsense, my dear fellow!' Tom answered. 'How can that be so? My boys are specially selected and specially trained, and the Christian homesteads they go to are carefully chosen and farmers paid to keep them until they are fit to find jobs for themselves.'

'Exactly, mah friend. And what happens when there are born Canadians who cannot find work on the land?'

'But that isn't possible,' Tom returned. 'Why, look at the size of the country. You could put the whole of England and Wales into one of its smallest provinces. With all those millions of idle acres it's only logic to assume that there must always be a shortage of labour.'

'Ah wonder,' Haddock said ruminatively. 'Ah wonder. Ah look at things in historical perspective, mah friend. So far from being a creature of logic man is such a dull animal that those vast lands of Canada may one day be unable to support even those few million that live there. Of course it is not yet fully developed, but later, when the evils of industrialization creep in, the evils of unemployment will rear up there too, and where will the Canadian unemployables emigrate? – Not back to England, surely?'

Tom flung down the pencil exasperatedly on the table. He saw his own and the children's problem so clearly that the Black Doctor's argument seemed to fog the issue and have no bearing at all on his tasks. His mind refused to roam round the Universe, bridging space and time; he had quite sufficient to occupy his waking moments right here in this mission building alone. That was the trouble with Haddock, he flung his nets too far. Worrying about the time when Canada would be overcrowded! Why, the whole idea was preposterous, fantastic!

'My dear fellow,' he iterated finally, 'you are too clever and too pessimistic. I can't foresee any of those eventualities occurring in my lifetime or yours. Meanwhile the problem of the outcast children is with us here and now. I refuse to worry about the possibility of there being unemployment in Canada in the future, when I have all my work cut out right at this moment to rescue even those derelicts of the street that my mission can accommodate, while still leaving scores of hungry children homeless. If my means are incapable of covering effectively that particular province to which I have dedicated my life, how can I attempt to tilt at the whole social structure? It is beyond me, beyond any of us puny mortals. Only God can do that by instilling Man with a change of heart, and remaking him to mirror His own precious spirit.'

'Maybe,' said Haddock. 'Maybe. But God takes too long, mah friend. Ah believe Man can do something about it too.'

'Remember the Bible, Haddock,' Tom interrupted. 'Put not thy faith in princes.'

'Ad didn't say princes, mah friend, Ah said Man.'

'And I say God,' Tom answered. 'I pin my faith in the Lord. With David I say, "I have kept God always before me."'

'Not always,' Haddock commented slyly. 'You didn't wait for God to hunt in the slums for outcasts – you went and ferreted them out for yourself. And you didn't get funds solely from God, like Müller,' he added, 'you got them from Man. And all that money that comes in is not enough, can never be enough. True, you are doing good work according to your lights, but to me it is the wrong work, because it leaves so much undone. Ah see your boys every Sunday morning in their natty uniforms and pill-box hats marching back here from Church service at the Edinburgh Castle. How proudly the band leads the way, and with what gusto the lads break ranks to buy their penny bottles of ketchup at Common's little shop right opposite mah surgery. Yesterday's orphans, and look at them today. – Fine! Inspiring! But look again, mah friend, at those shabby youngsters skipping in front, all ages, all sizes, a tattered vanguard thrown up by the streets, and behind a pitiful rearguard, not of orphans, not of the homeless, but children with parents and houses to sleep in. Yet they follow your boys enviously because those orphans have luxuries they don't possess, good food, regular meals, stout clothes, and bottles of ketchup. It is indeed an ironic commentary on our civilization that a child has to become a homeless orphan in order to enjoy some of the things that should be his by right of being a child alone!'

Tom raised his hand resignedly. Haddock's arguments roamed continually to a stage where Barnardo saw no point in following him. That children living with parents were being ill-treated was no excuse for abandoning entirely homeless ones. For those others something would have to be done too – only later. It was quite a different problem that Haddock would insist on lumping with his own engrossment.

'It's no use continually bringing in those outside implications,' Tom said. 'I have told you before that I am no politician. The fact remains that those other children have homes, whatever they are like, and parents to afford them some sort of protection, but my children have been rescued from the gutters, and apart from my mission, very little in that direction is being done by anyone else. So long as there is even one homeless child I shall devote all my time to this problem. When that is satisfactorily solved I may be tempted into wider fields as the Lord leads me. Until that time, and, my dear fellow, I know that that unfortunately means for a good many years to come, I shall have sufficient to do to direct the work of the East End Juvenile Mission.'

Haddock straightened himself uncomfortably in his chair.

Now the unsavoury part of his visit had to emerge from this ideological discussion.

'And that, mah friend,' he hinted gently, 'brings me to the real purpose of mah call.'

'So it wasn't just to convert me to your philosophy?' Tom inquired with a smile.

'No. Ah want to ask you, as an old friend, is everything well with your mission?'

'Good heavens, my dear fellow! Of course all is well – except,' he added, 'that if I had six times the cash I could do ten times the work.'

'Ah am glad to hear that,' said Haddock gravely. 'Truly glad. For Ah have heard disquieting rumours lately in the East End.'

'About the mission?'

'About that,' Haddock assented. 'And about you too.'

Tom nodded, thoughtfully fingering his pince-nez.

'I know it, Haddock. I know it only too well. The rumours have even invaded this building in anonymous letters, some going so far as to threaten me with physical violence.'

'Well!' Haddock said emphatically. 'Can't you do something about it? You can ignore malicious gossip, but when it comes to being attacked in the Press it's time you put your foot down to protect yourself.'

'Against whom?' asked Tom. 'Against what? The proof of my innocence is that I can afford to maintain a dignified silence.'

'Ah wish others could see it like that,' Haddock broke in impatiently. 'But most folk are only too ready to discover evil, and your "dignified silence" merely seems an admission of guilt. You can have no idea of the calumnies that are floating around. You have, Ah expect, read the letters in the papers, but you would be horrified at some of the things Ah have heard various people say.'

'They say?' Tom answered soberly. 'For them I shall adopt

the motto of one of our most distinguished families. "They say – What say they? – Let them say!" Let them say!' he repeated with quiet determination.

There was a timid tap at the door, and his secretary entered, in response to Tom's invitation.

'Mr Cadman to see you, sir,' he announced.

Tom puckered his brows and glanced hurriedly at his watch. 'Good heavens!' he exclaimed. 'I had no idea it was so late.' He rose to his feet as the secretary vanished, and approached Haddock with his right arm extended in a friendly gesture of farewell. 'Don't think I'm throwing you out, Haddock,' he apologized, 'but every second of my time is apportioned, and there is a gentleman outside whom I can't keep waiting. You must certainly visit me again soon. Come and see me at Mossford Lodge in Barkingside. I shall have more time then, and you can fire away at me some more of your peculiarly Utopian doctrines.'

Haddock clasped Tom's hand firmly, the warm gentle smile suffusing his noble face. More than ever he looked as he had done ten years ago, like a cheerfully suffering saint.

'Utopian?' he ventured mildly, his rich voice emphasizing the variegated vowels. 'Utopian? Not a bit of it. It's common sense and sweet reasonableness, and one day, Tom, Ah'll even make you admit that mine is the only way.'

'Possibly,' said Tom, cocking his huge head obstinately to one side. 'But my way is good enough for me, and it's been good for nearly two thousand years.'

'That's what the troglodyte said when someone showed him how to fashion a tool of iron. Remember, Tom, we're marching forward. We're making history every day.'

'I don't deny it,' Tom returned. 'Yet I still find the best history in the Bible, and the best philosophy there too.'

'Well, good day!' said Haddock. 'Ah can see it's no use arguing with you just yet. Perhaps in ten years' time . . .'

Tom smiled tolerantly, secure in his own convictions.

'Perhaps!' he conceded graciously.

With a wave of his expressive hand the Black Doctor left the room. For a moment Tom stared at the door, as though Haddock were still before it. There went a man, in his own way an idealist, and as obstinate and single-minded as he was himself. For all Haddock's persuasiveness, his position had not altered a jot, he still stood firm, foursquare with the Gospel. On the one side, Haddock might call on age, experience, history and reason, while he had only faith and God. Only those two, but for him they were enough. He walked back to his table and thoughtfully pulled at a hanging bell. Immediately his secretary entered.

'I'm ready for Mr Cadman now,' he said.

CHAPTER 18

A few minutes' walk brought Haddock back to his surgery. Rachel was ready saddled, standing docilely beside Ernest in the gutter. There was not a word of complaint from Ernest as the Black Doctor mounted his horse, although he had been away for longer than he had intended. Those were two faithful servants he had, the perennially youthful Ernest and the ageing mare; it would be one of the most difficult tasks of his life to replace either, and he hated to think of the surgery without Ernest or himself without his horse.

He had a patient to see in Jubilee Street. Fortunately it was merely a slight chill that had seemed to be developing into a fever, and he found on his arrival that the man had practically recovered, convinced, with that pathetic submissiveness and blind faith of the extremely ignorant, that Haddock had saved him from the jaws of Death. In the Mile End Waste, after his brief visit, the Black Doctor stopped at the trough in the low-galleried courtyard of the Spotted Dog and allowed Rachel to drink her fill. The ostler clattered over the cobbles from the stable, and tipped his hat to Haddock. Appraisingly he ran his hands over Rachel's sleek hide, he knew her well, and she lifted her muzzle from the trough and recognizing him whinnied a greeting.

'Wearin' well, ain't she, doctor?' the ostler remarked approvingly.

'Very well indeed, mah friend,' Haddock replied.

'Looks good fer twenty year more – 'pon me soul she do an' all!' said the ostler.

'Ah hope so,' Haddock answered fervently. 'Ah hope so.'

Rachel picked up her proud head and shook it daintily,

then slowly turned to Haddock as if to intimate that she was ready now for any further tasks her master might set. Ruminatively the Black Doctor gazed at the oak-panelled gallery. This old coaching inn had a long history. Dick Turpin had slept there on more than one occasion, and before him countless provincial families had stepped down on its cobblestones for the first time in London, men who came with money and lost it, and others who arrived without a second shirt and found the city streets paved with gold. And it had had travellers going in the other direction, and once a year the procession left here for Fairlop Oak. Some ancient ritual was commemorated in those annual visits, what it was Haddock didn't know and had never troubled to find out. It was a pleasant sight with all the costers in their decorated traps and donkey-drawn carts setting out on the ceremonial drive to Barkingside. Beneath that same ancient oak they held cockfights on Sundays, during the day, and in the evening prayer-meetings, and on the festival day all the carts and 'mokes' returned to the Mile End Waste decorated with green boughs which had been broken off in adjoining Hainault Forest.

Perhaps the ritual dated from a pagan era, perhaps from the time of the first divorcement of urban man from the soil, with this gesture as a tardy reconciliation. Such links with the countryside were getting fewer and fewer, and Haddock regretted to see their passing. Like most of the old festivals such as May Day their significance would diminish year by year until they fell into desuetude, unless the slumbering conscience of the masses would resurrect them into vigorous life again as a reminder that once the people had belonged to the good earth, and once the earth and all it contained had belonged to them.

Barkingside was where Tom lived. Mossford Lodge, that was the place, about a mile this side of Fairlop Oak. Tom was still worrying the doctor, he could not get those shameful calumnies out of his mind. Perhaps he could see Mrs Barnardo there and have a talk with her; if Tom wouldn't listen to reason it was possible that she might be more amenable and would persuade her husband to take firm steps to deal with his detractors. He would not be unwelcome, for after all Tom had invited him, and he had seen the young Mrs Barnardo once addressing a crowd of rough costers beneath Fairlop Oak, and from the firm and sympathetic way in which she had handled the meeting that passed, strangely enough, without a blasphemous comment, he was sure that she would not misunderstand the purpose of his visit.

As if he had communicated his intentions telepathically to Rachel, he found the mare ambling slowly down Bow Road. Slapping her haunches smartly he stirred her into a brisk trot that took him on towards Bromley-by-Bow. Past Stratford Rachel loped easily and, cutting right across some desolate stubbly brown fallow fields, he bore towards the open country. Past the fast growing village of East Ham he took a bridle-path that led him through the low-lying Essex farms to Barkingside.

At Mossford Lodge a man led Rachel off to the stable for a well-merited feed and another servant showed him through the hall and announced him at the door of the drawing-room to Mrs Barnardo. Haddock found her dressed in a flowing black lace dress embroidering some stiff linen, looking as competent at that feminine task as she had been at the sterner one of subduing a crowd of scoffing rowdies. She rose to her feet to greet the doctor, and although only an inch or so taller than her husband, she gave the appearance of regal stateliness by reason of her slender figure.

'Good evening,' said Haddock. 'Ah hope Ah have not disturbed you.'

'Not at all,' Syrie replied with a smile. 'Pray be seated, doctor.'

'You know me . . . perhaps?' Haddock asked, drawing up a chair opposite her.

'Indeed I do,' said Syrie graciously. 'Who hasn't heard of the Black Doctor – more especially Tom Barnardo's wife?'

'Ah am glad of that,' Haddock replied, inclining his head in acknowledgement of the compliment. 'Ah have come to have a chat with you – about Tom.'

'About Tom?' Syrie said. The embroidery dropped in her lap and she looked across at her companion in alarm. 'I . . . I hope nothing's wrong.'

'Nothing at all, mah dear lady,' Haddock answered reassuringly. 'It is only that having known your husband for so long, Ah take a professional interest in his health. Ah have seen him today, and Ah have told him he is working too hard.'

'I have told him that too,' said Syrie. 'Although I am no doctor. But it's no use talking to Tom about overwork. He has such colossal energy that he does two men's work every day, and comes up fresh next morning for more.' She tentatively inserted her needle into the linen, a plume of scarlet silk flowing like a gaudy kite's tail from its eye, and letting it stick there refocused her attention on Haddock. 'You haven't come all the way from Stepney just to tell me that, I'm sure. Come now, doctor,' she urged him gently, 'be frank with me. Tell me the real purpose of your visit.'

'Frank Ah will be,' said Haddock. 'And perhaps Ah shall tell you things that may hurt you if you don't know about them already, but Ah want you to understand that Ah'm doing this only out of mah great regard for Tom.'

Syrie sat bolt upright, her body tensed.

'Go on, please,' she begged him. 'I understand. Don't be afraid to tell me whatever it is you want to tell.'

'Thank you,' said Haddock. 'Well then, for some time past there have been rumours in the East End that your husband's mission is not being conducted as it should be, that the boys are half-starved and ill-treated – even that your husband misappropriates the funds. These and other charges have also appeared in open letters to the Press and . . .' The

Black Doctor glanced at her solicitously. 'Shall Ah go on?' he asked softly.

The tension of Syrie's body relaxed. 'Indeed you may,' she said. She picked up her embroidery again and drew the long needle through the taut linen. 'But I know all about that, doctor. You must know my husband, so you can be certain that he would have no secrets from me, and even if he had desired to keep me in ignorance, I should have known without his telling, for I have not been spared anonymous letters that reach me here in my own home, reviling that "whited sepulchre", that "sink of iniquity".'

Haddock shook his head sadly.

'Ah am sorry to hear that,' he commented. 'But Ah must admit it makes it much easier for me.'

'Doctor . . .' said Syrie quietly, 'what would you suggest?'

Before Haddock had time to reply, the door opened and Tom entered the room. So surprised at his sudden arrival were his wife and the Black Doctor that for a moment both stared at him in silence, Tom himself taken aback at the unexpected sight of the doctor's presence. There was a strange feeling of tension in the room as though several cross-currents of electricity had fused between these walls, making a sheer dramatic hiatus where the three-pronged silence became more pregnant with feeling than speech.

Tom was the first to recover himself. He walked across the room and, bending over his wife, kissed her affectionately on the cheek. Then he turned to Haddock.

'Glad you accepted the invitation, my dear fellow,' he said as though Haddock's presence were the most natural spectacle in the world. 'But if you'd have let us know, we'd have got something ready for you.'

Haddock raised his hand, comprehendingly. 'Ah'm sorry,' he apologized. 'Ah know Ah have put you both out.'

'No, no,' said Tom sincerely. 'Not at all. You are always welcome, believe me. This house is yours at any time that you care to call.' He leaned over his wife's chair, placing his arm fondly round her shoulders. 'That's so, isn't it, my dear?' he asked.

Syrie nodded, then as if she had forgotten about Haddock, she fixed her troubled gaze on Tom.

'You're home early, my dear,' she said.

Tom straightened himself uncomfortably.

'Yes . . .' he replied hesitantly. 'I . . . I felt rather tired.'

'*You* tired!' Her sceptically raised eyebrows dismissed his excuse. 'Tom!' she insisted firmly. 'I want to know what's wrong.'

Haddock, who for the past several minutes had been squirming irresolutely in his seat, rose to his feet. He realized now that he could hardly have chosen a more inopportune moment for his visit.

'Excuse me,' he said haltingly, in a worried tone. 'Ah must be going. Ah can see this is no time for a stranger to stay. Ah shall pay my respects on a more propitious occasion!'

'No!' Tom answered determinedly, waving him back to his chair. 'You had better stay now, Haddock – sit down, my dear fellow. I assure you you're not in the way.' He paced about nervously as his friend resumed his seat. 'I can guess why you came here, so you may as well hear the rest. I have bad news. The mission has been placed on the Cautionary list of the Charities Organization Society.'

'Really!' said Haddock, sitting up involuntarily in his chair.

'On the Cautionary list, Tom?' Syrie asked. 'What exactly does that mean?'

'Mean? – It *means* there is an official doubt as to whether the East End Juvenile Mission is worthy of public support, but it tacitly implies that the Homes are a fraud, and that I am a swindler.' He started pacing the room again, clasping his hands behind his back till with an impotent gesture and an exclamation of disgust he flung them up in the air, tossing his coat-tails about him in angry disarray. 'Me – a swindler misappropriating funds!' be brought out bitterly, addressing himself to Haddock. 'Living on the fat of the land. – Why, this Mossford Lodge of ours is a wedding gift from a friend, and my wife's own income partially runs it, while my allowance goes to the Homes. A couple of years ago I had a gift from my father of one thousand, five hundred pound, and where did that go? Into the East End Juvenile Mission! I am a poor man precisely because of the Homes. For them I threw away two careers. There was a future for me in commerce, but I preferred offering myself for the service of the Lord in China, and then I abandoned a medical career although I am a registered practitioner. And giving up all this for the children's cause, I become a faker of photographs when the lads who come to me are so filthy that they first have to be bathed and given clothes before I can talk with them, and if the photographic reconstruction of their former state is not faithful then it errs only because it can't convey the real degree of their destitution. A door is unwittingly nailed up on a boy for half an hour while a smith mends a lock, and he becomes a prisoner for three weeks! I incarcerate them in dungeons and feed them on bread and water! Faugh! –What nonsense! And yet these tales carried by dismissed servants and degraded parents, unworthy of the name, are taken up, repeated and believed by respectable Christians!'

'That's it,' said Haddock. 'There's the danger sign. These rumours may have started with irresponsible scandal-mongers, but the whole point is just that now honest, well-meaning people have come to believe that they are performing a public duty by lending their names in support of these charges.'

'Charges! Public duty!'Tom exploded again. 'I am preying on the public! A charlatan, a mountebank, a fraud because I call myself a doctor without possessing an MD degree. But I am a licentiate and Fellow of the Edinburgh Royal College of Surgeons, and that degree is universally recognized as sufficient recommendation for registration as a doctor. True,

doctor in my case is a courtesy title, but if every other practitioner in the East End had to show his Doctor's degree before
he called himself by that name, how many would be eligible
for that distinction? Would you even be eligible yourself,
Haddock?'

The Black Doctor smiled modestly. 'As it happens, mah
friend, Ah *did* take mah MD at that same University of Edinburgh, but you are none the less right in surmising that ninety
per cent of our colleagues are no more "doctors" than you.'

'There!' Tom exclaimed. 'You see how manifestly unfair it
all is. It is degrading for everybody concerned. But it has come
to a head now, it must be stopped once and for all. –What can
I do, Haddock?' he asked appealingly. 'My dear fellow, what
is to be done?'

'Done? It's obvious, mah friend. You must sue those
responsible. Your only remedy is libel action.'

'No . . .' Tom shook his head wearily. 'No . . . no. That's
impossible.'

'Impossible?' said Haddock. 'Why impossible? You have a
clear-cut case.'

'I know,' answered Tom wearily. 'I know, but just the same
I couldn't do it. Perhaps you remember that when I first knew
you I was a member of the Open Brethren in Sidney Street.
Well, I am still attached to Brethrenism, and our religious
principles refuse to allow us to enter into litigation on any
pretext whatsoever.'

'You surely don't mean that, Tom!' Haddock protested.

'I certainly do.'

'Even when your honour is at stake?'

'Even so.'

'And your Homes, and the children?'

'I'm sorry, Haddock,' Tom faltered. 'It hurts me terribly . . .
I don't know what to do. But I feel I can't go to court even
if it means the end of what has taken me all those years to
build up.'

'Well, Ah'm sorry too,' said Haddock gravely. 'Ah find it hard to understand you, and Ah am your friend – think of what the rest of the world will say.'

'They say – let them say!' Tom exclaimed impatiently with a flash of his old fire.

'But letting them say any more means the end of your mission, mah friend. You can't let them say!'

'I can't go to court, either.'

'You mean you won't.'

'Have it your own way,' said Tom obstinately.

'Ah'm to take that as final?' Haddock asked hopelessly, knowing with certainty what would be the unequivocal reply.

Tom nodded.

'Yes . . . I'm sorry, Haddock.' His voice showed once more the strength of feeling that was torturing him. 'You know what my mission means to me, but my religious faith means still more. Perhaps there is some other way,' he said dully, as though he only half-believed those words himself. 'I am sure God has not forsaken me.'

'Ah wish *Ah* was so sure, mah friend. Ah am not a lover of your mission, but Ah would hate to see it go under this way, and hate still more to see you crushed with it. Think it over,' he urged. 'Just this once, mah friend. Forget your principles and sue!'

'No . . . no . . .' Tom repeated resignedly.

'But supposing *they* sued?' Haddock threw in suddenly. 'Would your principles allow you to defend yourself?'

'Most certainly,' said Tom. 'If I were called before a bench, of course I should do my utmost to clear my name. – Do you really think they would take this matter into court?' he asked eagerly.

Haddock laughed harshly, as though his resonant voice had momentarily lost its joyous, throbbing timbre. 'Why should they?' he demanded. 'That was merely a hypothetical query, mah friend. Why should they go to court? The onus is on you.

They are doing well enough outside, and from your silence it appears ostensibly that they are right. It's not enough to think "Sue and be damned!" You sue and let your enemies be damned!'

'They are not my enemies,' said Tom. 'I forgive them, for they know not what they do.'

Haddock rose to his feet.

'At any rate, Ah know what Ah should do,' he said abruptly. 'Tom, you're a fool. Ah'm going now. Perhaps your wife will knock some sense into you. Good night!'

Syrie's eyes followed the Black Doctor to the door. Automatically she picked up her embroidery and pulled her needle through the linen to complete an unfinished stitch. Haddock's words had started a train of thought in her brain. She knew Tom well enough to be certain that once his mind was made up on a course of action no power on earth could shift him. If he was determined not to go to court, no calumnies could force him to sue, and meanwhile rumour piled uncontradicted on rumour, undermining his whole life's work, with his opponents, encouraged by his silence, baying like thirsty bloodhounds on a hot scent. She could not bear to see him sacrifice his life on the altar of a shadowy principle, for he was bound up with the Homes, the mission *was* his life, and it had been placed on the Cautionary list!

This last blow was as cruel agony to her as though she had seen someone hack off his arm. It had gone far enough. She would not wait to see this jewel of a man dismembered piecemeal. There had to be some other way. If Tom would not attack his enemies, at least he could defend himself; if he would not start any litigation he would certainly not remain a passive defendant if his opponents were plaintiffs. She came from a wealthy family and had influential friends. Perhaps they could, without Tom's direct intervention, obtain a rule of court to have an impartial Board of Arbitration set up composed of eminent jurists brought together by mutual consent of the parties.

Tom could have no objection to facing such a tribunal, especially when his detractors appeared against him. If only that could be done! It seemed the only way, and behind her delicate, yielding feminine exterior, under cover of her engrossment in an intricate embroidery design, Syrie's sharp brain was already sifting the names of people she could approach, just as uncompromising in her determination as Tom was unflinching in his.

Suddenly she became aware of him beside her, kneeling at her feet. Gently she laid the patterned linen aside, and drew his head up on to her lap. In all those years he had not changed. He was the same impetuous single-minded young visionary whose dreams she had soothed in her arms that sunny spring day in Richmond.

'It's good to be beside you again, Serena,' he said. 'I come home to you, my dear, and I come to comfort. When I got the news in my office, I was bewildered, and almost in despair, but I went down on my knees and God gave me courage, and now I am with you and I have confidence again.'

She patted his head gently.

'Don't worry, Tom,' she murmured. 'This is just another crisis. We have struck bad patches before and got over them. It will pass. Life, after all, isn't one rosy dream after another.'

'Dream?' he whispered. 'Dream?' A faint shudder convulsed him. 'Serena, this is a nightmare!'

She smiled comfortingly into his eyes as though he were a frightened child.

'It will pass, Tom. It will pass. In the morning the nightmare Caliban will seem just Puck with a hunch.' She ran her soft fingers tenderly through his hair. 'You'll see, Tom, you'll see!' she assured him.

CHAPTER 19

Brad read through his *Times* with the greatest of good humour. Occasionally passages in the report pleased him, and he chuckled heartily and read them again. He was seated in his usual secluded corner in Seeley's, facing the large mirror, but now he was sorry he was not in the more populous lounge where at a moment such as this he could cheerfully have outraged the conventions of the staid old habitués by reading these passages out loud. He had loosed a hare that events had startlingly clothed in reality, and Zachariah had completed the course in full cry. Nobody now suspected his hand in the rumours, or Zachariah's, for all the publicity had been taken over by earnest zealots who had rushed into print with their charges. Brad was glad that he had remained in the background, but he could easily imagine the Reverend Quelch's impotent fury at the infidels who had stolen his thunder and his iconoclastic glory.

'Enjoying yourself?' broke in a familiar voice.

Brad looked up as Tony dropped into the easy chair opposite him.

'Indeed I am,' Brad replied cheerfully. 'Well met, friend. Allow me to let you enter the fun.' He tossed the paper over to Tony. 'Look at that,' he chuckled. 'What do you think of Saint Thomas Barnardo now?'

Tony dropped the newspaper on to the table without a second glance.

'Now?' he answered with a casual shrug of his shoulders. 'I think about him just what I have always thought.'

'But read that, old chap,' Brad urged. 'And then tell me what you think.'

'I've read it, thanks,' said Tony dryly. 'Early this morning. Probably before you got out of bed.'

'Now! Now! Tony!' Brad protested. 'Dammit! I'm not quite the bad lot you imagine. You can be easily mistaken, old chap,' he argued half-sardonically. 'Look what you thought of Barnardo and note the things that have come out in court.'

'I don't believe those tales,' Tony replied shortly. 'Not a word of any of them.'

'Come! Come!' said Brad mockingly. 'You can't dismiss facts just like that. You are supposed to be a champion of rational thought just like your dear old uncle Gannet, and yet you let sentiment influence your judgement. My father always held that you rationalists were really the most incorrigible sentimentalists, and, begad, I'm beginning to think he was right!'

Tony flicked his cigarette ash irritably into a massive bronze tray. Brad, in spite of his oily charm, usually had the effect of annoying him. Even the way he spoke about non-controversial subjects had an uncomfortable knack of getting under his skin, and this time Brad was definitely wrong and had dropped the blandishments of his personal fascination to jibe openly at the sincerely held opinions of his companion.

'There's nothing sentimental about my evaluation of Barnardo and his work,' Tony said firmly, raising his voice to mask his anger. 'I met the man, and had first-hand experience of his Homes. That was sufficient to convince me. It could convince anybody.'

'In spite of all this evidence that has come out at the arbitration?'

'In spite of that!' Tony asserted, unshaken.

'And you call yourself a rationalist,' Brad jeered. 'Why, if you discovered Barnardo stealing your watch, you'd swear he was merely borrowing it to tell the time.'

'Now you're being ridiculous,' said Tony. 'That hardly falls into the same category as the evidence at the trial.'

'No?' Brad queried with a sarcastic smile. 'You don't

think so? When for twenty days these charges have been hurled at him, fully substantiated by forty-seven witnesses?'

'One moment,' said Tony. 'Not so fast. Barnardo has witnesses also, and he has not yet had a chance to defend himself.'

'Defend himself!' Brad sneered. 'Why, I never heard or read of a more damning series of indictments in my life. If he manages to wriggle out of them, I shall take off my hat to him as a bigger and cleverer rogue than even I imagined!'

'He won't have to wriggle out of anything,' said Tony, controlling his temper with difficulty. 'I am convinced he'll have a perfect answer to every single charge.'

Brad leaned back in his chair and threw up his hands with a baffled gesture.

'I only wish you were prepared to back your convictions,' he answered.

'I am,' said Tony quietly.

'In the only rational way – with hard cash!'

'Nobody suggested I wasn't prepared to do that either – I'll wager you a pony he clears himself completely.'

'A pony!' Brad scoffed. 'Is that all your hero's honour is worth?'

'No,' said Tony grimly, 'but that's all the loss I think your pocket is capable of sustaining!'

Brad sat up, flushed. It was now his turn to be angry.

'That's an insult, Tony,' he flung at him. 'Dammit, I won't stand that!'

'Swords or pistols then?' his companion returned suavely. 'Perhaps if you kill me you'll have an excuse for wriggling out of a bet – is that it?'

'It isn't! And damned well you know it! And to show you I mean that, we'll make the stakes not twenty-five pounds but fifty!'

'Five hundred if you like,' said Tony unconcernedly.

'Done!' Brad answered. 'Guineas?'

'Very well,' said Tony. 'Guineas it is!'

Brad's anger slowly evaporated as the full significance of the wager struck him. This little encounter was turning out a very good thing. Not only was his old enemy in the dock, but he stood to gain five hundred guineas from his conviction, and the way the evidence was going that appeared to Brad a foregone conclusion. It was indeed a pleasant prospect to have Barnardo, a decade later, paying indirectly tenfold for the loss of his watch and his purse.

The dark figure of the waiter glided through the passage and halted stiffly like a starched black and white wraith at the table.

'Oh, Hawkins,' said Tony, recalling the waiter as with the ingrained wisdom of long service he was about to make an unobtrusive departure, 'stay for a moment, will you? We – Brad here, and I, have just had a little bet.'

The waiter inclined his head obsequiously. 'I understand, sir,' he assured him. 'I have often officiated in affairs of this kind between gentlemen – of course you know that I am entirely trustworthy, so if there is a question of holding some small stake –'

'There is,' said Brad. 'Five hundred guineas!'

'Five hundred guineas!' Hawkins looked at the two young men in amazement, his expression so startled that Brad burst into an irrepressible chuckle. At once the waiter's face resumed its grave mien. The gentlemen were always right, and if they wanted to pull his leg, a little joke came also within his terms of service. He permitted a faint, comprehending smile to flit across his features, then with mask-like imperturbability waited for further instructions.

'Listen,' said Tony. 'You've heard of Doctor Barnardo?'

'Indeed, sir! – But who hasn't?'

'Well, we're having a little wager on the result of the trial. The day after the award we meet here at seven in the evening to settle up. You're a witness that the bet is on.'

Tony turned to his companion. 'Is that satisfactory, Brad?'

'Quite,' he said. Brad stretched out his long legs and ensconced himself more comfortably in the easy chair. 'Now, Hawkins, bring me a bottle of Seeley's Special,' he ordered.

'Very good, Mr Brad.'

The waiter turned, and with his peculiarly silent method of progression disappeared. Brad looked after him, tolerantly, hugely pleased with himself. Everything was coming up trumps. Yesterday he had been wondering by what miracle he could replenish his dwindling resources and restore some of his almost vanished credit, and now came succour, ironically enough through the person of his most hated foe. He sank naturally into the carefree, jovial mood that he usually took such pains to simulate. Lightheartedly he thumped his fist on the table.

'Wine! – The situation calls for a drink, Tony. We'll sink our animosity in some of Seeley's Special – eh, old chap?'

'So there's no duel now?' asked Tony with a whimsical smile.

'Not on your life!' said Brad emphatically. 'First I have to relieve you of five hundred golden guineas!'

The trial was a grim struggle, and Tom did not disguise the fact that he was fighting for his mission, his own life, and the lives of thousands of homeless children. It began in the summer, and when the prosecution's case rested after three gruelling weeks, the defence took up eighteen days in rebutting the charges, calling sixty-five witnesses. Six barristers were engaged, a leading QC and two juniors on either side, the Arbitration Board comprising the Recorder of Leeds, an eminent juridical expert, the Canon of Rochester, and the former member of parliament for Glasgow.

After all the evidence had been placed before them, the arbitrators sat in secret to consider their judgement, and at length, after five weeks, they reached a verdict. In October, four months after the commencement of the trial, they published their findings in a lengthy report of 10,000 words. Barnardo was triumphantly vindicated.

On the 15th of October there appeared a long leading article in *The Times* surveying the Arbitrator's report. The writer found that there had been no mishandling of funds, and a member of an eminent firm of accountants testified that the books were in perfect order. As to charges against Barnardo's moral character, these had proved to be merely gossip of the most malignant sort. The children were well fed and well treated, and their educational standard was at least as high as that of the best board schools, and the leader writer concluded his article by finding in the words of the Arbitrators that 'The East End Juvenile Mission is a real and valuable charity, worthy of public confidence and support.'

Brad pulled out his watch. It was a quarter to seven. For the tenth time that day he ran his eyes over *The Times* article, always forcing himself to read again those last few phrases – 'A real and valuable charity . . .' It meant that he was utterly ruined, and every fresh perusal of those lines only rubbed in his critical position, yet he was impelled to torture himself again and again by the irresistible attraction of those coldly printed words.

He dropped heavily into his favourite seat at the club. Very shortly now, Tony would arrive and the whole lamentable business would be settled. Now Brad hardly knew whom he hated more, Tony or Barnardo, and it seemed to him that all his troubles, even his precarious financial position, could be laid at their doors. One thing only gave him any satisfaction, that Tony would never get a penny of his money. He had determined on a drastic course of action, yet if he could get in one last blow at Barnardo, he felt he could relinquish the rest of the world's pleasures without much reluctance.

'Ah – good evening, sir,' said Hawkins, coming up silently behind him.

'Oh! Good evening –' Brad answered, in a preoccupied fashion. 'No sign of my friend Tony, I suppose?'

'Not yet, Mr Brad. It still lacks a quarter to seven.'

'Oh! . . . So you remember . . .'

'Indeed I do!' the waiter answered. 'And I am glad to see the doctor's got off. Aren't you, sir?'

'Should I be?' said Brad ruefully. 'When it's practically cost me five hundred guineas?'

The waiter smiled understandingly.

'So you're bringing that up again, Mr Brad. I know I'm a bit stupid, but it was only a joke the first time, sir.'

'You're right,' said Brad slowly. 'It isn't a joke now. Forget it, old chap, just my perverted sense of humour. Bet tell me, Hawkins,' he continued thoughtfully, 'how many Wintringhams have you known here at Seeley's?'

'Well,' the waiter replied. 'There was your father, of course, and when I first came here I still have a faint recollection of seeing your grandfather – a fine old gentleman he was too – if I may say so, sir.'

'Well! Well!' Brad murmured. 'All things come to an end. Look at me, Hawkins, I'm the last of the line. There won't be any more Wintringhams at Seeley's.'

The waiter smirked subserviently. 'It's much too early yet to tell,' he answered. 'You'll settle down one day, Mr Brad, they all do. You'll find yourself a wife, and before you look round there'll be half a dozen more young Wintringhams plaguing my old bones for Seeley's Special.'

Brad smiled and shook his head. 'No, I'm the last. Of that I'm certain, Hawkins,' he said with a heavy air of finality. 'I shall die a bachelor!'

'I hope you don't mean that, sir,' the waiter said earnestly. 'When you get as old as I am, Mr Brad, you'll miss your children – and your children's children frisking round your knees.'

'Don't worry,' Brad answered, a wry smile playing about

his lips. 'I won't ever get as old as you. A short life and a gay one – that's my way of reaching a happy ending.'

'You are far too young to speak about endings of any sort,' Hawkins protested. 'Perhaps you've been crossed in love, Mr Brad, and that makes you talk this way. Get it off your mind, sir. Next week you'll forget all about it, and next month you'll be laughing at yourself.'

Brad shook his head. 'No. You don't understand, old chap. I've never been in love with anybody except myself. It's something else, Hawkins. I'm fed right up. I need a change, and, dammit! I mean to have one!' He took his gold watch out of his pocket and slipped the heavy chain through the hole in his waistcoat pocket, the ornate ebony and gold Albert fob dangling to his knees.

'Here,' he said, gathering it up with a graceful movement. 'Take this. I haven't given you a "pourboire" for quite a time – keep it to remember me by.'

Hawkins seemed quite overwhelmed by this magnificent gesture. He looked first at the watch and chain, the smooth strong links glinting like an oiled yellow snake as his unsteady hand rocked them in serpentine motion, then he shot a peculiar glance at Brad to see whether this were not another example of his 'perverted humour'. Brad, however, appeared perfectly serious, so with a deep smile of gratitude, Hawkins thrust the jewellery into one of his capacious pockets.

'Thank you very much, sir,' he said. 'Very much indeed.' He leaned still lower, stooping over Brad until his long nose almost brushed the young man's shoulder. 'You're not leaving England, Mr Brad?' he asked, as though this were a matter of very great concern to him.

'I . . . Well . . . I am,' Brad answered hesitantly. 'Yes, I am. Very shortly.'

'Where to, sir, may I ask?'

'You may,' said Brad. 'You may, but honestly I don't know quite where I'm going myself.'

'Is it a tour then? – The Grand Tour perhaps?'

'Perhaps . . .' Brad answered thoughtfully. 'Perhaps.'

He sat up stiffly as though he had done with this vacillation and at last made up his mind. 'Bring me two bottle of Seeley's Special,' he said with apparent irrelevance. 'Hawkins! I'm going to celebrate!'

'Very good, Mr Brad,' said the waiter with a low bow.

As soon as Hawkins had gone, Brad brought out his slim notebook and the gold pencil that had served him so well for many an assignation. Tearing out a page he wrote a rapid message.

Dear Tony,

You were right. I haven't five hundred pence, let alone five hundred guineas. I can't pay you in cash, but I shall honour my bond with my life. Goodbye! – *And yet I know Barnardo is guilty!*

He read through the note with satisfaction. That last sentence pleased him immensely. Like Galileo recanting at the stake – and yet it moves! Quite the heroic touch, and something for the papers to chew over. A doomed man would not lie, especially with his last words, and perhaps tomorrow would see his note sweep the Arbitration Award from the headlines. He chuckled, and as an afterthought heavily underlined his accusation and folded the paper in two as the waiter approached. With the greatest deference, still mindful of that princely gift, Hawkins placed one bottle and a glass before Brad, and with the tray poised in his hand lifted his eyebrows in inquiry.

'There,' said Brad, indicating the opposite chair. 'Just leave it there, thanks.' He watched Hawkins place the bottle and glass punctiliously on the chosen spot, and as he turned away, Brad slipped the note beneath the bottle.

'Oh, Hawkins!' he called. 'Don't go away for a moment.'

'Yes, Mr Brad?' the waited asked.

'Don't let that wine go wasted,' said Brad. 'I want you to see that Mr Tony has it with my compliments.'

'W . . . Why . . . ?' stuttered the waiter with a puzzled air. 'Won't you be here, sir?'

'Oh, I shall be here,' Brad returned cryptically. 'I have this little wager to settle – only you never know how a chap like Tony will take it.'

'Very good, sir,' said Hawkins.

He moved down the passage and glanced at Brad with a quizzical expression that showed how much his normal composure had been shaken; then, still mystified, he vanished.

Left to himself, Brad looked round once more at the familiar walls as if to carry their soothing lines away with him. With a half-sigh he bent down and drew a flat, narrow, highly-finished morocco-leather case on to his knees. Slipping back the heavy bronze clasp he lifted the lid to reveal two long duelling pistols embedded in red silken cushions, their slim barrels resting face-to-face exquisitely parallel like a delicately balanced piece of machinery. His tense fingers closed over one butt, then as if the feel of it displeased him he changed his mind and chose the other. With a practised movement he grasped the grip in his palm and pressed the smooth cold circle of steel to his burning forehead. Opposite him a silent figure went through identical movements. His finger curled round the trigger, Brad paused and gazed at his image with reluctant admiration. His face had never appeared so striking, his finely trained moustache never so attractive.

'It's a pity,' he said out loud, 'to send such a handsome fellow to the devil!'

Next day, *The Times* leader writer went back to the Award, not having exhausted his encomiums on Barnardo. In the same issue, in very small print, tucked away in an insignificant corner was a small report of the suicide in Seeley's Club of one Bradley Wintringham – Gentleman.

CHAPTER 20

Summer came again. The trials and tribulations of the past year were over but not forgotten, and the publicity of the Arbitration had proved a blessing in disguise. Now the East End Juvenile Mission had become generally known as Dr Barnardo's Homes and the financial support that accrued during the previous few months, eclipsing by far every sum received over the same period, showed that the general public heartily endorsed the Arbitrators' verdict of 'a real and valuable charity.'

Tom had grandiose plans for the future. A board of trustees had been appointed to share with him the labours of directing what was rapidly developing into almost a National Institution. Already he had clashed on several occasions with the newly elected trustees over matters of expenditure, but with his enormous experience of the problem Tom had always been proved right. He had long abandoned two of his original three principles, but when, even with their vastly increased income, it was a question of the trustees allowing the Homes to run still further into debt or calling a halt to the policy of admitting derelict children at any hour of the day or night, Tom stuck obstinately to his guns, and in spite of head-shakings and prophecies of financial disaster his banner 'No Destitute Child Ever Refused Admission' still remained furled triumphantly aloft.

May again. On such a bright morning his friends had left him twelve years ago on the *Lammermuir* bound for China. Tom had travelled down from Barkingside by carriage, and the weather being so fine, he had dismissed the coachman at Poplar, intending to cover the rest of the distance on foot.

Twelve years ago. Then, he had been a stranger in this district, a child groping in a murky underworld of ugly buildings peopled by raucous ruffians, hoping for the day when he could cut through the gloom and set his face to the brightness of the East. Now he knew that he would never see China, and the ruffians had turned out to be his most loyal friends, while the East End had captured him with a peculiar, lively fascination of its own. Still, if the Lord had put him down to slum work as his particular vocation, he had the vicarious satisfaction of knowing that he had sent proxies to the Orient, several of his boys having already gone there as missionaries. Rescued from the streets themselves, and now bringing glad tidings to the heathen; after all, it did not matter who carried the torch, so long as the everlasting flame burned undimmed.

Tom glanced at his watch. He was earlier than usual today. Replacing it in his pocket he looked about him with a sense of enjoyment as if the familiar landmarks gave him pleasure, and with a springy step he set off blithely towards Stepney Causeway. Everything was going well, so well he felt on this sunny morning that he could take a bit more of suffering humanity to his bosom. Approaching the docks, his thoughts turned towards the host of workers whose lives were bound up with the ships and wharf-side warehouses, and he reflected that he need search no farther for more worthy subjects of his pity.

But what could pity do? Without an attempt at amelioration, pity was merely an added hurt from the donor, and an insult for the receiver; it fell, not as the gentle rain from Heaven, but like flailing hailstones on a bruised and wilting crop. Those heroes, for example, who every day went down to the sea, not in ships but floating coffins, scandalously overloaded. Tom, burdened by all his more personal tasks was yet not inattentive to the many social developments taking place around him. He still found time to keep in touch with all the latest discoveries in medicine, and from the scientific and sociological spheres drew out everything that might be useful to him and his work. The latest principles of psychology and education found practical expression in his Homes, and an intensive study of Scottish Poor Law relief methods had largely aided him in the success of his Boarding-out system. In the same way the young man had followed keenly Plimsoll's fight in Parliament to have the load-line lowered, until barely two years ago the Plimsoll line had finally found its way on to the statute book. Yet that had not prevented unscrupulous shipowners from evading the law with a complete disregard of men's lives so long as their profits were enhanced, even, apart from overloading, going so far as to paint the rotten timber hulks to resemble steel, and bribing inspectors to overlook the deception. For what little relief they had gained the sailors had to thank their indefatigable champion Plimsoll, yet it struck Barnardo ironically that even with regard to that noble statesman's efforts, the ingenious arguments of his friend Haddock would no doubt unearth some ulterior motive for Plimsoll's philanthropy.

From the seamen who risked their lives on the sea his train of thought turned logically to the men who loaded the ships and unloaded them. Casual unskilled labour for the most part, employed at the gas-factories and other industrial under-takings in the winter and seeking their chance to pick up a crust at the docks during the summer months. The docks were positively the last refuge of the honest workmen, and having seen the conditions of their employment Barnardo wondered that many more of them did not stoop to petty crime.

The whole system at the wharves was barbarous, degrading men to the level of animals, and just like uncontrollable animals it kept them behind iron cages while they waited for admission to the docks. The foreman would come out and, superciliously surveying the clamorous rabble behind the bars, select the men he required for the day, and while those fortunate ones passed triumphantly through the narrow gates to their underpaid, back-breaking jobs, the rest would trickle sullenly back to the street, leaving behind the weaklings who had been trampled underfoot in the mad scramble to catch the bully's eye. Yes. The sailors needed many more Plimsolls, but the dockers in their more prosaic occupation were not less entitled to an honourable place in the sun.

From a distance there seemed to come a vocal echoing of his thoughts. Gradually the sound came nearer and Tom recognized a throaty dirge, and behind its rhythm the impulse of marching men. A demonstration of some sort was approaching, a form of public protest that was becoming only too frequent of late, the assertion of hungry workers brought out into the open to demand their elementary rights. Some unknown docker or dockers with the inherited genius of folk-song as guide had produced the jingle that accompanied their tread, and it was a true expression of their thoughts, stating without intrusive poetic imagery the most striking part of their grievances.

> 'We are the unemployed workmen
> Starving all week through,
> We do not shirk,
> Any kind of hard work,
> But alas we can't get it to do.'

Soon the ragged army came into view, hundreds of shabby men marching in ranks four and five deep, their faces from a distance grim and grey as their clothes. Tom moved to the edge of the pavement and waited until they drew abreast. They had stopped singing now, and walked in a tense silence broken spasmodically by an excited shout from a marcher that was taken up in a deep-throated chorus by his comrades. There seemed to be no individual thoughts in this long grey column, no separate arguments breaking up the corporate feeling and dissipating it in futile knots; the dockers moved along as if animated by a single overpowering desire, a body of lean men welded by misery into one gigantic unit. Like some mighty cacophonous concerto a strident solo voice broke forth from one end of the ranks, then the other, and was tossed to the men, who seized it eagerly and orchestrated it with angry basses and percussions.

'Gawd Strike the Bosses Dead!' and the answering roar in varying tones with a Coda from the back ranks as the vanguard subsided . . . 'STRIKE THE BOSSES DEAD' . . .

'Wotcher finkin', guv?' interjected a robust voice at his side.

Tom turned half-left and noticed that one of the men had stepped from the ranks and was perched unsteadily on the kerb beside him. It was Splodger, hardly recognizable in a fairly clean jacket and newish corduroys, the only remnant of his familiar garb, the dirty deerstalker cap. His left hand clutched a long pole on the top of which was impaled a scrawny red herring with beneath a sheet of cardboard bearing the roughly written laconic caption 'Docker's Dinner,' while his right fist was thrust belligerently deep inside the pocket of his whole-falls.

'Oh hello, Splodger,' said Tom. 'I didn't see you.'

'In course yer didn't, guv,' the coalie replied as the young man gazed at him quizzically. 'But I seen you. An' naow I *do* know wot yer finkin'!'

'Do you?' said Tom interestedly.

'Aye. I do. Yer finkin' 'ere's 'ole Splodger agin – an' drunk as usual.'

'And are you drunk?' Tom inquired.

'Not on yer life!' said Splodger vehemently. He leaned over Barnardo and puffed a sudden freshet of breath into his face, the nauseating gust reeking of tobacco, but unmistakably without a trace of alcohol.

'There. Yer believe me naow?'

'I didn't disbelieve you before,' Tom answered.

'Sorry. I fought yer did – an' I ain't touched a drop fer

nigh on two days. I allus told yer when there was somefing doin' ole Splodger would be there!'

'And this is what you've been waiting for?' Tom asked.

'Naow!' Splodger exclaimed. 'Not on yer life! This ain't nuffing yet. One o' these days, an' not so very long neether, there's going ter be a real bust-up – and then yer'll watch the fur fly, guv!'

'Oh!' said Tom. 'So it's not yet. But where are you off to now, and where are all these fellows going?'

'Victoria an'Albert,' Splodger replied. 'We come aout solid at the East Indian, naow we're going ter git the uvver docks ter jine us.'

'And supposing they won't?'

'They will,' said Splodger. 'It's only a wonder they ain't come aout fust.'

'Do you think . . . Will there be any trouble?' Tom asked in a worried tone.

'Mebbe,' said Splodger heartily, as though he quite relished the prospect. 'Mebbe. I 'opes there is. I'm itching fer a charnst ter 'ave a go at some o' them peelers, and so is the uvver blokes. Tell yer wot, guv,' he chuckled. 'Come alongside o' me an' I'll see yer gits a nice weighty brick ter 'eave.'

'No, thanks,' said Tom. 'I'm obliged for the invitation, but I have some work to do.'

'Me too,' Splodger answered. 'An' I wouldn't miss mine fer a barrel o' the best – an' jest naow I wouldn't change wiv no one, neether.'

He stepped back into the road and elbowed his way into the tail-end of the demonstrators. Up thrust his pole in the air to joust at authority above the nondescript heads, and with a half-mocking wave of his hand he turned away, another docker, his jovial identity submerged once again in the grim temper of the marching men.

Tom watched them disappear round a bend in the road, then slowly resumed his interrupted journey. Splodger always bumped into him at a momentous crisis in his life, but this time it seemed that the coalie and his comrades were facing the crisis. The brilliant day did not seem so sunny now after all, for there was no cessation of misery in this East End. If only the employers were more generous, this vicious mood, breaking the soft spell of the weather, could never have manifested itself in the workers, and Tom was afraid that violence would achieve nothing but begetting violence on the other side. Nearly two thousand years since Christ, and Christians had not yet learned to live in peace together! Two thousand years. How long, O Lord – how long?

Before he passed beyond earshot of the demonstration, he found the Black Doctor reining in his horse beside him. Courtly as ever, Haddock doffed his top-hat, and in his deep gentle voice bade Tom 'Good afternoon.'

'Good afternoon,' Tom replied. 'Off to see a patient?'

Haddock stooped over Rachel's perspiring head and gently patted the delicate arch of her long, quivering neck.

'Not *one* patient, mah friend,' he answered. 'Hundreds. Ah am going to visit the docks,' he announced.

'The docks?' said Tom. 'Surely you are going the wrong way?'

'No. It's the Victoria and Albert Ah have in mind.'

'Oh yes,' said Tom. 'I understand now.'

'You saw the demonstration?'

'I did.'

'Well, then, you must know that when events like these are abroad in this part of London you won't find me very far from the scene of action, mah friend.'

'But I understood from one of the dockers that this was not very important, merely a preliminary skirmish.'

'It's something more than that,' said Haddock. 'Yet in a way that definition's true, mah friend. The docks have never handled more cargo, the shipowners have never been richer, yet the unskilled labourers who make all those profits possible are being shamefully exploited, and it will continue so until they learn that they hold the power in their own hands. Then the London and India Joint Docks Committee will really have something to worry about!'

'Do you think, Haddock,' the young man suggested, 'that something might be done in the way of mediation?'

'Mediation? – Not now, Tom, not in their present mood!' He curbed Rachel on a short rein as the reverberations of a sudden shout made her fidget nervously. 'You heard that, mah friend? – "God strike the bosses dead!" That means the gloves are off and they're determined to fight!'

Tom shook his head. 'Will it be a long dispute?' he asked anxiously.

'Depends. It all depends. Ah hope not. Ah pray sincerely that the Docks Committee will be forced to see reason soon.'

'And if not?'

'If not, then the men will go hungry a little longer,' said Haddock calmly. 'They're used to it. There's not so much difference in their larders whether they're working or not. It's simply a matter of drawing another hole in their belts.'

'But they're married, some of them,' Tom protested. 'They have wives and families. Must the children starve?'

'Ah'm afraid they must,' Haddock replied.

Tom was stung by the callousness of his answer, although he realized that the Black Doctor was the kindest of men. Something had deeply affected him to make him talk like this, but whatever Haddock's reasons for his apparently shameless acquiescence Tom could not admit such warped sentiments on any grounds whatsoever.

'That shan't happen,' said Tom firmly. 'Their families won't suffer, at least, not if I can help it. We have our own bakeries at the mission – I shall send them bread!'

Haddock smiled gratefully, and still a trifle condescendingly, as though Tom had not quite come up to his expectations.

'You have a great heart, Tom,' he said quietly. 'Ah am sure the men will appreciate it.'

'And yet,' Tom insisted, 'man does not live by bread alone.'

'Right,' said Haddock. 'But bread comes first, ma friend. You are upset,' he continued soothingly, 'and rightly so, Tom, yet believe me this is not completely outside your province, but an extension of your most intimate work. You saw them before, a ragged army marching past. They are your slum children grown up. Think it over, mah friend. Now, Tom, Ah'm off to the docks – goodbye!'

Pressing his knees into the resilient fat of Rachel's yielding sides, he swept off his hat again in a parting gesture, and smoothing his coat-tails over the well-worn polished brown saddle, the Black Doctor trotted off.

Once more Tom turned his footsteps towards the Mission. Three things had already pierced the charm of what had started off as a perfect day redolent with pleasing recollections. The demonstration, Splodger and Haddock, and somehow he had the unaccountable feeling that there was something yet to come. He could not help thinking of Haddock and his persistence that all these social problems were interrelated. Perhaps they were, but the link was of such a loose, elastic universality as to be non-existent for classification. For himself Tom saw no real connection between his children and the striking dockers, their only similarity being that both were products of the East End. He refused to dissipate his energy tinkering with reforms here, there and everywhere, when by continuing his single-minded application to one problem he could see it solved in his lifetime, or if not, at least well on the way to a satisfactory liquidation.

It remained a strange juxtaposition. Two doctors, each with a different vision. Posterity would prove which of them was right.

On Tom's table work piled up all afternoon. Steadily he went through his letters, corrected proofs, gave interviews to journalists or prospective members of his staff. The evening wore on, and around seven o'clock a special messenger brought him a letter marked 'Personal. Private!' Tom glanced through it rapidly, then replaced it in the envelope and rotated the stiff edges thoughtfully against the table, allowing the full significance of the missive to sink home. It was from the solicitor of the board of trustees placing his labours on a regularly remunerative basis.

Hitherto his work had been entirely honorary, but he could no longer allow the bulk of his wife's income to be spent on the upkeep of his home and the support of his growing family. Every year he had been offered gifts of money for his personal use by friends and admirers, but these he had invariably returned or donated to the funds. When he had first broached the subject to the trustees they had urged him to retain honorary status and accept gifts of money freely offered, but with characteristic bluntness Tom refused to take alms no matter how large or how delicately raised, insisting that the workman was worthy of his hire, and that he would not be ashamed to receive a salary for honest labour honestly done.

He rose to his feet and slipped the envelope into his coattails. It had happened. He was no longer independent, no longer the sole honorary director of his beloved mission, but the hired servant of a vast concern. It would make no difference in his attitude to his work, but it would involve a personal reorientation. This office of his had now become the board-room, and the mission that he had created with such herculean labours was no longer his, but had absorbed him. Perhaps even, he would one day become redundant and the trustees would dispense with his services. He dismissed the thought as beneath serious consideration from his mind; in any case, by his own ethics, if the workman was worthy of his hire, the corollary must also hold good. He could never envisage such an eventuality, for he understood very well how invaluable and irreplaceable were his services, but just the same he knew he would be a prey to nameless apprehensions until he had completely adapted himself to his new station.

As was his custom when perplexed or in difficulty he turned to his constant companion, the Bible. There, he usually found words of comfort, and opening the New Testament haphazard at the 14th chapter of John, he found them again.

'Let not your heart be troubled: ye believe in God, believe also in me.

'In my Father's house are many mansions: if *it were* not *so* I would have told you. I go to prepare a place for you.

'And if I go and prepare a place for you, I will come again and receive you unto myself; that where I am, *there* ye may be also.'

Tom's heart sang again – 'I know my Redeemer liveth!' Jesus had a hard path to tread, the hardest mortal man had known, yet He bore His crown of thorns uncomplaining on the rough road to Calvary. Against that peak of mental and physical suffering he was ashamed to place his puny trials. And it were not as though his life were being cut off in its very flowering; at thirty-three, when his Master hung crucified, he had the rest of his days before him.

Yet things were not the same. He had been independent for so long that he half-dreaded the closing of imaginary shackles that might curb the freedom of his work. It had been forced upon him, a simple and necessary step, but in all his life he had never found a decision more difficult to make. So it was over, and now he had to prepare himself to serve men where previously he had acknowledged no master but God.

His wife was surprised to find him returning home so early, but made him unobtrusively welcome, and although she sensed immediately that Tom needed her she showed no sign that she knew something was troubling him. Barnardo walked about the room in silence, undisturbed, while Syrie sewed placidly in her easy chair. Slowly, the never-failing spell of her presence crept over him and endowed the room with a restful charm that transformed it into a sealed chamber of mutual devotion insulated against harsh and hurtful thoughts.

'Well, Syrie,' he said at last. 'It's come.'

'What's come?' she asked quietly.

For answer he took the envelope from his pocket and without a word passed it over to her. Rapidly she read the letter through and gave it back to him.

'Isn't it what you wanted, dear?' she commented gently.

'It isn't what I wanted,' he replied. 'I wanted anything but that. It's what I've been forced to do.'

'Never mind, my dear,' she said. 'You'll find it was for the best.'

He knelt impulsively beside her, and she dropped her sewing and affectionately stroked the tired lines in his uplifted face.

'It will make no difference, Tom,' she assured him. 'The mission is your life, whoever runs it. You are dedicated to it, whatever happens, and now with your mind freed from financial strain, you'll surely find your work will benefit.'

'You think so, Serena?' he asked hopefully.

'I am certain of it, dear,' she replied. 'You have lost your honorary position, but that, after all, is only a name. To me, to all those hundreds in the mission, your status will always remain the same.'

He kissed her soft hand devotedly. From the earliest days of their marriage she had willingly effaced herself before his triumphs and was ever a rock of comfort in misfortune. A few moments with her and the situation in retrospect did not seem so full of mysterious pitfalls. He rose to his feet refreshed by the elixir of her sympathetic understanding, with renewed courage, and increased confidence. Thirty-three. He had at most, perhaps, thirty more years to live. In those three decades he had to pack half a century's work. He was determined to leave the East End cleansed of the greatest blot on its humanity, a vastly different and far better place than when he had found it. He would die content even at sixty if he could save a thousand orphaned children for every year of his life. That was a goal worth striving for – sixty thousand orphans saved from the gutters by the Grace of God and marked to the credit of Tom Barnardo – Doctor of the Lost.